Boston Scream Murder

Books by Ginger Bolton

SURVIVAL OF THE FRITTERS

GOODBYE CRULLER WORLD

JEALOUSY FILLED DONUTS

BOSTON SCREAM MURDER

Published by Kensington Publishing Corporation

Boston Scream Murder

GINGER BOLTON

KENSINGTON BOOKS
www.kensingtonbooks.com

KENSINGTON BOOKS are published by

Kensington Publishing Corp.
119 West 40th Street
New York, NY 10018

ISBN-13: 978-1-4967-2557-8 (ebook)
ISBN-10: 1-4967-2557-3 (ebook)

ISBN-13: 978-1-4967-2556-1
ISBN-10: 1-4967-2556-5

First Kensington Trade Paperback Printing: September 2020

10 9 8 7 6 5 4 3 2 1

Printed in the United States of America

ACKNOWLEDGMENTS

Thank you to my jolly troupe of critiquers and ladies-who-potluck—Cathy Astolfo, Alison Bruce, Melodie Campbell, Nancy O'Neill, and Joan O'Callaghan. We will always miss our honorary critiquer from the balcony and provider of freshly baked bread, the late Dave Campbell.

Many thanks to my many other supportive friends, including Krista Davis; Daryl Wood Gerber, who also writes as Avery Aames; Laurie Cass, who also writes as Laura Alden; Kaye George, who also writes as Janet Cantrell; and Allison Brook, who also writes as Marilyn Levinson.

Thank you to Kim Davis of Cinnamon and Sugar and a Little Bit of Murder, who not only tries recipes in cozy mysteries, but also photographs the results beautifully. Her hints improved one of the recipes in the back of this book.

Sgt. Michael Boothby, Toronto Police Service (Retired) took time to read my manuscript and make helpful suggestions, and I thank him for that and apologize for any of my characters who deviated from his suggestions.

Again, I had the privilege of attending the Malice Domestic Conference, a big, friendly, and happy party for those of us who love traditional mysteries. Thank you to the organizers and volunteers.

A special thanks to Janet Kellough and to Vicki Delany, who also writes as Eva Gates, for inviting me to be one of the featured authors at the 2019 Women Killing It Crime Writers' Festival.

Heartfelt thanks to agent John Talbot, who made Deputy Donut happen.

You folks at Kensington Publishing are the best. My wonderful editor, John Scognamiglio, encourages me and makes me laugh. Carly Sommerstein shepherds my work from manuscript to book, arranges thorough copyediting (and then I make changes; don't blame the excellent copy editor for my errors), and patiently answers my questions. Larissa Ackerman makes certain that my books do not go out into the world without appropriate fanfare. She and Michelle Addo coordinate and organize the Kensington CozyClub Mini-Conventions—fun for authors and readers! Kristine Mills designs the best covers ever, while artist Mary Ann Lasher brings Deputy Donut the cat to warm, fuzzy, adorable life and paints delicious-looking donuts that are also, for *Boston Scream Murder*, suitably creepy.

My family and friends put up with my distracted muttering as I mentally reenact and reject scenes and madly edit and tweak.

To booksellers, librarians, and readers—thank you for supporting Deputy Donut the mystery series. And Deputy Donut the cat. May you be warmed by hot beverages, donuts, fur babies, and stories.

Chapter 1

Even from the kitchen in the back of Deputy Donut, the three of us could hear the man at a table near one of our café's front windows. "Boston is the best city on earth!" he boomed. "You can get fresh seafood anytime, day or night. And I mean *fresh*. Not like here in Wisconsin."

Boston. I had to smile. Tom Westhill, Nina Lapeer, and I were making Boston cream donuts, but Halloween was only five days away, so we were calling them Boston scream donuts. Spreading fudge frosting on one, I mentally defended our town. Fallingbrook wasn't on an ocean, but the north woods near the Great Lakes had other advantages. I muttered to Nina, "That new customer should try fresh Lake Superior yellow perch. Or whitefish."

Nina cast a sideways grin down at me. With the rounded tip of a wooden spoon's handle, she made indentations resembling frightened eyes in the fudge frosting on a Boston scream donut. "Who is he, Emily?" The longest eyelashes I'd ever seen framed her brown eyes. Her spiky dark brown hair was mostly hidden underneath her Deputy Donut hat, a police hat with a fuzzy donut where the badge would be on a real police hat.

"From the sound of things, he's the Boston Screamer."

She burst out laughing. "It's a good thing I wasn't drinking coffee. I might have spewed it over an entire tray of donuts."

I looked over the half wall separating the kitchen from the serving and eating counter and the rest of the dining area. "I don't think I've ever seen him before. What did he order?"

Pressing the end of the spoon handle down at an angle to make an oval in the fudge frosting, Nina gave the scared-looking donut a perfect screaming mouth. "Guess."

"A Boston scream donut?"

Nina jabbed a skewer into the frosting twice, and the screaming face had nostrils. "You got it. Well, he said 'cream,' not 'scream.' But as you said, he's screaming"—she made an air quote with her free hand—"about Boston."

"About seafood in Boston. Does he want us to serve lobster and scrod donuts?"

Manning the deep fryers behind us, Tom chuckled.

Nina deftly used a knife to carve mitten-like hands cradling the sides of the donut's screaming face. "When I took his order he was telling the other men at the table about duck boat and walking tours of Boston."

Backlit by one of our two large front windows, the Boston Screamer was barely more than a silhouette. I asked Nina, "Do you think the retired men have recruited him to join them?" The retired men met at that table every weekday morning. They weren't normally quiet. That morning, they were listening to the Boston Screamer instead of talking.

Nina gently placed the frosted top half of a Boston scream donut onto the filling-coated bottom half. "Do the retired men invite new members to their table?"

I spread filling almost to the edge of the bottom half of another donut. "I don't know. They came here as a group when Tom and I opened Deputy Donut three years ago, and although other men have sat with them, none have become part of the group." I raised my knife from the filling I was spreading. "I wonder if the Boston Screamer is Cheryl's date."

Nina opened her eyes wider than usual. "Cheryl has a date? I thought she was a confirmed bachelorette, or whatever you call a woman in her sixties who has never married."

"Cautious. She's trying one of those dating sites for over-fifties. She plans to meet the man here, where she'll be surrounded by friends."

"Isn't she a little old for him?"

"She's about sixty-five. How old would you guess he is? You talked to him."

"Listened."

"Listened. How old?"

"I can't tell with old people."

Behind us, Tom warned her, "Watch it."

Nina turned toward him. "You're not old. Policemen retire young, right? Even police chiefs?"

"Thank you." Tom was sixty-two, but despite the salt-and-pepper hair hidden underneath his donut police hat, he looked younger, and I suspected that he was in much better physical shape than a lot of men thirty years his junior.

Nina pressed a screaming mouth into another fudge-frosted donut top. "You're welcome. The Boston Screamer could be sixty-five or seventy, but don't men who register on dating sites specify that they want to date women who are much younger than they are?"

I nudged a tray of filling-covered donut halves toward her. "I don't know, especially about sites for over-fifties."

"Have you ever tried a dating site? Like, for your age?"

"Certainly *not*!" Tom said. "I'm a happily married man."

"I meant Emily," Nina said.

"I haven't." I had married Tom's son, Alec, when I was twenty-one. I'd been widowed six years ago when I was twenty-five, about the age Nina was now. I asked her, "How about you? Have you tried matchmaking sites?"

"Yeah, but everyone on them was probably as old as that guy yelling about Boston." She looked toward the front door again. "Where are Cheryl and the other Knitpickers? It's after nine."

I glanced through our office windows toward the driveway leading to the parking lot behind Deputy Donut. My cat,

Dep, who had given her full name to our coffee shop, stayed in our office. At the moment, instead of watching the kitchen and dining room through our interior windows, she was perched on the back of the couch and staring toward the parking lot behind the building. "They're probably outside urging Cheryl to come in."

While Nina and I had been talking, I'd heard the word "Boston" shouted at least five more times. I told Nina, "It must be time for me to go see if the retired men might need more coffee."

With a teasing lilt, she accused, "You want to see if the Boston Screamer is good enough for Cheryl. You don't want her to be hurt." Although Nina looked all angles, elbows, and spiky hair, she was as softhearted as anyone could be.

I had to smile. "I don't want any of our customers to be hurt, especially loyal regulars like the Knitpickers."

Nina warned, "The Boston Screamer is going to call you 'little lady' in the first ten seconds of talking to you. He called me that, and no one has described me as little since about kindergarten. Plus, he was sitting down, and I was standing. Looming over him."

I complained dramatically, "No one has ever called me tall, and no one is ever likely to."

"Little and cute can't be *all* bad."

"Thanks." Smiling, I carried a pot of coffee around the half wall, past the end of the eating and serving counter, and into the dining room.

We had made changes recently. We still had the wide-planked wooden floors and the white walls with their faint peach tint, we still displayed artwork from The Craft Croft on our walls, and we still had our chairs with their seats and backs upholstered in comfy coffee-brown leather, but we had replaced our sliced tree-trunk tables. Tom, his wife, Cindy, who was Alec's mother, and I had painted the tops of plain round tables to look like donuts. No two tabletops were the same, and they were all cheerful. Glass protected our painted donuts and made cleanups easy. In corners around the room, friendly-looking ghosts and witches lounged on chubby pumpkins and twisty gourds.

The Boston Screamer was dressed as if for a date, in khakis and a white dress shirt. I decided that he must be about Cheryl's age or older. He was shorter than the other men around the table, and muscular without carrying an extra ounce of fat. He held out his mug for a refill. He didn't look like a dangerous desperado out to hurt his dates. His nose was well-defined, sharp without being pointy, and his chin was determined and square. His eyes were an extremely pale shade of blue as if they'd been bleached by the sun on boats off the shores of New England.

He asked loudly, "Are you the little lady responsible for this Boston cream donut?"

My smile widened. Nina had been right about the words he would use, but her time estimate had been about eight seconds too long. Refilling his mug, I answered, "Three of us— my partner, our assistant, and I—develop the recipes for our donuts, including the one you're eating."

"It's pretty good," he said. "Acceptable, actually."

I managed not to laugh at the backhanded compliment. "Thank you."

He pointed a finger at me. "If you double the chocolate frosting, your Boston cream donuts will be about perfect. And you need to be more careful. Mine looks like someone stuck their fingers into it."

"We did that on purpose, with a spoon handle and a skewer, not our fingers. Before you bit into it, there was a face. It's a Boston scream donut, because Halloween's coming up."

He looked down at his plate. "I get it. Very clever. Still, you could charge more for them with that one improvement, thicker frosting. I was a bank manager before I retired, and I know how small businesses can get themselves into trouble by skimping on quantity and substituting gimmicks for quality. There. That's some free advice for you, little lady."

I thanked him again.

"And I have to congratulate you and your colleagues on your outfits. The black slacks, white shirts, and white aprons with your logo on them are good branding. Do you know what branding is?"

"Yes."

He glanced at my head. "The fur donuts on your hats are a little over-the-top." I grinned, but he didn't seem to notice that what he'd said could be funny. He went on, "I get it. Deputy Donut. A donut on a deputy's hat. And even the cat in your logo is wearing one. The tilt to the cat's hat is a nice touch."

"Thank you. The donuts on our hats are not real fur."

"I knew that from the first glance." He leaned forward and spoke, for once, quietly. "I was told that the people working here would know who Cheryl is."

Chapter 2

✺

The Boston Screamer glanced around our charming and friendly café. "I don't see anyone resembling Cheryl's picture."

I reassured him. "She should be here any minute."

"Okay, good. Get me another Boston cream donut on a fresh plate for her. Double the chocolate frosting on hers and don't poke anything into it or make it look like a screaming face. I want to make a good impression."

This guy was amusing me, but needing to be polite to customers, I managed not to laugh.

"And bring her some of your coffee. What did the young lady who took my order say today's special was? I want the best premium coffee you can bring me."

"It's a blend from Guatemala, a dark roast. The flavor is mellow, but people tell me that the caffeine level is high."

"Excellent. But don't bring them until Cheryl gets here. I don't want the donut to be stale or the coffee to be cold. It's freshly brewed, right, and hasn't been sitting around getting scorched and bitter?"

Now I really had to struggle not to laugh. "Right," I said.

"And you'll bring me the bill, for both of us."

"Okay." I was almost certain that he was too micromanaging for Cheryl.

He asked, "Have you ever been to Boston?"

"Once, when I was twelve, on a summer vacation."

"Isn't it a great city?"

"I liked it."

"You probably don't remember much about it. You should go back for a visit. You should consider moving there. I worked in Boston the summer I was twenty-three, in a restaurant. Best summer of my life. The seafood! I must have eaten a ton of seafood that summer alone."

Still uncharacteristically quiet, the other men at his table were watching him as if he were a rare specimen in the New England Aquarium.

The Boston Screamer sipped at his coffee, put it down, and glanced around our dining room again. "This place looks good. Who was your decorator?"

I wasn't sure that the Boston Screamer could see Tom from where he was sitting, but I pointed toward the kitchen. "The man in the kitchen in the donut hat and I did it ourselves. He's my business partner."

"Business partner, as in you and he own this place together?"

"Fifty-fifty. We opened it after Tom retired. He was Fallingbrook's police chief."

"Aha. Tom Westhill." The Boston Screamer nodded, the complacent gesture of a man who knows or knows of everyone in town. "I've heard he's a good man. So that's why you named it Deputy Donut."

"It was the cat's name first."

The Boston Screamer tightened his lips to a pinched frown. "Health regulations don't allow cats in public dining areas."

"She doesn't go near the food. She stays in our office. Look through the window from the dining area into the office. We made it a kitty playground with ramps, catwalks, kitty staircases, tunnels, and carpeted columns."

He rose to his feet and gazed toward the rear of the building. "Creative. I like all the windows and your use of foodie colors—coffee and chocolate browns, peaches, apricots, tangerines, butter, and whipped cream."

This time my smile was genuine. "We did that on purpose, but you're the first person to comment on it, complete with foodie words. The colors go with the cat, too." Dep was a torbie, a very special tortoiseshell tabby with rings on her sides that resembled donuts. She was watching us from the back of the café-au-lait couch. She wasn't puffed up, but she was alert, as if she hadn't yet decided whether the latest Deputy Donut customer was a friend or a foe. She could be persnickety about which customers I should or should not serve.

The Boston Screamer gave me an approving nod. "And there's an emergency exit from your office. Where does that go?"

Wondering if he had a particular reason for checking on the location of emergency exits, I answered, "To the parking lot. And there's another back door, too, from our storeroom. You have to go through the kitchen."

The Boston Screamer sat down again. "Good. I admire people who plan well. Did you and Chief Westhill design that office?"

"We designed the entire shop. Tom's wife, who teaches art at Fallingbrook High, helped us paint the tabletops."

"What about the kitchen? Commercial kitchens can be tricky. Didn't you hire a professional designer?"

"We designed it ourselves."

Smoothing the Deputy Donut logo on his paper napkin, he asked, not shouting but not whispering, either, "How would you like to earn extra money on the side?"

I didn't know where this was heading, but I was glad that the retired men were witnessing the conversation and that I still wore my wedding ring. "We cater, too," I said quickly. "Donuts and beverages, and we can stack donuts into shapes for cake-like desserts or provide a donut wall."

"Hmm. I have a party coming up."

Uh-oh. I was planning a party for friends on Saturday, which was Halloween, after the trick-or-treating. I hoped his party wasn't that night. I attempted an encouraging smile.

The Boston Screamer didn't need encouragement. "It's tomorrow, my seventieth birthday. It's being catered, but I'd like you to provide three dozen donuts and an urn of this superb coffee, by the time the party starts tomorrow at noon. The donuts shouldn't be stacked into shapes or anything silly like that. I want double thickness on the chocolate frosting, and no holes in the frosting. Not Boston scream but Boston cream. When your birthday's only four days before Halloween, you don't want Halloween decorations upstaging you. But the important part is not my birthday. It's Boston."

"Then maybe you'd like tea."

He pointed a finger at me. "You're quick. I like that. Think you can be quick enough to make three dozen donuts and deliver them out at Lake Fleekom at eleven fifty-five tomorrow morning? Do you know where Lake Fleekom is?"

"Yes."

He explained, anyway. "It's only ten minutes away."

I glanced toward the kitchen again. All three of us were scheduled to work the next day. "We can do that," I said.

"Here's what I also have in mind, in addition to my Boston tea party." His lips twitched in a fleeting grin. "I have a cottage that I occasionally let renters use. The interior's outdated, and last week's tenants damaged it. I need to patch the walls and repaint, and I'd like to renovate the kitchen so that the ladies would love to cook in it. I'm not much for cooking. My late wife did all that, and here it is twenty years later, and I'm still not into cooking. Thank goodness for you folks and your restaurants and takeout."

"You're welcome."

"I'll get contractors in to do the work, but I'd like you to give me some ideas about the latest trends in colors and kitchen design. I do have a few ideas, so you wouldn't be starting from scratch. For renters to feel at home, I should remove the pictures of my late wife. Also, I'd like to give the whole place an updated New England vibe, make people feel like they're at a seaside cottage. Meet me there this evening, if you can. Bring Chief Westhill along if it makes you feel safer."

"This evening's fine." I did not want to go alone to a strange man's cottage, but Tom worked long hours and enjoyed spending at least some time at home with Cindy. I asked, "How about if our assistant, Nina Lapeer, comes along instead of Tom? She's an artist."

"The young lady who served me when I first came in? Did she help you paint these donut tables? They're very well executed."

"Thank you. We did that before we met her."

"That's okay, anyway. Bring Nina along. An artist, you say?" He didn't seem to require an answer. "I've heard from my banking clients how that goes. It doesn't pay, and she has to do jobs like waitressing to buy supplies and make ends meet. But I can tell by the way she uses makeup to show off those cheekbones and the planes of her face that she has artistic talent. After all my years as an executive, I can spot the ones who might expend enough effort to succeed."

I pointed to the largest painting in the room, a jumble of sailboats, rowboats, and canoes in an impressionistic style, seen from above, all in moody tones of indigo and blue. "She painted that one."

Sipping coffee, he gazed at it. "Is she represented by a gallery?"

"The Craft Croft."

"I know the place." He pointed south. "It's a few blocks that way, down Wisconsin Street. Tell Nina she needs to aim higher than artisans' co-ops. She should try for galleries in larger cities."

Pleased at his compliments for Nina, I ignored the slight to The Craft Croft and to Fallingbrook, which was big compared to nearby towns and villages. "I think that's what she hopes to do. She's good, isn't she?"

"Very. And I know a little bit about art. She shouldn't be wasting her time here."

Fortunately, I didn't need to find a diplomatic answer to that. The Knitpickers were outside the front door, surrounding a woman as if persuading her to come inside.

At first, I didn't recognize Cheryl. Last I knew, her curls had been white. Now they were shades of sun-kissed sand. One of Cheryl's friends opened the door. "Cheryl's coming in," I told the Boston Screamer. "I'll introduce her to you."

He stood up. "I'll move to another table. Excuse me, gentlemen. I enjoyed our talk."

That was no wonder.

Taking his mug and plate, he moved farther back to a table for two. I went to the front door and welcomed the Knitpickers.

Although never having had children, let alone grandchildren, Cheryl reminded me of a grandmother. She had a way of beaming when she smiled, even though her biggest smiles often caused her round, rosy cheeks to nearly hide her eyes. Today, not only had she dyed her curls light brown with blond highlights, she was wearing a new outfit—gray slacks, a floral blouse, and a purple cardigan that matched the flowers on the blouse and the frames of her glasses, which I'd also never seen before.

She seemed to be trying to appear brave. However, looking into her blue eyes, I was certain that she was nervous. The entire effect—hair color, new outfit, apprehensive expression—made her look younger than usual.

I extended a hand toward her. "Cheryl, come with me. There's someone here who wants to meet you."

Cheryl's friends settled themselves at their usual table near the retired men. The Knitpickers weren't paying a lot of attention to the retired men or to the knitting they were pulling out of bags and baskets. They were watching Cheryl.

I led her to the table where the Boston Screamer was stand-ing behind the chair across from his. He pulled out the chair.

"This is Cheryl," I told him. Not knowing his name, and not about to introduce him as the Boston Screamer, I let him introduce himself.

"I'm Richmond P. Royalson the Third," he informed her. "Call me Rich." Emphasizing the shortened form of his first name, he flashed an expensive-looking gold wristwatch. "Have a seat, Cheryl. I've ordered for you."

Chapter 3

✌

I gave Cheryl a reassuring smile. "I'll get your coffee and donut."

In the kitchen, Tom and Nina were watching old-fashioned unraised donuts dancing among golden bubbles. Although Rich was conventionally handsome, I preferred Tom's sturdy good looks. I said just loudly enough for him and Nina to hear, "The Boston Screamer's name is Richmond P. Royalson the Third, call me Rich. Does that ring a bell?"

Nina shook her head.

Tom lifted the basket of donuts out of the oil and spoke quietly. "About twenty years ago, his wife drowned in Lake Fleekom."

Nina and I moved closer to Tom.

He hung the basket on the side of the fryer to drain. "I was a patrol cop and not involved with the investigation, but I remember it." He lowered another basket into the oil. "That fall was colder than this one, and the lake was slushy. She overturned her canoe. There were no witnesses. She was supposedly a good swimmer, but she was wearing heavy clothing and boots. Between hypothermia and waterlogged clothing, she didn't make it to shore. The last I knew, Royalson was the manager of the Fallingbrook Mercantile Bank. I never met the man."

Nina tilted her head. "I would have thought that bank

managers and police chiefs would, I don't know, hang out together or join the same men's clubs."

"Not this police chief," Tom stated emphatically. "I prefer being home with my wife and my woodworking toys. I mean tools."

Near the front of the dining area, Cheryl smiled stonily at the widower waving his arms and shouting words like "Boston," "New England," and "lobster." I told Tom and Nina, "He wants a Boston cream donut for Cheryl, not a Boston scream donut, and he wants us to double the fudge frosting. He ordered today's special coffee for her."

Nina turned toward the coffee makers. "I'll get the coffee."

I sliced a round raised donut without a hole in it and slathered a double load of frosting on the top half. It was impossible to eat these extravagant treats neatly, and the cream filling I dolloped on the lower half wasn't going to help. I carefully balanced the top of the donut on the cream filling. Nina took the coffee and donut to Cheryl while I spread extra fudge frosting on the top halves of donuts. They did look and smell even better than the ones with less frosting.

Nina returned from Cheryl and Rich's table. She carved screaming faces into the thicker fudge frosting. She and Tom agreed that we could easily make the extra donuts for Rich's party the next morning in time for me to deliver them at eleven fifty-five.

Tom told us, "You two will be careful visiting Royalson at his cottage this evening, won't you." It wasn't a question.

Holding her wooden spoon by its bowl, Nina pointed the frosting-covered handle at him. "I'll be perfectly safe with Emily. She has all that extra training from her days as a 911 operator."

"That was a few years ago," I pointed out. "And our training wasn't exactly about defending ourselves from people who were obsessed with crab cakes and lobster bisque."

"But you've kept up with first aid," Nina reminded me.

"I hope we won't need first aid!"

Nina turned back to Tom. "And I loved martial arts when I was a kid. Emily and I will look after each other."

Tom backed playfully away from the fudge-covered spoon handle. "Good. Take that death-by-chocolate spoon with you, and I won't have to tag along."

I asked Tom, "Do you think Rich might have had something to do with his wife's death?"

"It was ruled an accidental drowning. Don't go asking him if he had anything to do with it."

"Would I do such a thing?"

Tom pierced me with those dark eyes. "No!" he answered so firmly that I had to laugh. "Certainly not."

I glanced over at Rich. He was sitting with his back to me, but I heard the word "Boston" again. Facing him, Cheryl dabbed frosting off one corner of her mouth and winked at me.

When Rich and Cheryl left Deputy Donut, Rich was the perfect gentleman, holding the door for her. Before it closed, I heard again, "In Boston . . ."

The retired men and the other Knitpickers departed around noon as usual. We fed assorted fried goodies like deep-fried dill pickles and arancini, delicious Italian rice and cheese balls, to a lunch crowd that included police officers and firefighters.

Although the Knitpickers met in Deputy Donut weekday mornings and seldom showed up other times, Cheryl returned by herself later in the afternoon. She sat at a table for two, facing the door as if watching for someone. Did she already have a second date with Rich?

I asked what she'd like.

"Just a coffee. That donut I had this morning was filling."

"Too much fudge frosting?"

Those blue eyes twinkled. "Can there be?"

"Rich requested the extra frosting. Also, he asked me for suggestions for redecorating his cottage and renovating its kitchen. Nina and I will meet him there after work this evening. Would you like to come along?"

"No, thanks. I heard enough about Boston this morning to last the rest of my life. He's not bad, but I don't have to have everything mansplained." She lifted an index finger to her lips. "Sh. I arranged to meet a different man here this afternoon. I didn't expect so many choices from one dating site." She stared toward the door for a second. "Wow," she whispered. "This one looks as good as the picture he posted on the site."

The man coming into Deputy Donut was tall and broad shouldered. His new-looking khakis and brown-striped shirt fit him well. At first, I was afraid that he might be a lot younger than Cheryl, but as he approached, I realized that his brown hair was graying at the temples. He had the amiable sort of face that made me feel like I already knew him. His most striking features were his hazel eyes and the smile wrinkles that deepened when he shook Cheryl's hand. "Sorry I'm late," he said. "I'm Steve." He ordered a coffee and looked at the card on the table listing the day's special donuts. "What's a jack-o'-lantern donut?"

I explained, "It's an unraised pumpkin donut with orange frosting and candy corn eyes."

Cheryl asked, "What about the mouth?"

"That's the hole in the donut." Between the open mouths and the way Nina had been placing the eyes, the expressions on our jack-o'-lantern donuts ran the gamut from comical to benign to scary. Well, almost scary.

"I'll try one," Steve said.

Rich Royalson walked in.

A pixie-like woman clung to his arm. Although the younger woman's short hair, turned-up nose, and complexion with its sprinkling of freckles were girlish and cute and her sleeveless wool dress showed off arms that were firm and muscular as if she worked out, she appeared to be about fifty. Rich had told me that he was turning seventy the next day. He was old enough to be the woman's father.

The way she was clinging to him was not daughterly.

Reminding myself that gaping at customers wasn't polite, I closed my mouth.

Rich glanced toward Cheryl, turned red, gave her a curt nod, and hustled the woman to a table on the other side of the dining room.

Cheryl lowered her head. For a second, I thought she was embarrassed or maybe even hurt, but when she looked up at me, I realized that her shoulders were shaking with laughter, not sobs. She gave me another wink. I was glad she'd already told me she wasn't interested in Rich. Still, I hoped that the new guy wouldn't hurt her. Steve seemed younger than Cheryl. Would he drop her as quickly as Rich apparently had?

In the kitchen, I chose a cheerful jack-o'-lantern donut for Steve and poured his coffee. When I set them in front of him, he was asking Cheryl what he should see in Fallingbrook.

Rich ordered Boston cream donuts and coffee for himself and his date. I plated a couple of fudge-frosted and pastry cream–filled donuts before Nina could carve screaming faces into them. Rich and his date sat with their arms stretched across the table toward each other and their fingertips touching. *It's like Valentine's Day in here,* I thought, *instead of almost Halloween. . . .*

I gave them their plates and returned to the kitchen for mugs and a pot of coffee.

The front door opened with a bang.

A blond man in dirty-looking jeans and a torn, sleeveless hoodie over a T-shirt strode to the table where Rich was making eyes at his date. "How dare you!" the blond man shouted. He appeared to be a little younger than the pixie-like woman, perhaps in his midforties. Biceps bulged beneath his shirt sleeves.

Rich and his date thrust their chairs backward and stood up. Her chin up and her eyes blazing, the woman demanded, "What are you doing here, Derek?"

The man she'd called Derek snarled out one side of his mouth, "I'm just here to warn your new boyfriend." He turned toward Rich and raised his voice. "She's only after your money."

I set the mugs on the nearest table and carried the heavy pot of hot coffee closer to Derek. Despite the whimsical hat on my head, I attempted to look formidable. "Please, sir." No one seemed to hear me.

Rich boomed, "I've known Terri for a long time. She's the love of my life. I'm thrilled that we managed to reconnect."

Derek yelled, "She tricked me! She got me to rent your cottage for all of last week, encouraged me to have a party there, and called you and reported me so's you'd come and toss me out and she could seduce you and pretend to be the victim of a party that she threw. You owe me for the two nights I paid for that cottage and didn't get to use." He peppered his speech with swear words. His blue eyes bulged. His hands balled into fists at his sides.

Rich's face became a deeper red than it had been when he walked in and noticed Cheryl. "And you owe me for the damage you and your drunken friends did to my cottage. The rental contract clearly stated that there were to be no parties. None. And no more than four people. You were letting a fifth person sleep on the couch. You don't get a refund, and you don't get your damage deposit back, either."

His fists now up near his waist, Derek took a step closer to Rich.

Customers were staring at the three enraged people. This was not the atmosphere we liked in Deputy Donut. Besides, someone might get hurt.

The carafe in my hand was becoming heavy. I held it in front of me like a shield. "Sir," I said to Derek, "if you're not going to sit down and stop harassing other customers, I'll have to ask you to leave."

Derek turned one hand into a fake revolver, pointed it at Rich, and stated, "You're going to be sorry for stealing Terri. And she's going to be sorry she ever snuck around behind my back and made a fool of me." He marched to the door.

Chains on the backs of his scuffed black boots clanked. He slapped the door open with one hand against the glass and stomped outside.

Shoulders shaking, Terri ran toward the ladies' room.

The other customers in Deputy Donut had been quietly observing the drama. Now they chattered, leaning toward other tables to talk to people whether they knew them or not. Wherever Derek had gone, his ears must have been burning. Cheryl caught my eye, gave her head a quick shake, and mouthed, "Wow."

I retrieved the two mugs, went to Rich's table, and poured coffee for him and his date.

Rich's face was almost purple, and a pulse beat in his neck. He handed me an envelope and spoke quietly but jerkily, as if his anger was affecting his breathing. "The directions to my cottage and the key to the back door are in the envelope. The renovations are a surprise for Terri. I have a date with her tonight, so I can't meet you at my cottage. Is your talented assistant coming with you, Nina Lapeer?"

"Yes."

"Excellent! I called one of my former banking clients and told him about her. He has important contacts in the art world, and he trusts my good taste. He's interested in seeing Nina Lapeer's work. What do you think of that?"

I gave him a genuine smile. "I like it. Thank you."

"Hey, I do what I can to help others, especially up-and-comers. That painting of hers that you're displaying—is it for sale?"

"It is."

"I'm going to think about where I could put it. It's too big for any wall in my cottage, but maybe it would fit in my house. What do you think about that idea?"

"It's great. You can contact The Craft Croft to make the arrangements."

"Will do. It should be a good investment. That's the name of my game—quality investments. I've done very well with them, so when it comes to renovating my cottage, money's no object. You and Nina can suggest whatever luxuries you think renters and Terri and I might like, especially in the kitchen. And Nina should keep in mind that I could be in the market for a smaller painting, maybe to go on the wall above the fireplace."

"I'll tell her." I would have to thank Cheryl for causing Rich to visit Deputy Donut.

"I'll have a look at The Craft Croft to see if I want to buy any of her other work. Meanwhile, you're bringing donuts to my party tomorrow at eleven fifty-five, aren't you?"

I tucked the envelope into one of my apron's wide front pockets. "Yes."

"You can return the key to me at the party. Tonight, while you're figuring out what I should have my contractors do, take a platter out of one of the upper kitchen cupboards near the sink. It's a big platter, so it's probably near the bottom of the stack. Be careful. It's fragile, but it's decorated with sailboats and will be perfect for you to arrange your donuts on. Now, what do you think of that? Perfection!"

I wasn't sure what I thought of a version of perfection that involved platters at the bottom of undoubtedly teetery stacks of breakable dishes, but I answered, "It sounds good."

"After the party, you and Nina and I can meet at the cottage and discuss your ideas, and if she has any suitable paintings, she should bring them. Tomorrow night at seven? My party will be over by then." He quoted what he would pay us. "Plus, I might buy a painting. Or several."

I decided that I didn't mind spending the next two evenings playing with decorating and renovating ideas. It should be fun, and Nina could use the publicity. If what Rich had said about telling a former client about her work was true, he'd already been promoting her. I gave him a big smile.

Terri came toward us. She frowned. Her redone makeup did not conceal her red eyes and puffy eyelids.

Rich patted my arm. "Mum's the word," he whispered.

I started toward Cheryl and Steve's table.

Rich pulled out Terri's chair. She didn't sit down. "What were you two talking about?" Her voice was shrill.

Rich answered quickly and loudly, "Tomorrow's party. But don't you worry your pretty little head about it."

"Let's leave, Richie. I don't feel safe here. He might come back."

"Rich," he corrected her.

"Rich."

I asked Cheryl and Steve if I could bring them anything else. They didn't have time to answer. Instead of escorting Terri outside, Rich brought her to Cheryl and Steve's table. "Cheryl, meet Terri. Terri, meet Cheryl." He looked point-edly at Steve. "And you are?"

"Steve Quail."

"Well, Steve Quail, congratulations on dating such a sweet little lady. And Cheryl, I hope there are no hard feelings. Since the time two weeks ago that you and I arranged our date for this morning, I reconnected with Terri. I thought I'd lost her years ago. I didn't want to disappoint you, Cheryl, by breaking my date with you, so I came here to meet you this morning, anyway. Isn't it great how things turn out?" Cheryl opened her mouth, but before she said anything, Rich an-nounced in hearty and patronizing tones, "You've already found someone else."

Both Cheryl and Steve blushed. Cheryl regained her com-posure first. "It's okay, Rich."

Rich squinted at Steve. "Have we met before? I was a bank manager, with dozens of people coming into my corner office every day."

Steve looked as uncomfortable as I might be if someone as boomingly annoying as Rich publicly claimed to have a con-nection with me. But then, Steve's blush at Rich's assumption that he and Cheryl were already a couple hadn't yet subsided. "I don't think so," Steve said.

"Tell you what," Rich burst out. "We can all be friends. I'm having a birthday party tomorrow out at Lake Fleekom. First house you come to at the lake. Noon, for lunch and the afternoon. Why don't you two join us? No presents, only good wishes."

Terri nodded. "Yes." She didn't exactly sound sincere.

Cheryl glanced at Steve as if for confirmation, then said quietly, "Thank you, Rich. That would be nice."

Terri reminded Rich, "We were leaving."

He escorted her out. She had not touched her coffee or her lavishly frosted Boston cream donut.

Chapter 4

✿

Terri wasn't the only one who didn't finish a donut. Steve ate his jack-o'-lantern donut, but after he and Cheryl left, I discovered that the two pieces of candy corn that Nina had used as eyes on his jack-o'-lantern donut were underneath his plate's rim.

We closed for the afternoon at four thirty as usual and made the yeast dough we would need the next morning, including enough for Rich's Boston cream donuts. I told Nina and Tom that Rich had said he'd talked to a former client who had contacts in the art world.

Nina glanced at me and away again. "Sweet," she said softly.

Tom asked, "Did Royalson give you a name?"

"No, why? Did you ever arrest any Fallingbrook art connoisseurs?"

Tom studied the ceiling as if Fallingbrook had large numbers of criminal art connoisseurs and their names were written up there. "I can't think of any at the moment."

Nina wasn't afraid to tease him back. "Don't worry. I won't spend the millions I expect from my paintings like, oh, about next week."

"You're irreplaceable here," Tom told her. "But by about your second million, we'll understand if you want to devote all of your time to painting."

Nina smiled. "As if. But thanks."

We placed the yeast dough we'd made into our proofing cabinet and set the temperature and humidity to allow the dough to rise perfectly overnight.

Nina walked home with Dep and me. Dep wore a halter and leash and was good at keeping the pace—her pace. Falling leaves tempted her to practice her hunting skills, which weren't very good at the best of times. She did catch one leaf. After it landed.

We all trotted up the stairs to the porch of Dep's and my sweet yellow brick Victorian cottage. Just inside the front door, I took off the wiggly cat's halter and leash, gave her a quick hug, and set her down on the pine planks of the living room floor. She scampered toward the back of the house where she could, if she wanted, find her food, water, toys, and litter tray. Or she could relax on a wide, cushioned windowsill above a radiator cover in the sunroom and watch squirrels bury acorns.

I locked the house, and Nina and I headed to the driveway. Pointing at the kayak on top of my car, she teased, "You know that the reds of your kayak and your car clash?"

"Yes, and that a kayak on the roof of a fast car makes it look like a slow car. And act more like one, too."

"You're never going to drive top speed, anyway."

I backed carefully out of the driveway. "Don't count on it."

"Are you expecting a flood? Or were you planning to paddle to this guy's cottage?"

I pulled out onto the street. "Good idea. I've never gone kayaking on Lake Fleekom. You can balance on the back of the boat with your feet in the water." More seriously, I added, "I've been keeping my kayak on top of the car since midsummer, when I bought it. That way, I can race off for some last-minute kayaking whenever I want to."

She eyed me slyly. "With your handsome detective."

"Or by myself. And Brent is not mine. I'll probably get him to help me put the kayak away for the winter, though.

He said I could store it in his garage." Someday, I hoped to have a garage built beside my own house. "That would be better than trying to heave it over the wall around my yard."

"You could open a gate."

"There aren't any. I have to go through the house to get from the front yard to the back. It's inconvenient, but nicely safe for both Dep and me." I turned onto the main road and told Nina that Rich wanted her to pay attention to his cottage's interior to figure out if any of her paintings would go with the new décor we would plan for his cottage.

"How high are the ceilings?"

"I don't know, but he said that your painting in Deputy Donut is too big for his cottage but might fit in his house."

"The one in Deputy Donut is one of my smaller ones. I don't know if I could paint a canvas that didn't require a ladder to reach the top. And I'm saving for an even taller ladder."

She read Rich's instructions aloud. I turned off the main road and drove down a hill. Lake Fleekom, shimmering in the early evening haze and mostly surrounded by trees, was below us. Even if Rich hadn't said that his house was the first one we would come to on this road, I probably would have guessed that the imposing two-story stone mini-château with lots of roof angles and chimneys was his.

Nina leaned forward. "That house probably has a few rooms with nice, high ceilings. Look how tall the windows are."

Sturdy stone posts supported a wrought-iron fence. Ornate gates at both ends of the circular driveway were closed. They were also almost useless—anyone could drive around the ends of the fence, which didn't extend far beyond the gates. A white party tent was set up near the back of one side of the house, but the grounds sloped down toward the lake, and I could see only the two top peaks of the tent.

But I wasn't going to Rich's home until morning. Tonight, we were exploring his cottage.

Nina read aloud, " 'Turn right.' " She laughed. "Good call. That's the only direction you can go."

I had expected the road to divide into two branches in front of Rich's place, with one branch going left around the lake, and the other going right, but there were only woods to the left. We passed another house, a timber frame one with no fencing in front, and then the road curved left. Not far beyond that, we entered thick woods with boulders approximately the size of commercial fridges and freezers.

Imitating Rich's boisterous voice and attitude, Nina read, " 'At this point, you have to slow down. The pavement ends and the county doesn't keep the road perfectly maintained.' "

We bumped along a gravel road for a half mile before we came to a clearing beside the lake. I read the sign aloud, LAKE FLEEKOM COUNTY PARK. About two dozen cars might fit in the small park's gravel lot. In a grassy area, an open pavilion featured a stone fireplace and sheltered about ten picnic tables and benches. An old-fashioned water pump was nearby, and I caught a glimpse of outhouses tucked near trees surrounding the lawn. Pointing at the gently sloping sand beach, I said with satisfaction, "There's a place to launch my kayak."

Nina offered, "I'll wait in the picnic shelter."

With pretend reluctance, I agreed to drive the rest of the way to Rich's cottage. It couldn't have been far. From what I'd seen, Lake Fleekom was big enough for a kayaker to enjoy exploring, especially if the kayaker liked to nose around every cove, but it wasn't huge. We passed what appeared to be someone's driveway, two ruts with grass between them that disappeared into the woods between the road and the lake. More woods formed a canopy over the road. Rich's cottage was nestled in the forest on the lake side of the road.

The cottage was cute, if a little unexpected, with its white siding, blue shutters, and dormers in the pitched roof. Nina laughed. "We should have guessed it would be a Cape Cod. Unless there's no second floor and those dormers are the fake kind perched on the roof above a cathedral ceiling, the walls can't possibly be tall enough for my paintings."

"Let's go see. He told me the key is for the back door." I pointed toward a charming flagstone path that wound between tall pines toward the right side of the cottage. Unlike the grounds of Rich's house, which almost shouted "estate home," this property was like other northern recreational properties with pines, poplars, and white-barked birches that would provide a shady haven on warm days. The air smelled fresh and crisp. Crows cawed and blue jays scolded. At the rear of the cottage and beyond a treed and rocky slope, the lake reflected the pale tangerine sky. I could barely make out the gleaming party tent on the far shore. Closer, a grayish aluminum canoe was upside down on a weathered wooden dock.

A large screened porch spanned half the back of the cottage. The door to the porch was unlocked. We stepped into a summer retreat where four dining chairs surrounded a table and comfy lawn chairs invited guests to relax.

Nina ran her hand down the side of a glass-fronted wooden cabinet next to the door leading into the cottage. "Look. A custom-made cabinet containing handcrafted canoe paddles." The name ROYALSON had been wood-burned into the shaft of each paddle.

Agreeing that the cabinet and paddles were beautiful, I fit the key into the lock. After jiggling the key and shoving at the door's upper corner, we managed to enter the kitchen. The cottage had that smoky, damp-linoleum smell of closed-up cottages with wood-burning fireplaces. Except for a couple of holes punched or kicked into walls—possibly the damage that Rich had accused Derek of doing—the interior appeared to be well maintained.

Nina burst out laughing. "If Richmond P. Royalson the Third wants Wisconsinites to feel at home renting here, he should consider decorating with the Packers' green, gold, and white, not the red, white, and blue of the New England Patriots."

She took a notebook out of her shoulder bag and started a list. The kitchen was serviceable, but we both would have preferred hardwood or tile to the worn Patriots-red linoleum on the floor. We agreed that new solid-surface counters would be prettier and easier to clean. Rich had said not to worry about cost. Nina added sleek new cabinets to her list. The work triangle was fine, but new appliances and a shiny sink would make cooking more appealing.

In the hallway next to the kitchen, Nina put her hand on a doorknob. "What's in here?" She opened the door. "Oh! A cute little powder room with a huge window. You can sit on the throne and look out at the lake."

The powder room had obviously been redone recently, but the dark red ceiling and navy blue walls above white tiles were a little oppressive. We agreed that the powder room didn't need anything besides paler hues on the walls and ceiling. And maybe white plantation shutters for at least the bottom half of the window.

At the top of the stairs, we found a full bathroom, complete with a tub fitted with a shower. Again, the fixtures and tile were new, but the colors of the walls and ceiling were suitable for a nine-year-old Pats fan.

Two bedrooms, one with a queen-size bed and the other with a pair of twin beds, flanked the bathroom. The ceilings at the front and back of the cottage sloped down to walls that were only about five feet high. Taller people would be able to walk in the centers of the rooms and into the dormers. The hardwood floors needed only refinishing. Bedside rugs would be comfy for toes on cool mornings, and curtains and bedlinens could be modernized.

Nina suggested, "We could recommend a nautical theme and colors."

"Not Packers colors?" I asked.

"If he didn't use anybody's team colors, he could rent to people from all over the country or the world, no matter what team they rooted for or didn't root for." She bent to look at a photo on a dresser. "Who is this woman whose photos are all over the place?"

"She must be Rich's late wife. He admitted that displaying lots of her pictures probably wasn't a great idea for a rental cottage."

"Or for bringing a new girlfriend to stay. This must be the wife that Tom said drowned in Lake Fleekom twenty years ago. None of the pictures look newer than that. They've kind of faded, and the fashions are that old and older." Nina bent forward and studied an arrangement of photos on the bedroom wall. "She was pretty, wasn't she?"

I agreed. "Good bones, like her cottage." In the oldest photos, Rich's late wife was barely out of her teens. She'd been blond and blue-eyed with clear skin and a great figure, and she'd stayed classically lovely as she aged. In the newest photos, she looked about fifty years old, which meant that she and her husband had been close in age. Many of the pictures from approximately the final ten years of her life had been taken in and around this cottage. In one of them she was in an aluminum canoe like the one we'd seen on the dock. She was smiling and waving her paddle at the person taking the photo.

Feeling sorry for the woman who appeared to have loved life but hadn't made it past middle age, I followed Nina downstairs to the combined living and dining room. Nina made a note about refinishing the hardwood floors and retaining the wood-burning fireplace. Like the walls, the mantel was due for a new coat of paint. I pointed at the blank space above it. "That's where he would like one of your paintings."

Nina cocked her head. "I don't know if I could paint anything that would look right in a Cape Cod, unless we gutted the building and did away with the second story. I suspect he would prefer to keep his bedrooms and full bathroom, though. I would. I love this place!"

"Even though your paintings don't suit it?"

"I paint them, but they're for colder, harder, bigger spaces."

"Like art galleries and museums."

"You've got it. I paint the pictures, but I wouldn't necessarily want to live in the sort of place where they'd look best. Cape Cods are about the coziest homes around." She rubbed her palms together. "Let's ask if he'll let us choose new furniture." She pointed at a corner next to one of the two front windows. "It looks like he's already started decluttering."

Books had obviously been removed from a bookshelf and heaped on a colonial-style maple table. "Or something," I muttered. Maybe Derek and his buddies had emptied the shelves.

Nina pushed the books into a neater pile. "Why leave them in a mess when he could have stacked them? Oh!" She pulled four stapled-together packets of paper out from underneath books. She scanned them. "Emily." Her voice was rough, as if a pine cone had become lodged in her throat.

I peeked around her arm. "Wills?"

"Two of them, two copies each. Richmond P. Royalson the Third and a woman named Terri Estable are making each other their sole beneficiaries. Wasn't his date this afternoon named Terri?"

"Yep."

"Fast work. Rich had a date with Cheryl this morning and one with Terri this afternoon."

I told Nina that Rich had explained to Cheryl and her date that he'd reconnected with Terri after he'd arranged his date with Cheryl. "And he also yelled at Derek that Terri was the love of his life."

"I heard that. So, his drowned wife was . . . what?"

"A different love of a different life?" I turned to the last pages of the wills. "How odd. The wills aren't dated and signed."

Nina shoved the wills back where she'd found them. "It's strange, but if he likes my paintings or finds me a buyer or two, I'm not going to complain."

Near the other front window, the writing surface of a slant-front desk was folded up in its closed position. Below that sloping expanse of maple, one corner of a small maroon book stuck out of the top drawer, preventing the drawer from closing. I opened the drawer, pulled out the book, and was about to put it back neatly. A slightly yellowed last will and testament was underneath where the book had been.

I called to Nina. Together, we paged through the will. It was nineteen years old, probably signed and dated shortly after Rich's wife's death. The beneficiaries were Richmond P. Royalson Junior and Alma Ruth Royalson. "Rich's father," I concluded. "And his mother? Or his sister?"

I put the will where I'd found it. The maroon book was a hard-bound notebook filled with blue-lined white pages. One word was printed in heavy black marker on the first page. RENTALS.

I flipped toward the back of the book and found the most recent entries, also printed in heavy black marker. I summarized, "A man named Derek Bengsen rented the cottage starting the Saturday before last, and he and his friends were kicked out on Thursday, five days into their week, like the Derek who came into Deputy Donut claimed."

"Does it mention Terri?"

"No, but this must be the same Derek who accused her of wanting him to rent this place and encouraging him to throw a party here so she could get Rich to rescue her."

Nina added, "And feel sorry for her, reconnect with her, and discover that she was the love of his life."

Rich's estimate of the damages caused by the partyers included a hefty amount of lost rental income while the cottage was being cleaned and repaired. Derek Bengsen's address was near my friend Samantha Andersen's town house. I closed the book, laid it on top of the old will, and closed the drawer.

Nina looked up at splatters on the ceiling. "I wonder if Derek and his buddies did that, along with the holes in the kitchen walls."

"Probably, or Rich would have had it cleaned and repaired before they came."

Nina planted her fists on her hips. "Maybe. Some landlords charge renters for damage that was already there. If renters don't point out the damage when they first encounter the rental property, they let the landlord keep the deposit, you know? Like the amount had already been charged to the renters, so they feel like they've already spent it, although they haven't."

"Where were you when I was trying to figure out who had committed murders in Fallingbrook?"

"In my studio, wrestling with canvases. But I heard about those cases. That's why I wanted to work at Deputy Donut. Well, in addition to the donuts and coffee . . . I knew that whatever happened, I'd be safe around you and Tom."

"Ha. Good luck."

"Safe from everything except calories."

"The way you run around the shop, that will never be a problem." Her donut-eating was like Tom's and mine. We had to taste our creations, but we seldom ate entire donuts. I turned toward the kitchen. "Speaking of large quantities of donuts, I guess we should go look for the platter Rich wants me to bring to his party."

In the kitchen, I opened doors on the left side of the upper cabinets while Nina checked the cabinets on the right.

She yelped, "Ow!"

Chapter 5

I whirled to find out what was wrong.

Nina was rubbing the back of her head.

Above her, a large and very deep cast-iron skillet was swinging from a hook in the ceiling. The skillet's ridiculously long handle had allowed the pan to bump Nina and turn the skillet into a creaking pendulum. It looked about to hit her again or fall off the hook or both.

I yelled, "Watch out!"

She reached up with both hands. Holding the skillet by its pan, she attempted to resettle the handle on its hook, but the handle slipped off. She made a show of being pulled down almost to the linoleum by the skillet. "Ooof. It's heavy."

"Are you okay?"

"Yeah, it barely touched me. It just surprised me. But feel how heavy." She transferred some of its weight to my outstretched hands.

I couldn't help laughing at the ungainly thing. "It's ridiculous."

Biting a lip, she studied it. "Whatever is it for?"

"I don't know. Could that long handle let people use it over an open fire? It's big enough to use as a deep fryer." Maybe I was exaggerating.

Nina got into the spirit. "Pioneer donuts!"

"That's where they got the name 'old-fashioned' donuts."

Nina flashed me a stern look. "Groan. Can you help steady it while I try to put it back where it belongs?"

"Where it *doesn't* belong. That's another thing to tell Rich. Even if he and Terri are too short to run into that thing, his tenants might be as tall as you are. I doubt that anyone could use that skillet in a kitchen, so why keep it in here?"

"*You* might call it a skillet," she said solemnly. "I call it a kill-it."

"An overkill-it."

We managed to hang the unwieldy thing up. Whoever had last cooked with it over an open fire had not cleaned it, unless bashing it into the wall next to the fridge and leaving a soot-rimmed and skillet-shaped hole counted as cleaning. We had to scrub about a ton of soot off our hands. And scour the sink afterward.

Finally, we returned to opening the upper cabinet doors to hunt for the platter Rich wanted us to use for the next morning's Boston cream donuts.

Nina breathed, "Wow." She examined her palms and must have found them spotless. With great care, she lifted a pottery bowl off a stack of platters. The bowl was an abstract of an open clamshell. It was glazed in iridescent pastels—aquas, pinks, blues, and ivories. She set the bowl on the counter. "It's handmade." Gently, she turned it over. "It's a Cindy Westhill, signed and numbered. It's number one of only ten, which makes it even more valuable. It's dated, too, just over twenty years ago. Is she any relationship to you and Tom?"

"She's his wife, my mother-in-law."

Nina blew a whistling breath between pursed lips. "I knew that Tom's wife was an art teacher who helped you paint the tables in Deputy Donut, and they're beautifully done, but I didn't realize that his wife was the potter I learned about in art school."

"And I didn't know that art students studied her work."

Nina raised her head and stared around at the dark blue kitchen cabinets. "You know what?" Without waiting for me to answer, she went on, "The colors that your mother-in-law used for this bowl would be a perfect palette for a seaside New England cottage, even though the cottage is not in New England or anywhere near the sea."

I would have high-fived Nina if I hadn't been afraid of flapping our hands too close to the valuable bowl. "Perfect." My one-word answer reminded me of Rich. I added, "I'll take photos for reference."

She gazed lovingly at the bowl. "For reverence."

With our phones, we photographed the bowl from all angles, both with flash and without, until Nina got what we both thought was a faithful reproduction of the bowl's hues.

We carefully removed plates and platters that the clamshell bowl had been on. The platter next to the bottom was decorated with seaside scenes. "This would fit Rich's party theme," I said, "but he specifically mentioned sailboats. I see only one sail, and it's on the horizon."

The largest platter was still on the shelf. Nina took it out and set it on the counter. "This is probably the one he meant. It has lots of sailboats."

Agreeing, I set the seascape platter on the shelf. We stacked the other platters and plates on it. Nina eased the clamshell bowl onto the top of the pile. "I would display that in my home," she said, "not in a rental cottage where it could be damaged by people like Derek and his friends."

"Maybe Rich won't rent it to people like that again, especially after he renovates. And maybe he and Terri will use the cottage themselves, instead."

Nina closed the cabinet. "That could be fun—going all the way to the other side of the lake to their cottage for a weekend."

"Or for a romantic lunch of donuts fried in a three-ton skillet over an open fire."

She looked out the kitchen window toward the screened porch and the lake. "They could come by canoe. Paddling across the lake is more romantic and probably as quick as driving on that gravel road."

"It did have a few ruts."

"You know what?" Nina asked. Again not waiting for a reply, she said, "Terri might hate the renovations and decorations we suggest."

I groaned. "She'll probably paint everything green and gold."

"Or black," Nina added ominously, "to match the soot stains from someone bashing the skillet into the kitchen wall."

I had to pull hard to close the back door, and then I had to fiddle with the key, but I finally managed to lock the door. I double-checked. It was firmly locked. As we left the porch, I noticed that someone had punched a hole in one of the larger screens closest to the building. Was that another casualty of Derek's party?

I dropped Nina off at her apartment, a combined artist's studio and loft above Klassy Kitchens, a shop selling top-of-the-line kitchen cabinets and fixtures. It was near downtown Fallingbrook and within walking distance of Deputy Donut. I didn't think Nina owned a car. Easing herself out of mine, she said she would look in Klassy Kitchens for ideas for Rich's cottage.

I drove home and went inside. Alec and I had painted the living room walls white.

The furniture and accessories were jewel tones approximating the ruby, sapphire, emerald, and topaz stained glass above the front windows and door.

Dep let me know that I had been gone too long.

I picked her up and hugged her. "On Wednesday, we won't have to work."

"Meow!"

I rested my cheek on her warm fuzzy head. "You're right. I might not be here all day on Wednesday. Brent and I often go kayaking Wednesday afternoons." My handsome detective, Nina had called him. He wasn't mine, but he was handsome, and he was a detective. He had been Alec's best friend and partner at work, first as patrol cops, and later as detectives. Grief had driven Brent and me apart for the first three years after Alec was killed, but during the past three years, Brent and I had returned to being friends who enjoyed meals together. And kayaking. Dep squirmed. I set her gently on the floor. "You're not a boater at heart, are you, Dep?"

Tail up, she bounded toward the back of the house. I followed her through the dining room. It was mostly white because the room's only windows were stained glass above built-in bookcases on both sides of the fireplace.

Alec and I had gone a little overboard on our kitchen. We had installed an oversized fridge and a double-oven range with six burners. The cabinets were pine to go with the woodwork in the rest of the house, and the floor was covered in terra-cotta tiles in shades of pumpkin, smoked paprika, and dark-roast coffee beans.

Dep ate her dinner from a chocolate-brown bowl that Cindy had made, complete with kitty paw prints and Dep's full name, Deputy Donut, in white. I told her, "You're a lucky cat, Dep, with your own personalized Cindy Westhill dishes." Dep's only answer was to tilt her head and crunch delicately on a piece of kibble. I grilled a mozzarella and pesto sandwich and ate it at the granite-topped kitchen island.

After dinner, Dep accompanied me upstairs to my combination office and guest room. The white walls, which Brent had originally helped Alec paint, were still waiting for the perfect artwork. I would find it someday, especially if Nina scaled down the size of future paintings.

At the computer, I found the obituary for Richmond P. Royalson Junior. He had died twelve years after his son changed his will in favor of him and Alma Ruth Royalson. Alma was Rich's mother. She and Rich were the only family members listed as surviving Richmond P. Royalson Junior. Alma's obituary was also easy to find. She had died only a couple of years ago, at the age of ninety-four.

From Rich's rental book, I knew Derek Bengsen's address, so of course I had to look for Terri Estable's. I found a

T. Estable in the town house complex where both Derek and my friend Samantha lived.

I went back downstairs and read in the wing chair in the living room with Dep purring on my lap until bedtime.

When I closed my eyes in my calming white and Wedgwood blue bedroom, I saw the lovely hues of the clamshell bowl that my mother-in-law had made about the time I was eleven and her son, my late husband, Alec, was graduating from college. Although Alec and I both grew up in Fallingbrook, we had not yet met each other.

Alec. I would always miss him.

Picturing the hues that Alec's mom had put together when he was a teenager was comforting, and so was the purring cat nestled behind my knees. Rain pattered on my bedroom windows.

By morning the rain had ended, but the clouds had not completely rolled away. The first thing I said to Tom in Deputy Donut was, "I didn't know that Cindy was famous for her pottery. I knew I liked her work, but . . ."

Nina chimed in, "We discovered one of her bowls in Rich Royalson's cottage last night. It should be locked in a glass case in a museum."

I added, "Alec never told me she was famous."

Tom turned on one of the fryers. "Alec was away at college at the height of her fame. Besides, nothing about our parents is abnormal, while at the same time, everything is. And from the moment Alec began talking, he was determined to be a policeman like his dad." He grinned. "*I* was the star in his eyes. Besides, Cindy did not necessarily want to keep up with all the latest trends in pottery."

Nina measured flour into the bowl of one of our large mixers. "Artists can be stubborn about following our own vision and not caring about the market." Those dark eyes glinted with self-deprecating humor. "Or pretending we don't when all we really want is to become rich and famous."

With three of us working, making an extra three dozen donuts for Rich's birthday party was easy. Nina and I wanted to carve screaming faces into the thick fudge frosting. We restrained ourselves.

The Knitpickers and retired men came in and sat at their regular tables, across from each other and near the front windows. The retired men loved to tease the Knitpickers and vice versa, and Cheryl got a lot of teasing about Rich Royalson. She defended herself by telling them about Rich coming in later with a different woman, and about Steve, who, she said, was a better match. She had to endure even more teasing for dating two different men in one day. She didn't stay as long as usual. Apologizing about needing to go home and change for Rich's party, she left around eleven.

Shortly after eleven thirty, we packed an urn of fresh Guatemalan coffee, Rich's sailboat platter, which we had wrapped in layers of plain newsprint, boxes containing three dozen Boston cream donuts, plus paper napkins and cups, into the Deputy Donut delivery car. The car was a 1950 Ford four-door sedan painted black and white like a police car, complete with our Deputy Donut logo on the white front doors. Instead of a light bar like real police cars had on top, a huge donut with white fiberglass icing was lying flat on the roof. The sprinkles were tiny lights that could be made to sparkle and dance.

Rich was lucky. The sun had come out, and his seventieth birthday was surprisingly warm for the twenty-seventh of October. Driving to Lake Fleekom, I didn't turn on the rooftop donut's sprinkle lights, which wouldn't have shown up in the sunshine. I also didn't broadcast a recorded siren, music, or even my own voice making announcements over the megaphone-shaped loudspeaker mounted in front of the donut. I drove as sedately as one could in a car with an oversized donut on the roof.

Both of Rich's gates were standing open, and the circular driveway was empty. I guessed that Rich's vehicles were inside the three-car garage on the right side of his house. Apparently, no guests had arrived early.

I swooped into the driveway in a grand manner and parked my vintage Ford close to the front steps. It was eleven fifty-four.

In a hurry to deliver the donuts and coffee and return to Deputy Donut to help Tom and Nina, I ran up to the elegant stone porch and pushed a button next to a massive carved wooden door. Inside, chimes boomed, a long and involved tune.

No answer.

I tried the chimes again. Reverberations, echoes, but no people.

Rich was probably in back, either in the tent or gazing out over the lake. I'd find him and ask where he wanted me to put the donuts and coffee. I walked around to the side of the house. The tent was set up on a flat expanse of lawn next to a beach. In its own sheltered valley, Lake Fleekom was only now being touched by the morning's first sunbeams. Fingers of mist twisted upward from the water. On a gray day, the scene might have looked spookily perfect for Halloween week. On this sunny and blue-skied day, it looked romantic and magical, an enchanting backdrop for a party.

The clunk of a paddle against a canoe gunwale carried over the water through the mist. I loved making donuts and sharing them with people, but I wished I had my kayak and could, right that very moment, paddle through that mystical mist.

Stepping over extension cords snaking from the house to the tent, I made my way down the grassy slope. Black and silver balloons, garlands, and birthday wishes hung on the outside of the tent. More of them decorated the inside.

Near the back of the tent, six round tables, each with six chairs, were covered in white tablecloths and set with white napkins, gleaming cutlery, and sparkling glasses. Rectangular tables near the front, also covered with white tablecloths, were ready for last-minute food additions. Little tented cards announced what would go where. One labeled LOBSTER ROLLS was beside a plastic wrap–covered bowl of buns. They were similar to hot dog buns, but sliced through the top instead of the side. Oysters were on ice, ready to be shucked. One slow cooker sent out the delicious smell of baked beans, while another contained equally fragrant seafood chowder. The label near an empty chafing dish said LEMON-BAKED SCROD.

A handwritten guest list was taped to a section of tablecloth hanging over the side of one table. The list was about twenty names long.

I didn't find Rich, but I did see tented cards for Boston cream donuts and for gourmet coffee next to a sheet cake in a large, clear-topped box. The cake was decorated with sailboats. Beside it, a small stand of business cards for Cat's Catering was labeled TAKE ONE. The logo for Cat's Catering was similar to ours, a cat silhouette. Their cat didn't wear any sort of hat, let alone one like the donut-festooned cap on my head.

Maybe Cat's Catering and Deputy Donut could work together sometime. I picked up a card, slipped it into my apron pocket, and turned around to go back to the car for the urn of coffee.

A well-stocked bar was beside the furled-back tent flap to my left.

Richmond P. Royalson the Third was crumpled on the ground between the bar and the tent flap.

Rushing toward him, I nearly tripped over the seascape platter I'd seen in his cottage kitchen. Pieces of it were surrounded by slices of Boston brown bread, the dense bread traditionally steamed in cans. Plastic wrap that must have covered the bread lay nearby.

I dropped to my knees beside Rich and felt his wrist for a pulse. Nothing. I tried his neck. Still nothing. His skin was much too pale and much too cool.

Instantly, I felt guilty for nicknaming him the Boston Screamer.

He was never going to scream again.

But in that moment, I might have screamed, even though, as far as I knew, no one who was capable of hearing was anywhere near me.

Chapter 6

꒰ꜛ꒱

From my kneeling position, I noticed something else on the ground behind the bar—a long-handled cast-iron skillet like the one that Nina and I had rehung the night before in Rich's cottage.

I stood, yanked my phone out of my apron pocket, tapped 911, and gave the dispatcher Rich's address. "There's a man here without apparent vital signs. Please send an ambulance and police officers." I glowered at the skillet. "I think the man might have been attacked." My voice cracked. I wanted to be outside that tent. I wanted to be far away. I wished I had never agreed to bring donuts to Rich's party. I wished I hadn't come. . . .

A paddle banged against a canoe again, maybe farther away than the first time. Even if mist hadn't concealed any boaters who might be out on the lake, I wouldn't be able to identify a boat or a person through the tent's vinyl windows. They blurred and distorted everything.

"The officers and ambulance are on their way," the dispatcher said. "Stay on the line, please."

"Okay." My phone against my ear, I bent to study a piece of paper near Rich's hand. The paper was wrinkled, as if Rich had been clutching it when he fell. A black felt-tip marker lay nearby.

Without touching the paper, I read what I could. It was a

to-do list written in thick marker like the printing in the rental notebook at Rich's cottage. Items were checked off in the same black ink: turn on electricity to tent at ten twenty-five, *check*; send Terri away at ten twenty-eight, *check*; caterers preliminary visit ten thirty to eleven, *check*; donuts and coffee at eleven fifty-five, *blank*; guests begin arriving at noon, *blank*; caterers return with last-minute food by twelve twenty-five, *blank*.

The top of the list was too wadded up to be readable, but I knew not to disturb what I strongly suspected was a crime scene, and I didn't dare touch the list or smooth it to decipher it.

I moved to the tablecloth where the guest list was taped. With the back of one fingernail, I lifted the bottom of the piece of paper. Nothing was written on the other side. Why did the guest list have only about twenty names while there was seating for thirty-six people around tables in the back of the festive tent?

I had clearly heard Rich invite Cheryl and Steve, but their names were not on the list. Had Rich gone around inviting people at the last minute? Maybe he had ordered food and seating for more people than had accepted his invitation, which could have been why he'd been eager to invite Cheryl and Steve although he barely knew Cheryl and had merely been introduced to Steve.

The guest list was in an airy, feminine handwriting that was nothing like the dark printing and check marks on Rich's to-do list and the printing in his rental notebook. The first name on the guest list was Terri Estable. The curlicued top of the *T* swept, tentlike, above the entire length of her name.

Hoping to catch a glimpse of the canoe I thought I'd heard, I eased out of the tent. I kept the phone next to my ear while I walked across the flat lower section of the lawn to Rich's high-tech dock. Setting my sneakered feet down as quietly as I could on the synthetic planks, I made my way to the end of the dock. Ripples tapped at its supports. Out on the lake, thick mist hugged the surface of the water. The air smelled cold and watery. Beyond the cloud-like fog, I could see only the tops of trees around other sides of Lake Fleekom. Mist filmed the neighbor's dock and the tall cedar hedge separating that property from Rich's.

I turned around. Maybe if I stared hard enough to bring the hazy forest beyond the tent into focus, my hearing would sharpen also, and I would be able to distinguish the subtle sounds of a possible attacker slinking away through the underbrush.

A car door slammed. My heart racing and the soles of my sneakers pounding the dock, I ran back to land. The police already?

In a lacy pink dress and shiny black patent heels, Cheryl was mincing down the hilly part of the lawn toward the tent.

I called out, "Stay there!" I hadn't run far, but I was out of breath.

The 911 dispatcher asked, "Are you all right?"

My hand hurt from clutching my phone. "I'm fine. The deceased was throwing a party that was to begin at noon, and a guest has arrived. I'm going to try to keep her and the others away from the deceased."

"Excellent. If there might be an attacker around, don't take risks."

I promised that I wouldn't and went up to meet Cheryl, who had obediently stopped when I told her to and was gazing uncertainly at me. "The party is canceled," I explained.

Those usually benign and grandmotherly blue eyes could be shrewd. "Something terrible has happened, hasn't it, Emily?" She reached out and gave my free hand a consoling squeeze.

I closed my eyes for only as long as it took to inhale. "I can't talk about it, but I need to stay here. Would you mind telling anyone else who arrives that the party is canceled, and they should leave? That doesn't include first responders but does include any caterers who might arrive. Tell the caterers not to unload anything."

"I'll do my best." She was still holding my hand. "You take care, Emily."

I thanked her. We let go of each other, and she started up the hill toward Rich's driveway.

Feeling sorry for myself because I couldn't have kept the empathetic woman with me for company, I returned to the doorway of the tent and stared at the beautiful setup for a seventieth birthday party that would never happen. The inside of the tent was silent except for occasional burbles from the slow cooker of Boston baked beans.

Earlier, those beans had smelled delicious. They no longer did.

"Need a hand?" someone asked behind me. I whipped around. It was Cheryl's date, Steve. Like Cheryl, he was dressed for an afternoon garden party. He was wearing new-looking loafers, black slacks, and a dark burgundy dress shirt.

Doing my best to dissuade him from coming closer, I walked a few steps away from the tent's entryway. "Can you help Cheryl?" She was up on the driveway beside the driver's window of a white van with the Cat's Catering logo on its side. She shook her head. More cars pulled into the circular driveway, and I thought I heard a motorcycle. Its engine revved and went quiet. "She looks a little frantic up there," I said to Steve. "She's trying to send the caterers away and tell other people that the party is canceled."

"Why?"

I didn't know how much Cheryl had told him about what I'd said, so I gave him only a short answer. "I'll explain later."

"Okay." He turned around and sauntered up the hill.

Wearing dirty jeans and a faded black T-shirt, Terri's ex-boyfriend, Derek, barreled toward him. Steve extended both arms as if to stop him, but Derek dodged around him and charged toward me.

Bracing myself for an attack, I considered diving into the

tent and fending Derek off with that long-handled cast-iron skillet, which if I was correct, had already been used as a weapon that day. But it was part of the crime scene and should not be disturbed. Besides, it was too heavy for me to fling around with anything resembling precision. I would probably end up twirling myself and the skillet across the beach and into the lake.

Derek tossed a lock of blond hair off his forehead. "What's going on?"

"Don't come any closer," I warned with all the authority of a short person wearing a police hat with a donut attached to the front.

The voice in my ear said, "The police are almost there."

"The party's canceled," I said.

Derek's eyes were half covered by his upper lids. "What party?"

From near the lake behind me, a woman demanded, "What are you doing here, Derek? You're not invited. Go away." I recognized Terri's shrill tones and turned around.

Wearing a red life jacket over a red fleece hoodie, jeans, knee-high rubber boots, and binoculars on a strap around her neck, Terri was striding toward us and away from a red canoe pulled up on the shore next to Rich's dock. The canoe hadn't been there before I talked to Cheryl. Terri must have beached it almost silently.

Derek held his palms out toward us. "I'm leaving." His hands were mostly clean, but black lined the creases. The stains looked a lot like the soot that Nina and I had scrubbed off our hands the night before after doing battle with the long-handled skillet in Rich's cottage.

I was sure that the police would want to talk to Derek. "Wait in your car," I suggested. "Someone will explain."

He sneered. "I don't have a car. And I don't know what's going on here, but I'm not getting involved." He stomped up the hill toward the driveway. The heels of his boots were worn down at the sides.

Terri turned to me. Her cheeks were flushed, and her lips were thin with anger. "What are you doing here?"

I guessed she didn't know that Rich had ordered donuts and coffee from me. "I . . . Rich asked for our coffee and Boston cream donuts."

She glared at me but didn't say anything. Had her canoe paddle been the one I'd heard banging against a gunwale a couple of times since I arrived? She could have clobbered her long-lost and suddenly new boyfriend with the skillet, the plate of Boston brown bread, or her paddle, and canoed away quickly and noisily. After she was sure that someone else would be here and would therefore appear guilty, she could have slipped quietly back to shore and acted innocent.

I wasn't certain, but I thought that the canoe I'd heard being bumped with a paddle was aluminum. Terri's canoe looked like fiberglass with wooden gunwales.

I knew it wasn't nice to question her before she learned the truth about Rich, but I wasn't sure that what had happened to him would upset her. Maybe she already knew. I didn't ask why she went canoeing in huge rubber boots. According to Tom, heavy boots could have been at least part of the reason Rich's late wife drowned in this lake. Instead, I asked her, "Were there other boats on the lake?"

"I heard some boats while I was out there, but it's too foggy to see more than a few feet away, and I don't know who else might have been paddling around." She touched her binoculars. "I go birding in my canoe whenever I can, but today, when I had my first chance to canoe on Lake Fleekom since Derek got us kicked out of the cottage we rented, it was too foggy to see many birds. It was cold, too."

We rented? According to Derek and the rental records that Nina and I had found in the cottage, Derek was the renter, in name at least. Terri wrapped her arms around the red life jacket. It almost perfectly matched her canoe. She continued shivering.

I wasn't cold, but I was close to trembling, too, from shock.

Above us near the driveway, a motorcycle roared away.

I asked Terri, "How many homes and cottages are on this lake?" I tried to sound casually friendly and conversational despite the phone plastered to my ear.

"Ten or twelve, I guess, from what I could see before Derek and his friends got us kicked out, plus there's a county park with a beach where people launch rowboats and canoes. This lake's too small for motorboats." Her gaze darted from me to the tent to the back of Rich's house to the driveway. "Do you know where Rich is? He sent me away so he could surprise me after the caterers arranged everything inside the tent." She pointed up toward the driveway. "They're leaving, so they must be done." She looked down at her rubber boots. Their toes glistened with water. "I suppose I should go change, but I'm sure he won't mind if I just peek into the tent first."

Whether she cared about Rich or not, I didn't want her to see him or interfere with the apparent crime scene. Feeling terrible about him and also about keeping his death a secret from her, I blocked her from going closer to the tent. "The party can't go on."

"What?" she screeched. "Why not?"

A man pushed through the hedge between Rich's yard and the neighbor's. How did police keep crime scenes pristine before backup arrived? People were coming from everywhere, even out of the bushes. The man strode across Rich's lush lawn to us. He was tall and muscular. His paint-stained work pants and sweatshirt made me guess that he was not dressed for Rich's party. Maybe, like Terri, he had not yet changed. Judging by the gray in his hair and the wrinkles in his neck, he was about Rich's age.

"What's wrong, Terri?" he asked. His brown eyes looked concerned. A small spray of cedar stuck out of his hair above one ear.

Terri reached up, pulled the debris out of his hair, and dropped it on the lawn. It could have looked like an intimate gesture if she hadn't seemed too distracted to notice what she was doing. "This caterer says the party can't go on." Maybe she was also too distracted to realize that the intimacy of her gesture could have given away that she was close to Rich's neighbor after only recently reconnecting with Rich.

And perhaps as much as two hours after Rich might have been attacked . . .

I guessed that the police would want to talk to these two, especially Terri, and they'd also want to be the ones to inform her of Rich's death so they could gauge her reaction. I pointed up the hill at a cozy grouping of lawn chairs near a deck spanning the rear of Rich's house. "You two could sit up there until everything's sorted out."

Like Terri's ex-boyfriend, the neighbor looked strong enough to fatally wield that skillet. The blue, yellow, and white splotches on his outfit were probably paint, but what about the red and brown ones? I didn't want to stare at them but couldn't help it. He held a hand out toward Terri, "I'll wait with you, Terri." Maybe he knew what was in the innocent-looking party tent and why I didn't want Terri to see it.

Terri ran her hands through her pixie-cut brown hair. She barely seemed to hear either of us. "Rich said I should put my canoe away when I got back. I'll do that."

I knew I should try to stop her, but the sound of sirens, still far away, distracted me. Unless the hills and valleys around Lake Fleekom were throwing echoes in strange directions, the sirens were coming toward us.

Terri shrieked, "Is there a fire?" She glanced up toward Rich's house as if expecting flames to spew out of upper story windows. Because the house was set into the hill, there were three floors in back. The neighbor put his arm around her. She sagged against him for a second, then detached herself and marched down to her canoe. She lifted it to her shoulders and carried it above her head up the hill. The neighbor retrieved her paddle from the beach and followed her to the back of the house. She lowered the canoe and slid it underneath the deck. Although she was only about my size, she made it all look easy. I was certain her canoe weighed more than my kayak, which I tended to carry with both hands in front of me like the novice I was.

Rich's neighbor leaned the paddle against a pillar supporting the deck, led Terri to the lawn chairs, and helped her sit in one. She was still wearing her life jacket and binoculars. The neighbor eased down into a chair next to hers and stared down toward the tent. I had an uncomfortable feeling that he was watching my every move in an assessing and judgmental way.

Two police cars raced down the hill and tore into the driveway. I told the 911 dispatcher that first responders had arrived. She let me disconnect.

Finally, I could use my phone's camera. I ran into the tent, quickly snapped pictures of the guest list and the to-do list, and ran out again.

Two of the four officers emerging from squad cars were close friends of mine, Misty Ossler and Hooligan Houlihan. Beckoning, I called to them. They waved and trotted down the grassy slope toward me. The other two officers went out of my sight, toward the front door of Rich's mansion.

I stared up at the tall stone structure. Was anyone inside it? Did Rich have servants? Family?

Terri was standing, the back of her hand against her mouth. The neighbor had stood, too, and again had his arm around Terri. He was glaring at me as if he'd watched me dash into and out of the tent and had figured out that something was very wrong. Maybe the neighbor had attempted to kill Rich, was afraid he hadn't succeeded, and didn't want me or anyone else reviving him.

I wished that reviving Rich were possible.

Misty grasped my arm. "What's up?"

I babbled, "I brought donuts to Rich Royalson's birthday party and found him lying inside the tent. I think he's dead,

and it looks like he could have been attacked with a skillet."
I pointed. "He's behind that flap, between it and the bar."

A bit taller than her auburn-haired, freckle-faced patrol
partner, Misty was also senior to him in the police department. She preceded him into the tent.

An ambulance screeched into the driveway. Samantha
jumped out of the driver's seat. I called to her, and she ran
down the hill while her partner, a man I didn't know, opened
the back of the ambulance.

I pointed to the tent doorway. "Misty and Hooligan are in
there with him. I think we're all too late."

Samantha gave me a concerned look, patted my arm, and
went into the tent.

I glanced at Terri again to see if she showed any signs of
recognizing Samantha, who, I thought, lived near her.

I couldn't tell if she recognized Samantha, but she probably recognized Samantha's EMT uniform, and she and Rich's
neighbor had to have recognized Misty and Hooligan's uniforms. Terri cradled her cheeks in her hands. She looked
about to scream.

Samantha's partner wheeled a gear-covered stretcher down
to the tent. He left the stretcher outside and carried gear inside.

I heard Misty radio headquarters and request a detective.

She didn't need to. An unmarked police car pulled up behind the marked cruisers. A tall and handsome man wearing
a dark gray suit unfolded himself from the driver's seat.

Brent Fyne, the man Nina called my handsome detective.

Chapter 7

Although the most devastating night of my life had been six years before, again seeing Brent in an emergency situation brought it back to me in a painful flash.

That evening I had traded shifts with a recently trained dispatcher so that I could have dinner with out-of-town friends. While we were at the restaurant, Alec and Brent were shot. If only I'd been at work, maybe I could have arranged for help to arrive sooner for my fallen husband. Brent had told me that, despite his own injured arm, he had radioed for help even before a bystander called 911, and that I shouldn't blame myself. I wasn't sure I could help letting guilt eat away at me. Brent also blamed himself and mourned the loss of his best friend. Our rational selves knew that neither of us could have prevented Alec's death. Our emotional selves hurt.

In the half second I was remembering that, I was running up to the hill toward him. His deep green tie and unbuttoned jacket flapping, he strode down the slope. There was no wind, but his light brown hair looked windblown, as if he'd run out of the police station and jumped into his unmarked police car in a hurry. Usually the responding police officer made the decision that a detective was needed, as Misty had, but by that time, Brent had been pulling into Rich's driveway.

He grasped my upper arms, shot a glance toward the mist-covered lake, and murmured, "I'd rather be kayaking."

Despite the grim tightness of his lips and chin, those gray eyes were comforting. "Me, too."

But we couldn't wander off together into that magical mist. Brent let me go and took out his notebook. "You called this in, Em?" Had he rushed out here because he knew that I was the one who had called about a deceased person?

His concern nearly unhinged me. "Yes, I found Rich." My voice shook. "His skin was already cold."

"Who else was here?"

"No one that I know of, but someone was here before me, his attacker. Also several people showed up so quickly that they had to have been nearby when I discovered him. He's Richmond P. Royalson the Third."

Brent raised one eyebrow in question.

I summarized how I'd met Rich Royalson and why I was at his lakeside home on that sunny October Tuesday instead of in Deputy Donut. I described the people who had arrived soon after I did. "Cheryl, the Deputy Donut customer who arranged the date with Rich at Deputy Donut, and her date, Steve, are still in the driveway." Pointing up at the deck at the back of Rich's house, I explained Terri's previous and new-found relationship to Rich. "The man hovering with her near the lawn chairs came from the next yard, so I guess he's Rich's neighbor. And Terri's ex-boyfriend Derek showed up just before Terri did, but he left. On a motorcycle, I think." I told Brent about the quarrel that Derek had initiated in Deputy Donut and about the threats he'd made against both Rich and Terri. "He told them they'd be sorry for the way they treated him. And just now, Derek had dirt in the creases of his palms, as if he'd handled something like a sooty skillet." I described the skillet I'd seen beside Rich's body. "It or one like it was hanging in his cottage last night." I explained why Nina and I had explored Rich's cottage.

"When did you leave Deputy Donut this morning, and when did you arrive here?"

"I must have left there a little after eleven forty. I was due here at eleven fifty-five, and parked my car at eleven fifty-four. I found Rich a minute or two after that." Brent would be able to pinpoint the exact second that I had called 911.

Brent gave my shoulder a quick, encouraging squeeze. "Stay here." He took out his phone, tapped the screen, waited, and then said into his phone, "Tom? It's Brent. Emily's fine, but she's a witness to a possible crime, and we're going to talk to her for a while. She should be free to return to Deputy Donut in an hour or so. Can you tell me when she left there this morning?" Brent gave me a friendly nod. "Can anyone else confirm that? Let me talk to Nina, then." He asked Nina the same question. "About eleven forty-five? Great. Thanks."

Brent disconnected and said, "So . . . about the earliest you and the hundred and ten horses under your hood could have gotten here would have been eleven fifty-five."

I folded my arms. "Those horses got me here at eleven fifty-*four*."

"Speeder." He held out his hand. "Did his skin feel colder than mine does right now?"

I rested my fingers on the back of Brent's hand for a second. "Definitely. And he was pale."

He slanted a sad look down at me. "I don't suspect you."

"Thanks," I managed. "I didn't think you did."

He called headquarters and asked them to send an officer to Deputy Donut to take Tom's and Nina's official statements confirming when I'd left work.

While he was talking, Samantha and her partner pushed the wheeled stretcher up the hill. Nothing was on it besides equipment. Samantha called to me, "See you Thursday, Emily!"

"Okay." At the moment, I didn't feel much like partying, and Samantha, Misty, Hooligan, and Brent probably didn't, either. Maybe by Thursday evening, we would feel more like ourselves. Our fire chief, Scott Ritsorf, was also invited to Samantha's potluck. The six of us always had a good time together. Thursday evening, with Rich's death still on the minds of most of us, we might lean on one another emotionally more than usual.

Brent disconnected and asked me, "Can you wait for me in your car? I'll join you as soon as I can."

"Okay."

Hooligan came out of the tent. Brent went the rest of the way down the hill to him, and they talked in low voices. Hooligan climbed toward Terri and the man I guessed was Rich's neighbor. Brent joined Misty inside the tent. The ambulance chugged up the hill, away from Lake Fleekom and the patient the EMTs weren't able to revive.

I trudged up to the donut car. The two police officers who had arrived when Misty and Hooligan did were chatting with Rich's arriving guests, probably taking names, addresses, and phone numbers before sending them away. Both officers were occasional patrons at Deputy Donut. Cheryl and Steve were already gone. I told one of the officers that Brent had asked me to wait for him in my car.

He glanced from my donut hat to my donut car, nodded, and waved the next car forward.

I climbed into the donut car's driver's seat and fiddled with the keys in the ignition. The car smelled like coffee and the chocolate and vanilla in the Boston cream donuts. Ordinarily I loved those aromas. I cranked down the driver's window and then flung myself across the wide bench seat to reach the handle for the passenger window. I rolled that window down, too, and opened the little vent on my side.

About a half hour later, Brent slipped into the passenger seat. "Can you finish telling me all about it, Em?"

"The ambulance left without him. He's dead, right?"

He ran his fingers through the hair above his forehead. "He has been for, I'm guessing, since before you left Deputy Donut. The medical examiner is on his way."

I described finding Rich and told Brent I hadn't been able to see the boat or boats I'd heard on the mist-covered lake.

"Tom said that Rich's wife drowned out there about twenty years ago."

"That case was before I joined the Fallingbrook Police Department, but I heard about it. You and I definitely need to go kayaking on Lake Fleekom."

"But not when it's slushy." I gave Brent every detail I remembered of Rich's two dates in Deputy Donut, of the quarrel between Derek and Rich, and of Derek's threats. I described the unsigned and undated wills in Rich's cottage; the previous will made out to Rich's parents, both of whom had since died; the notebook recording rentals in the desk drawer where I'd found Derek's last name, Bengsen; and the sooty gash in the kitchen wall. "Another thing we saw in Rich's cottage kitchen, besides the skillet that made that gash, was a platter like the one that is now in pieces near his body. That platter might have been the murder weapon, if there was one, but I'm guessing that the skillet would have done more damage."

Brent gave me a terse nod. "You didn't see the side of his head that was on the ground?"

"No."

"I'm betting on the skillet, also, but the postmortem will tell me more. The platter could have been broken by accident or in a fight."

Picturing Rich attempting to defend himself with one of his prize platters and some sliced Boston brown bread, I was overwhelmed by sadness for the man and his senseless death. I gave Brent the key and directions to Rich's cottage. "The donuts and coffee he ordered for the party are still in the rear seat. Want some?"

"A coffee would be great."

We got out. The two officers were standing at the ends of the circular driveway, in front of the open gates. A minivan was coming down the hill.

I opened the donut car's back door, moved the coffee urn to the edge of the seat, filled a paper cup, and handed it to Brent. While he sipped, I guessed, "Maybe there was another beneficiary in the years since Rich's mother died. Maybe Rich was about to change his will to the woman I pointed out to you earlier beside Rich's back deck, Terri Estable. Maybe his current beneficiary, whoever it is, couldn't let that happen." I waved my hand toward the stone building towering over us. "Rich seems to have been wealthy. He told me that he'd done well with what he called quality investments."

"We'll find out if a will was filed for him since his mother died. Hooligan got a statement from Terri Estable, but we need to have a more thorough discussion with her. From what you saw, it sounds like Royalson changed his will in a big hurry after he reconnected with the alleged love of his life. Could she and her ex-boyfriend, the one with the possibly sooty hands, have been only pretending to quarrel?"

"If so, they're good actors, but yes. However, if they planned it all, including murdering Rich, Derek was stupid to come to Deputy Donut first and threaten Rich and Terri."

"Criminals can do strange things. Did you and Nina have a good look inside the deceased's cottage last night?"

"We went into all of the rooms, but we didn't examine every nook and cranny. The skillet we saw was hanging in the kitchen, and a platter like the broken one was in a cabinet above the counter near that skillet, to the right of the sink."

"I'd like you to take another look around that cottage with me. Can you meet me there after you're done at Deputy Donut tonight?"

"Sure."

"Nina, too, if she can make it?"

"I'll ask her, but I'm sure she can. The two of us scheduled a meeting with Rich in his cottage this evening to discuss our suggestions for his renovation and redecorating project." I swallowed to dislodge another lump in my throat. Rich had been annoying at times, but he had obviously enjoyed his life, and although he had just turned seventy, he might have enjoyed many more years.

Brent explained, "I'd like you to check for the skillet, the platter, and for anything that looks different from last night. Also, I'd like you to show me the wills and the rental records."

"Okay." I pointed at the coffee urn. "Would the investigators like the coffee and donuts I brought for Rich's party?"

"We'd all like that. I'll see that you get the urn back."

He carried the urn to his cruiser while I brought the boxes of donuts and the bags of cups, napkins, creamers, sugar packets, and stir sticks. He put it all into the cruiser's rear seat.

I told him, "Rich's platter, the one I was supposed to arrange the donuts on, is also in my car. Would you like that?"

"I'll get it from you later. I might have a DCI agent with me this evening." For serious crimes, the Fallingbrook police called in the Wisconsin Division of Criminal Investigation. DCI detectives were called agents, and when they helped in an investigation, they took over and directed it.

I was certain that Brent was perfectly capable of running the investigation. "Do you think your chief will call them in this soon?" Other times, it had taken a couple of days.

"I'm going to ask for them right away."

"Are you going to put in the request yourself?"

"Yes, because you called it in, and you were the first on the scene."

I felt my face blaze. Brent and I weren't dating each other, but we'd probably been seen together, especially on nearby lakes and rivers in our kayaks and in restaurants before and after our watery adventures. We were friends, close ones, but only friends.

With his free hand, he touched my shoulder. "Don't worry. You didn't do anything wrong. You did everything right. See you tonight at Royalson's cottage." He headed down the hill toward the tent and his investigation.

I climbed into the donut car, waved at the police officer at the gate, and started back toward downtown Fallingbrook and Deputy Donut.

Brent had said I'd done everything right, but I hadn't. I'd gone back into the tent and had taken pictures of the guest list and the to-do list. There was nothing wrong with that, but Rich's neighbor had been watching, and he'd looked disapproving.

And I hadn't even thought of telling Brent that I'd taken those pictures.

Chapter 8

I told myself not to worry about those two quick snapshots. I seldom showed Brent my photos.

But my photos were not usually associated with crimes or possible crimes.

I'd merely wanted a better look at the to-do and guest lists without touching them. Besides, I hadn't needed to tell Brent about my photos. He would examine those lists himself.

Could this new investigation challenge Brent's and my friendship? I gripped the old steering wheel tightly. In addition to eating together and kayaking together, we occasionally showed each other affection in ways that were a little warmer than when Alec was alive. I liked Brent a lot, but Brent had been Alec's best friend. That complicated our relationship and prevented us from becoming as close as we might have been if Alec had never existed.

But Alec had existed, and I would always love and miss him.

I parked the old Ford in the lot behind Deputy Donut and went inside. For our lunch guests, Tom had battered and deep-fried green pepper rings plus bocconcini with fresh basil. I snacked on cheese and bits of pepper while I described the day's tragedy to Nina and Tom.

Nina readily agreed to the change of plans. "I'll be glad to help the police, but I'm sorry about Rich and that he's not going to see his place the way we envisioned it. He was kind of funny, the way he talked, even if he didn't know he was funny and wasn't trying to be funny."

I agreed. "He meant well, in his occasionally insulting way. And I'm sorry that he's not going to buy paintings from you or introduce you to influential people in the art world."

"I wasn't counting on any of that." She sounded a little wistful. "I figured that was mostly bluster." I wanted her to succeed in making a career of art, even if it meant she would no longer work with us at Deputy Donut. She was incredibly easy to get along with, as was our summer help, Jocelyn, who was now in college.

Jocelyn was coming home for Halloween weekend and was scheduled to help us on Saturday and Sunday. She hadn't been home since late August. The previous summer, she and I had shared unexpected adventures after a murder. We had also helped solve the murder. The bond between us was strong, and I could hardly wait to see the enthusiastic twenty-year-old gymnast.

Around three thirty, a man came into Deputy Donut. He didn't fit into any of our usual categories of customers. Our café attracted a lot of people besides our regulars and first re-sponders. During summers, tourists often came into Deputy Donut. When the leaves were in their full glory in the au-tumn, we had a steady stream of leaf peepers. Now that most of the leaves had fallen, we could expect hunters. Winter would bring people who enjoyed all sorts of winter sports.

The newcomer's suit appeared to have been tailored to fit his tall and heavily muscled body. His hair was dark. His nose was thin and pointed, and the skin of his closely shaven face looked like it had been pulled too tight. I guessed he was in his fifties. I asked what he'd like.

"Coffee."

The suit made me wonder if he was a detective. Maybe Brent had already succeeded in getting a DCI agent to Falling-brook. "We have a medium-roast Colombian, and today's special is a lively roast from Ecuador with fruity overtones."

"The latter." One of his eyelids kept closing and opening as if he were winking.

I couldn't see the bulge of a shoulder holster under his jacket. "Would you like to try one of our donuts? We have specials for Halloween week."

He waved his hand as if he would never allow donuts past his pale, narrow lips. I turned toward the kitchen. Dep was standing on the back of the couch in the office. She had made herself huge and was twitching her puffed-up tail and staring straight at the newcomer.

I stopped in front of her window, bent to put my face close to hers, and gave her a super-frowny look through the glass. She merely arched her back higher. Hoping she wouldn't make our new customer uncomfortable, I went into the kitchen for his coffee.

Nina whispered, "Who's the mystery man?"

"I don't know. Maybe a detective."

"Or a murderer," she said darkly. "Be careful."

I sidled up to Tom, who was mixing dough for the next day. "Do you recognize that man who just came in, the one in the tailored gray suit? Is he a detective?"

Tom glanced toward the man. "I don't know every detective in the state of Wisconsin."

"Smarty-pants." I poured a mug of coffee and turned around.

The man was not at the table where I'd left him. At first I thought that Dep must have scared him out of the shop. Then I saw him on the opposite side of the dining room, closer to the front. He was staring straight ahead.

Heading toward his table, I couldn't see any gun-holster bulges underneath the ankles of his neatly pressed pants. His shoes looked new and expensive.

I set the mug in front of him. Maybe Cheryl had found another man through the dating site. I might as well learn as much as I could. "I haven't seen you before," I prompted. "Are you new to Fallingbrook?"

He continued staring straight ahead. "No."

It was obvious that he didn't want to be drawn into a conversation, and I didn't want him to think that customers in Deputy Donut had to be chatty if they didn't feel like it. Besides, his careful lack of expression was so cold that I felt like ice crystals were forming along my spine.

I took orders from regulars and served them.

The mystery man didn't stay long. He went outside and turned south, walking quickly. If he'd been waiting for a date, it couldn't have been Cheryl. She was too reliable and kind to stand anyone up. He had left half his coffee behind, along with a lavish amount of cash. He hadn't waited for a bill.

In the kitchen, Nina confided, "He was staring at my painting. Maybe he's the art collector that Rich said he'd called."

I glanced toward the two different tables where the man had sat. "That could be it. He left one seat that might have been too close to your painting and went to one where he could get a view of it from across the room."

She stuck her lower lip out. "And he hated it so much that he ran out, never to return."

I held up one index finger. "He was hurrying, but he was walking south. Toward the Craft Croft."

"And toward the bookstore and a dozen other shops. Or probably toward his car, so he could get as far from my painting as fast as he could."

We closed the shop at our usual time and tidied for the Jolly Cops Cleaning Crew, who came in every night and did the heavy cleaning and replenished the oil in the deep fryers. Tom drove home to Cindy.

Nina had some calls to make and stayed in the dining area. I went into the office and sat on the couch. With Dep purring on my lap, I looked at the photos I'd taken in Rich's party tent. Because of the feminine handwriting, I suspected that Terri had written the guest list and had put her name first.

Derek Bengsen wasn't on the list, and Terri had told Derek that he hadn't been invited. My guess that about twenty names were on the list was close. There were twenty-two.

Why had Derek come to the party even though he hadn't been invited? Had he been at Rich's earlier that morning, carrying out his threat to make Rich sorry, and did he return to attack Terri, but I got in the way?

The to-do list didn't tell me a lot except that Rich appeared to have checked off the caterers' first delivery before he was attacked. According to the list, Rich had supposedly sent Terri away two minutes before the caterers had been due to arrive. Was Terri right that he had sent her away so that the arrangement in the tent would surprise her? Maybe he'd had another reason, like an expected visitor he didn't want her to know about.

Had that person killed him?

On his to-do list, Rich had given a range of time for the caterers' first visit of the day, ten thirty to eleven. Did that mean that he had expected them to arrive between those times or that they were supposed to arrive at ten thirty and leave at eleven? Either way, he had checked it off. A Cat's Catering employee might have been the last person to see him alive.

I'd seen the Cat's Catering van after it returned as scheduled, before twelve twenty-five. Returning to the scene made sense even if the caterer had killed Rich and guessed correctly that the party would be canceled. In order not to appear guilty, the caterer would have needed to pretend Rich's death was a surprise.

Despite those conjectures, I couldn't help picturing Derek, his rage when he was in Deputy Donut, and his obvious contempt for Terri when she confronted him after Rich's murder. And the soot in the creases of his palms . . .

Nina came into the office. We put Dep into her cat carrier. Dep had a lot to say about that indignity, none of it repeatable in polite company. We took the vociferous cat out through the back door leading from the office to the parking lot and slid Dep's carrier into the rear of the donut car beside Rich's carefully wrapped platter. Dep continued her disgruntled comments while I drove home and parked in my driveway next to my kayak-topped car.

We let Dep out of her carrier in the living room, said goodbye to her, switched the platter to the cramped rear seat of my small red sports car, and got into the front seats.

Out at Lake Fleekom, the mist was gone, but the sun had dipped below the trees. If mist rose now, would it be pinkish in the sunset's afterglow?

Rich's house was surrounded by police crime scene tape. Investigators' vehicles were parked haphazardly in the circular driveway and the straight extension that led to Rich's three-car garage.

We kept going, along the road as it curved right and passed the neighbor's house. No one was in sight. The road made a curve to the left and entered the forest. We reached the unpaved section and bumped along the lakeside road past the county park and the two-rut lane winding into the woods. Trees loomed over the road the rest of the way to Rich's cottage.

Two unmarked cruisers were parked outside it.

Chapter 9

❦

I removed Rich's wrapped sailboat platter from the rear seat.

Brent came around the corner from the side of the cottage. Behind him, a tall and slender woman confidently placed the stiletto heels of her boots on the pathway's uneven flagstones. Her sleek silver bob and teal wool suit with its flared, knee-length skirt screamed professional success. I guessed she was close to Brent's age, midforties. She was stunning, partly because of the premature silver, partly because of the perfect figure, and partly because of the authority in her posture and the way she moved. Brent introduced her as DCI agent Detective Gartborg. Unless the DCI had sent more than one detective, which they hadn't done other times, that afternoon's mystery man had not been a DCI agent.

Detective Gartborg said hello, didn't offer to shake our hands, and didn't tell us her first name.

She stared at the wrapped platter in my hands. "What do you have there, Emily?" Her voice was deep and musical.

"A platter that Rich Royalson asked me to bring to his party earlier today, but it turned out he didn't need it." That was an understatement. . . .

The woman held one hand up like a cop stopping traffic. "You're not to bring things into the scene."

Brent held out his hands. "I told her to bring it tonight."

That was not exactly how he'd worded it. He'd only said he'd get it from me later.

Giving it to him, I hoped that in the shadowy woods no one saw my blush. I was a detective's widow who spent lots of time around police officers and former police officers. I knew that civilians couldn't bring anything into a crime scene during an investigation. It didn't matter that Nina and I had taken the platter from the cottage only the night before, not that we could prove it. What mattered was that Rich's death was being treated as suspicious. Even though he hadn't died at his cottage, the skillet might have come from inside it. And Nina and I had seen those wills.

Brent carried the wrapped platter to one of the cruisers and placed it in the trunk.

Detective Gartborg gave Nina and me a stern look. "We have to establish some guidelines here. You two can come into the scene, but you are not to touch anything, remove anything, or leave anything behind."

I nodded.

Nina did, too. "We won't."

Brent returned to the three of us waiting awkwardly for him. "Come around to the back," he said. "We didn't need the key you gave me, Emily. The back door was standing open."

"We closed it last night," Nina told him. "I remember because Emily had trouble locking it."

Gartborg's heels clacked on the flagstones, and I pictured Rich and his late wife deciding where to set each stone. They must have loved this cottage and these pine-scented woods sloping down to the lake.

Gartborg turned around and asked me, "Are you sure you locked it?"

"Yes. I double-checked. It sticks, but it was locked." The lake was mirror smooth, reflecting the sky, which had faded to apricot.

Near the powder room window, Brent pointed at the ground. "Be careful. There's broken glass." Sharp pieces of glass littered the mossy dirt.

"That glass wasn't there last night," Nina said.

I added, "And the powder room window was intact." That explained why the door was open. Someone must have broken the window and climbed into the powder room, but when it was time to leave, he or she unlocked the back door from the inside and went out that way, which would have been easier and safer than scraping past pieces of glass sticking out of the window frame, especially if they were carrying that huge skillet. And they would have been in too much of a hurry to close the back door behind them.

Gartborg asked, "How do you know it's a powder room?"

Nina stared at her.

I answered, "I remember the layout. And I can see the top of the toilet tank from here." The window was, as Nina and I had noticed the night before, surprisingly large and low for a bathroom window.

Gartborg pointed the toe of one boot at a stone. "What about this stone, was it here?" It was rounded, slightly larger than my fist would be if I made one. Neither Nina nor I remembered seeing the stone, and neither of us could say for certain that it hadn't been there, either, but some of the other stones close to the cottage's foundation were partially buried and moss covered. This one was bare, as if it had been carried up from the beach.

Studying the ground near the broken window, I thought aloud, "There are several stones about that size that also aren't mossy lying around out here. There's probably another stone on the powder room floor, one that went through the window after it broke. It's as if someone stood back and heaved stones at the window from a distance. Some of them must have bounced off the house and landed here. The paint on the window frame is dented and chipped in places."

"It looks that way to us, too," Gartborg said. "Why would someone do that?"

She probably knew better than I did, but I guessed, picturing Derek, "He didn't want to be hit by flying glass?"

Gartborg corrected me. "Or she. Would a man use a skillet as a murder weapon?"

Aha, I thought. The postmortem might not have been done yet, but Gartborg seemed to have concluded, as Brent had, that a blow from the skillet had killed Rich.

"Why not?" Nina demanded. "Men cook, too, and they might be more likely than women to cook with the skillet we saw in this cottage, probably over an open fire. That skillet was heavy." She threw me a sorrowful look, and I remembered punning about the skillet being a kill-it or an overkill-it.

Those puns were no longer funny. I gave Nina a reassuring smile. I turned back to Gartborg. "Do we know that the person who broke the window was the person who attacked Rich? If so, that person might have been cut."

Gartborg pulled on a pair of disposable gloves. "We don't know. We couldn't find the skillet you described inside this cottage. Maybe you can." She opened the door to the screened porch and held it for us.

The door between the porch and the kitchen gaped open. Nina and I went inside ahead of the detectives. Together, the two of us said, "It's gone!"

I pointed up at the bare hook. "The skillet was hanging up there."

Gartborg asked, "Are you positive?"

Telling her I was, I showed the detectives the skillet-sized, soot-rimmed hole in the wall.

Gartborg asked, "Was that there yesterday before you two arrived?"

Nina and I both said that it was.

I added, "Flinging that skillet at someone with any amount

of force would take strength. Nina and I worked together to lift it up to its hook." Brent's eyes were on me. I figured I might as well be the one to say what I guessed he was thinking. "Nina's and my fingerprints will be on the skillet that was here last night. I'm guessing it's the one I saw next to Rich's body, but maybe other cottages around this lake have them, too. Maybe buying them was once a trend here. If the skillet I saw in the tent with Rich does have Nina's and my fingerprints on it, then it's the one from this cottage. And if it doesn't"—I raised one shoulder and let it fall—"it's inconclusive."

Nina pointed at the sooty hole. "Whoever swung the skillet at that wall probably also left his prints on it."

I eyed the broken and black-smudged drywall. "I'm guessing that would be Derek Bengsen or one of his friends. Maybe even Terri Estable. Which doesn't mean that one of them didn't also swing it at Rich's head in his party tent this morning."

Nina glanced around the kitchen. "Anyone who touched that skillet could have left sooty fingerprints other places. You won't have to dust for prints." She gave a wan smile as if not expecting her joking to go over well with the two detectives.

Brent smiled back at her. Gartborg stared at walls and counters as if hoping to recognize Nina's and my fingerprints on them.

"Our prints will be in various places around this cottage," I said, "but we did attempt to wash the soot off our hands after we hung up the skillet."

Gartborg asked, "Why did you take it down?"

"I bumped into it," Nina explained, "accidentally. It looked about to fall, and when I tried to put it more securely on its hook, it came all the way off. I was surprised at how heavy it was, and I got Emily to lift it, too. Both of us are strong."

"It was heavy," I agreed. "Derek or Rich's neighbor could have swung it. Rich's girlfriend, Terri, the one his will was made out to, is hardly bigger than I am, but she looks athletic. She was definitely strong enough to pull her canoe onto the sandy beach without a sound. And she flipped that canoe over and carried it on her shoulders up the hill to Rich's house. Then she lowered it as if it were nothing and shoved it underneath his deck. I gathered that she often goes birding in her canoe."

Gartborg asked. "And do you kayak a lot, Ms. Westhill?"

"Not as much as I'd like to." I was careful not to look at Brent or give Gartborg a clue that I ever went kayaking with the handsome detective she was directing in this investigation. If he wanted her to know that, he could tell her. "But I'm fit from running around our donut shop."

Nina chimed in, "And I'm fit from that and from manhandling huge canvases and tall ladders so I can paint the upper halves of the canvases. But that skillet was still heavy."

Brent said, "I didn't pick it up, but it looked substantial. Emily, where was the platter like the broken one you saw near the body of the deceased?" For once, he didn't shorten my name to Em.

"It was on the bottom of the stack in the cabinet above the counter to the right of the sink."

Gartborg pulled at the lower corner of the cabinet door with one gloved finger.

Nina gasped. "The clamshell bowl is gone!"

We described the bowl to the detectives. Nina told them about Cindy Westhill's fame as a potter and that the bowl was dated about twenty years before and numbered. She added, "It was worth a lot."

Gazing toward Brent, Gartborg's face hardened as if she thought she might have found a motive for Rich's murder. She wasn't going to pin it on Nina or me, though. We'd both been with Tom at Deputy Donut when I believed Rich was murdered, and no one was likely to suspect Tom of lying about that or anything else.

I stood on tiptoe and peered into the cabinet without touching anything. "The platter like the one that was broken inside the party tent isn't here, either." I explained to Nina that it was the one we'd left on the bottom of the stack, the one depicting one sail on the horizon.

Nina didn't have to stand on tiptoe. "I agree. That platter was larger than the others, and we'd be able to see its rim if it was still here. It's gone."

Gartborg asked Nina, "Was that platter valuable, also?"

"No," Nina answered. "It was mass-produced, like the one that Detective Fyne put into the cruiser outside. Those two platters might have some value as vintage collectibles, but they're not pieces of art like the clamshell bowl, and they're probably not unusual enough to have much value."

Brent finished what he was writing in his notebook and looked at me. I recognized the bleakness in his eyes. It showed up when he was deeply involved in a serious investigation and disappeared when he was relaxing or having fun. "Can you two show us the wills and the book with the rental notes that you told me about, Emily?"

Wishing I could make the bleak look go away, I led the others into the cottage's combined living and dining room.

The table where Nina had found the wills underneath a jumble of books was bare.

Nina raised her shoulders and held both of her hands, palms up, in front of her. "The wills are gone, and it looks like the books they were under are now back on the bookshelf. I found the wills when I started straightening the books."

Gartborg frowned at her. "Why would you do that?"

Lowering her hands to her sides, Nina stared toward the wall above the fireplace. Even if she did paint a picture small enough, it would probably never display one of her paintings. "I don't know. We were here to come up with ideas about redecorating and renovating. Those books were just heaped on that table, and I can think better if things are tidy."

Gartborg relaxed the frown wrinkles. "I get that." She stared toward Brent. "Those two wills could be anywhere."

"I'll check the wastebaskets," he promised. "But maybe the wills have been removed from the premises."

I pointed to the colonial-style desk. "The rental book was in the top drawer."

Gartborg opened the drawer and pulled out the maroon notebook. "This?"

I clasped my hands behind my back to prevent myself from touching anything. "That looks like it."

She peered down into the drawer. "Aha. Here are some wills." She pulled out stapled packets and examined them. "Three wills. Write this down, Brent. One is signed by Richmond P. Royalson the Third, and leaves everything to Terri Estable. Another is signed by Terri Estable and leaves everything to Richmond P. Royalson the Third. Both are witnessed. They're dated yesterday."

"Yesterday?" I repeated. "They weren't signed or dated last night when Nina and I were here. And there were two copies of each will."

Although I hadn't meant to sound doubtful, Detective Gartborg thrust the signed pages of the two wills almost underneath my nose. They'd been dated yesterday. Rich's signature was dark and heavy like the writing on the to-do list and in his rental book. Terri's was feminine with the curlicued top line of the *T* sweeping above its entire length.

"What time did you two leave here last night?" Brent asked.

I looked at Nina for confirmation. "About seven?"

"Around then. Maybe a little before."

Brent concluded, "They could have been signed last night after you two left."

"People don't always get the dates right." Gartborg's tone was cold, especially compared to Brent's. She examined another will. "The third is the one that Emily told you about, Brent, the nineteen-year-old will made out to Richmond P. Royalson Junior and Alma Ruth Royalson." Still wearing her gloves, she riffled through other papers in the drawer. "I don't see any other wills."

Brent was writing in his notebook, but I spoke more to him than to the DCI detective. "Rich or Terri must have put those wills in the drawer and taken the copies away. They probably straightened the books, and they could have taken the skillet, the platter, and the clamshell bowl away with them when they left. I mean, we don't know if the attacker got the skillet from here. Maybe Rich took the skillet to the tent for some reason."

Gartborg sighed as if she didn't want to hear civilians theorizing about things that she had already figured out. I realized I'd been doing it almost ever since Nina and I arrived. Brent had always seemed to appreciate my brainstorming.

He glanced up at me, nodded, and continued writing.

Gartborg pointed out, "If Rich took the skillet, he didn't need to break in."

I asked politely, "Could Nina and I have had his only key?"

"No," Gartborg said. "He had another one in his pocket." She asked Nina and me, "Can you two see anything else that has changed since yesterday evening?"

Neither of us could, and we all went upstairs to the slope-ceilinged second floor. We didn't see any differences up there.

Downstairs again, all of us went outside.

I breathed a sigh of relief. Nina and I had succeeded in not touching anything except with our feet.

Detective Gartborg turned to Brent. "You know the area. Can you arrange for someone to board up the broken window?"

He stared down toward the water. "I called someone before Emily and Nina arrived. They should be here any minute."

I followed Brent's gaze. The dock was bare. I asked, "Does anyone know what happened to the canoe that was on the dock yesterday?"

Chapter 10

"What canoe?" Gartborg asked.

"There was one there last night," Nina said. "An aluminum one, plain aluminum, not painted."

Hiding an appreciative smile at her eye for detail, I peered through the screen into the porch. "A paddle might be missing, too, from that custom-made cabinet next to the kitchen door. I didn't count them last night, but I don't remember that empty space." Two dowels that were meant to support the grip of the paddle were bare.

"I don't remember it, either," Nina said. "I think there were five paddles yesterday, different lengths."

Now there were four.

Brent asked, "Were they arranged that way last night, longest to shortest?"

Nina and I both said that they were.

Gartborg suggested, "We could be missing the longest paddle. Taller people use longer paddles, right?"

Brent nodded. I wondered if he was thinking what I was thinking: after one paddle was taken out of the cabinet, the others could have been moved, like if a short person wanted to make it look like the missing paddle was a long one. Terri was short.

Brent pointed out that whoever took the canoe could have simply grabbed the paddle that was easiest to reach when he or she opened the door. "Royalson was shorter than average, but he might have preferred a longer paddle. Maybe he went canoeing before he died. He must have been over here last night or earlier today. He could have been here with Ms. Estable and the witness, or the wills could have been signed and witnessed somewhere else, but someone put a copy of each will into that desk drawer after you two"—he nodded at Nina and me—"were here. Maybe he came by himself, put the wills away, and canoed back home, with or without the clamshell bowl, the platter, and the skillet."

Gartborg folded her arms. "I didn't see a canoe fitting that description at his home. Did you, Brent?"

"No. Only a red one under the deck." Brent turned to me. "You told us you saw Terri Estable put a red canoe there, right, Emily?"

"Right. You arrived a few minutes later. If her paddle had the name Royalson wood-burned into the shaft, I didn't see it, but it wasn't close enough for me to have seen it, anyway." I asked the detectives, "Did Rich live alone in that big house?"

Instead of answering, Gartborg questioned me. "Why do you ask?"

"It seems weird to keep important papers in a rental cottage. I thought maybe he was living with someone, and he wanted to keep the wills a secret from that person. But if he was living with anyone, it seems like it would be Terri Estable."

Brent said quickly, "She works in Gooseleg but she lives in a town house in Fallingbrook. Her ex's town house is in the same complex. If he is her ex."

I tried to hide my satisfaction at having discovered Derek's and Terri's addresses. "So, Rich did reconnect with Terri recently?"

"As far as we know," Brent said.

Nina crossed her arms and scowled. "He could have canceled the date with Cheryl. When he met her at Deputy

Donut, he already knew he'd rediscovered the love of his life. Stringing Cheryl along was rude."

I had to smile. "He was sort of comical about that, in a self-centered way. He said he hadn't wanted to disappoint Cheryl by canceling their date."

Nina stared down toward the lake, now the same dusky blue as the sky. "Terri was probably after him for his money. A personality like Rich's would be hard to live with."

I added, "Not to mention his booming voice."

Gartborg spoke sharply. "Estable's not going to have to, now."

I thought about the way people tended to repeat their mistakes, especially when it came to choosing partners. Terri might simply wind up with yet another difficult personality. However, from what I'd seen, Rich had been an improvement over Derek, so maybe Terri was heading in the right direction. Or maybe Gartborg expected Terri to spend many years in prison. Was Gartborg suspecting the two most logical villains—Terri Estable and Derek Bengsen?

Nina flapped a hand toward the dock. "Maybe the unpainted aluminum canoe that Emily and I saw last night fell off the dock and sank. Like, fell off sideways. Or there was a hole in it, and that's why it was on the dock and not in the water, but then someone pushed it in. Maybe a gust of wind caught it. Last night's storm was windy at times."

Brent turned toward the dock. "Let's go have a look."

Gartborg didn't move. "Let me know if you find anything interesting, Brent."

Brent, Nina, and I made our way down a stony path to the shore. Peering into the water on one side of the dock, we walked to the end. We couldn't be certain that the murkiest depths weren't hiding a canoe, but we didn't see one. And we didn't see a canoe when we sauntered back toward shore and looked down into the water on the other side of the dock, either.

Stepping onto the muddy beach, I noticed a partial footprint. I showed it to Brent. Remembering Gartborg's comment that standing far away and throwing stones at a window and using a skillet as a murder weapon seemed like things a woman might do, I said, "That looks like a man's shoe print."

Brent shined his phone's flashlight down at the mud. "It could be from a woman wearing oversized boots."

I pictured the people on Rich's lawn earlier that day. "Terri was wearing big boots when she came back from canoeing."

Brent gave me one of his warmest smiles. "So she was."

Nina reminded us that if Rich had canoed away from his cottage, the shoe print could have been his.

Brent wrote in his notebook and took pictures with his phone. "Thanks, Em and Nina. You two can go now." He called up the hill, "Kim, can you come take a look at this?"

Running up the bank, Nina and I passed Gartborg planting her stiletto heels carefully on probably slippery grass. She offered a just-between-us-girls smile and muttered, "I should have taken time to change into comfy shoes before I came out here." She raised her voice, "Coming, Brent, slowly and unsurely!"

We made it to the flagstone pathway and around the corner of the building, out of sight of Brent and Gartborg, before Nina whispered, "I think she likes your detective."

"He's not my—"

"Gotcha! But if you might ever want him to be yours, you'd better watch her."

I pretended a breezy nonchalance. "She's welcome to him. She's more his type than I am. Tall, sophisticated, gorgeous—"

"You're gorgeous," Nina said, "for a shrimpy person."

"Thanks."

"Didn't you like my New England vibe?"

I wasn't sure how to make my voice drip with sarcasm, but I tried. "Is that what it was?"

"New England. Seafood. Shrimp."

I opened the driver's door of my car. "Ha, ha."

We both got into the car. I turned it around and started back toward town.

Nina was quiet until we bumped past the county park and its cozy little beach. She slapped at the dashboard. "Do you know what I think?" She didn't wait for an answer. "The mystery man who showed up in Deputy Donut this afternoon and barely said a word had a grudge against Rich. He came to town, killed Rich, and went to the local donut shop to eavesdrop on conversations to figure out if he was a suspect. He could have seen you at Rich's this morning, even if you didn't see him. Maybe he was in those woods near Rich's house. When the mystery man finally recognized you this afternoon, he ran to his car and drove out of town as fast as he could."

"I guess I'd better call Brent and describe him. He could have been one of Rich's banking clients. Maybe Rich did something nasty to him."

"The mystery man's expensive suit didn't seem like the best outfit for a murderer to wear. He could have gotten it totally messed up. But it was fine for a birthday party, I guess."

"Or," I suggested, "he was wearing a more casual outfit when he killed Rich, but he went home and dressed in his most expensive suit because if people saw him in it, they would automatically think he wasn't a murderer. He seemed nervous. One of his eyes kept closing and opening, but I don't think he was winking at me."

"Maybe he had something in his eye."

"Like a crumb of Boston brown bread." I told Nina that Rich might have attempted to defend himself with a platter of sliced Boston brown bread.

She sat back and folded her arms. "It's too easy to pin the murder on a mystery man. He was probably just an art critic who became more critical when he saw my painting, and he had to get away from it before it made him sick."

"I doubt that."

"And I doubt that he's a murderer. It's much more likely that Terri and her ex-boyfriend Derek planned the entire thing—the drunken buddies and their party, the wills, and all. I think they worked together to kill Rich so they could have his house, his money, and his cottage."

"It's possible, but Terri didn't seem happy to see Derek when he showed up at Rich's birthday party. She yelled at him to go away. Also, you should have seen Terri with Rich's neighbor, a man about Rich's age. He and Terri appeared to be close. Maybe Terri and the neighbor worked together to kill Rich."

Nina summarized, "So, we're almost certain that Terri was involved in Rich's death, but we're not sure who her partner in crime was, if she had one."

We reached the paved section of the road. I accelerated.

Nina snapped her fingers. "If Rich didn't move his canoe, Derek or Rich's neighbor might have done it. Or both, one in the bow and one in the stern, especially if they found another paddle or brought their own. What do you bet that the neighbor has boats and paddles?"

"I didn't see any, but he has a dock." I slowed and steered around the road's right curve. "And no matter who took that paddle, Terri, maybe with Derek's help, could now be angling to get the neighbor to will everything he owns to her." We were passing Rich's neighbor's timber frame house. I slowed. "His house isn't a mansion like Rich's, but it's gorgeous. And it is also on a large and presumably valuable lakefront property."

"I like the neighbor's house better. I like the way the natural wood finish blends in with the forest and the lake. Rich's palace doesn't fit in."

"It probably wasn't meant to." It certainly didn't at the moment, with yellow police tape draped around the property. I drove up the hill and away from Lake Fleekom.

Ten minutes later, we were a few blocks south of the center of Fallingbrook. I stopped outside Nina's apartment and studio combination. Nina waved at the balding identical twin brothers staring out through the front windows of Klassy Kitchens. She turned back to me. "Harry and Larry showed me around their store last night. I saw cabinets, sinks, and fixtures that would have been perfect for Rich's cottage." She and I exchanged sad glances. She opened her car door. "I'll have to tell them I'm not in the market for kitchen stuff, after all. Have a good day off tomorrow, Emily."

"I feel like I had most of today off."

"Don't you sometimes go kayaking with your detective on Wednesday afternoons?"

"When the weather's good enough."

"It's supposed to be great again tomorrow."

"He'll probably have to work on the investigation."

She flexed her fingers like claws. "She's going to get those long pointy nails into him."

I ignored that. "Call if you need anything tomorrow."

"Tom and I will be fine." She closed the car door gently and headed for the front door of Klassy Kitchens.

I drove home. Sitting on the living room floor inside the front door, Dep raised her left front paw and peered at her wrist as if checking a watch and reminding me that I'd been gone a long time.

I picked her up and nuzzled the donut-like marking on her side. "I missed you, too, Dep."

She purred.

After we ate, we toured our yard in the dark. Dep didn't need to wear her leash out there. The wall that enclosed the yard was high and made of smooth bricks that didn't allow her to get a grip on them. She might have been able to climb trees or shrubs and jump to the top of the wall, but she had decided early in kittenhood that climbing trees and shrubs was not an enjoyable activity for a cat who couldn't figure out how to back down and didn't appreciate tumbling to the grass. Besides, I kept the foliage near the wall pruned so she wouldn't be tempted. She limited her climbing to the carpet-covered pillars, ramps, and kitty staircases in the office at Deputy Donut.

The two of us determined that nothing outside needed to be pounced on or batted around, so we went inside. I locked the back door even though no human could make his way into our yard without a ladder, a crane, a catapult, or a parachute. The security of that yard was one of the things that Alec had loved about the property.

After I was in bed, Dep stretched out, purring, next to my legs.

I was a matchmaker, always wanting my friends to pair off with people I thought they would love, but even though Detective Gartborg looked like the type of woman that Brent had dated when Alec was alive, I wasn't sure she was a good match for him. She seemed too hard-shelled and cold, although she did appear to like him, if bossing him around was a sign of liking.

"Brent and I are just friends," I said into the darkness. "And he and that DCI detective are on a first-name basis."

Dep jumped off the bed and stomped downstairs. Maybe I shouldn't have mentioned Brent aloud. When he wasn't visiting us and Dep heard me talking about him, she went to the front door and sat with her nose almost touching it.

"It's going to be a long wait, Dep," I mumbled. "Maybe a very long one."

Licking the top of my head, Dep woke me up almost as early as my alarm would have.

"Thanks, Dep," I murmured groggily. "We have the day off."

She meowed and jumped off the bed. Breakfast was leisurely, for me at least. Dep chased a catnip-filled salmon around the house. Later I sat in the sunroom enjoying the warm cat on my lap, the mild but flavorful Mexican coffee in my mug, and the view beyond the windows. Ornamental shrubs and grasses would give my flower beds texture and color during the colder seasons.

Brent called. "I'm sorry I can't go kayaking this afternoon. I have to work."

"No problem. I figured that might happen. What about Samantha's party tomorrow night?"

"I'm still hoping I can make it. How about kayaking next Wednesday?"

"Fine, as long as I don't have to attach an icebreaker to the front of my kayak."

He laughed. "Maybe we'll end up cross-country skiing, instead. Talk to you later. And take care."

I promised that I would. I did not, however, promise not to go kayaking by myself.

Chapter 11

Meanwhile, I could do something that might help solve Rich's murder and release Brent to spend more time partying with our friends, cuddling Dep, and kayaking—or cross-country skiing—with me.

I dug out the catering company's card that I'd pocketed in Rich's party tent. Cat's Catering was about a mile away. It was a warm and lovely day, perfect for a walk. I tucked a Deputy Donut business card into a pocket and said goodbye to Dep.

The beginning of the walk was through my Victorian neighborhood. It was always charming. This week, it was also fanciful. Jack-o'-lanterns grinned from porches and grimaced up at the sky from sidewalks while ghosts, skeletons, and webby things dangled from trees. More than one witch had missed her turn and collided with a tree trunk. Gigantic spiders and bats clung to walls and chimneys.

I cut through a wooded park. Cyclists, joggers, and dog walkers were making use of the paved pathways. In a fenced-in playground, toddlers climbed steps and ramps, pushed toy trucks through a sandbox, and swung on swings. "Watch me!" one shouted from the top of a miniature slide.

On the far side of the park, Cat's Catering was in a white-painted brick building trimmed with black cat silhouette logos like the one on their business card and on the van that

Cheryl had sent away from Rich's. Two of those vans and a similarly decorated SUV were in the parking lot.

I opened the building's front door. A bell jingled beyond the back wall of the reception area. Judging by the mouth-watering aromas of garlic and oregano, someone was about to enjoy an Italian feast. Books displaying menus and recipes were open on tables between comfy chairs.

A thirtyish woman wearing a white apron and a white paper chef's hat pushed open a swinging door. A large, bright, and well-equipped kitchen was beyond the door. She stopped at the reception counter, reached across it, and shook my hand. "I'm Cat." Her wide smile displayed a girlish gap between her upper front teeth.

Returning the smile, I placed the Deputy Donut business card on the counter between us. "I'm Emily. We have more in common than similar logos. I'm one of the owners of Deputy Donut. We often take donuts and beverages to events, like donuts that we put together into shapes resembling forts and princesses for birthday parties."

"I've heard good things about you!" The big voice went with her rawboned height and the direct gaze of her hazel eyes.

"Great! If you ever need cakes made of donuts or specialty coffees or teas for an event, think of us."

She picked up the card and studied it. "We might do that. And if anyone asks you for foods that you don't prepare, will you think of us?"

"I will. What you're cooking today smells delicious."

She tapped her fingers as if counting. "Stuffed mushrooms, ciabatta, lasagna, chicken piccata, roasted green beans and tomatoes, cannoli, and tiramisu. Wasn't your donut shop supposed to provide donuts and coffee to Rich Royalson's party yesterday? We were going to bring coffee, but he paid us for it, anyway. He said you were bringing special gourmet coffee."

"That was us. What a pity that none of the food you made got eaten. Your Boston baked beans and seafood chowder smelled delicious, and the table settings looked great. Did you bake the birthday cake, too?"

"We did." She looked about ready to cry. "We were able to give the women's shelter the food that we weren't allowed to deliver at Royalson's, but I wish we could have donated all of the food that didn't get eaten. I hate wasting food. To be fair, it wasn't Royalson's fault that some of yesterday's food got wasted. But it wasn't the first time that catering an event for Royalson caused us to have to give away food unexpectedly."

"What happened the other time?"

Her hands on the counter, she leaned forward. "We were supposed to cater last year's staff Christmas party at the Fallingbrook Mercantile Bank. Royalson had signed the contract, but at the last minute, he changed his mind and had a restaurant up in Gooseleg do the catering. To add insult to injury, instead of paying the cancellation fee he was contracted to pay, he said he had a win-win solution for the bank and for us. He told us that the Gooseleg State Bank needed last-minute catering for their party the night that Fallingbrook Mercantile was having its party, and he would recommend us to fill in. It turned out the restaurant that had been supposed to cater the Gooseleg bank's party had backed out." She stood straight and chopped at the air with one hand. "Well, guess why!"

I gave her a half smile. "They were catering Rich's bank's party instead?"

"You got it. The Gooseleg party was smaller, so we ended up losing money. At least the women's shelter got some Christmas cheer, but they get that from us anyway, and it's easier when we plan it all from the outset. Our losses weren't as bad as they would have been if Royalson hadn't given us the lead on that other party, but it was ridiculous. The other caterer probably had to scramble for enough supplies and food, while we had too much. I even tried swapping events with that other caterer, but they were adamant."

"Why did you trust Rich enough to cater another party?"

She flicked an invisible spot off the gleaming stone counter. "That was a fluke. In June, we were catering a family reunion out at Lake Fleekom County Park. Royalson rode a bicycle past as we were setting up, and he saw our van and remembered the name of our company, probably because of the way he treated us last December. Mistreated us, I should say." She gave me a half-hearted smile. "I try not to judge clients, but after that Christmas party fiasco, I didn't particularly like him."

"I can see why."

"Anyway, that day in June, he got off his bike, cornered me, and said he was glad to see that we were doing well. He said that canceling our Christmas party catering had been unavoidable, but he had a way of making it up to us. I don't know if it was guilt that made him ask me, right that moment, to cater his birthday party, but I like to think it was the smell of the baked beans and fried chicken we were unpacking."

I made a show of sniffing toward the kitchen. "Probably."

"Thanks. We have scrumptious recipes and super employees. I took on Royalson's birthday party job because I wanted to prove to him that we're excellent caterers. Maybe I also wanted to make him regret not using us in December and maybe consider hiring us next Christmas. But I wasn't about to be tricked again. I told him he had to pay me in full, ahead of time. He agreed. His check cleared and everything."

I gazed at a wall of photos of delectable-looking foods and beautifully set tables. "He made a good decision, contracting with you this time."

She heaved a big sigh. "Maybe not, considering what happened. I feel sorry for him. I don't know why he made that switch in December, but other than being totally boring by praising Boston ten times a minute while we were planning his birthday party, he wasn't that bad."

"He did seem obsessed about Boston." I told Cat about his ordering Boston cream donuts. "But the amount of frosting wasn't enough for him. We had to double it."

Cat grinned. "That sounds like him. He said he wasn't a cook, but at the same time, he always knew a better way to prepare every dish." Her lips turned down in a pout. "But it's sad. I can't help wondering what would have happened if he hadn't biked past the county park that day in June. Another caterer might have been able to arrive when Royalson wanted us to, and maybe they could have saved him."

"What do you mean?"

"He asked us to come at eleven, but we already had another engagement and arranged to arrive at Royalson's at ten thirty, instead, with plenty of ice to keep cold things cold and slow cookers for dishes that could stay warm there, like Boston baked beans. So, because we had to leave, there was a gap in time when he was there by himself and someone came along and . . ." She ran an index finger across her throat.

"When did you leave?"

"We're quick, and we'd set up the tent, tables, and chairs the day before. We left at eleven."

"No one was there when I arrived almost an hour later." I closed my eyes briefly and rocked back on my heels. "Well, Rich was there. I mean, his body was."

The hazel eyes opened wider in apparent shock. "Did you find him? Were you there by yourself?"

I nodded.

"You poor thing."

I hoped she wouldn't jump to the conclusion that I had killed Rich. "It was horrible." I also hoped she wouldn't realize that I was trying to figure out if she or someone from her company had killed him. There had been less than an hour between when she left and I arrived. Who had been there in the meantime?

That wide, mobile mouth dragged down in one corner for a second. "Also, I wonder what would have happened if we hadn't been the ones to set up the tent or if we or someone else had set up a tent differently. The way we oriented it, the doorway could be seen only from his side yard and maybe from the edge of his driveway closest to the tent. But what if the tent's doorway had been visible to his neighbor or to the lake?"

"Don't beat yourself up about it. The hedges between his property and his neighbor's are tall."

"But someone might have seen between the branches."

I conceded, "Maybe, if they were in the right place at the right time. Also, the lake was fogged over. Nobody could have seen much from any distance out on the lake."

"True. It was foggy when we left at eleven after our preliminary setup that morning, and it was still foggy when we arrived with the last-minute food before twelve twenty-five but were then sent away, food and all." She fiddled with a stack of brochures. "A tent with no side walls would have been cheaper for him to rent. Or we could have rolled up or pinned back the sides, but because of the time of year, he wanted the kind of tent we could heat if we had to. The prediction was so warm that we didn't bother with heaters, but for protection from breezes, we didn't fasten the sides back. We could have. We would have if the day had been warmer. I'm afraid that, by renting Rich our best tent, we accidentally gave privacy to a murderer."

How did she know that Rich had been killed inside the tent? Someone could have told her—the police, perhaps, or someone else who had been at the scene. The murderer? One thing was certain. I hadn't told her. I also wasn't about to ask how she knew.

Had this apparently empathetic woman killed Rich because he had caused her to lose money and waste food last December? It seemed like a stretch. Stranger things had happened, though.

Cat leaned closer and confided, "When we arrived at ten-thirty Tuesday morning, Royalson decided we should leave the tent walls in place. He was very much alive, then. Very. He showed us where he wanted everything, and we started spreading out tablecloths. A much younger woman, his daughter maybe, came into the tent and taped a guest list to one of the tablecloths. She put it on the part that hangs down, so it wasn't in our way, but I don't know. For parties that small, people don't usually check off the names of people as they show up, you know?" I didn't tell her that there were more seats in the tent than there were names on the list. She went on. "Royalson was carrying around his own list of what was supposed to happen when. He didn't stick it to any tablecloths while we were there. Royalson told the woman to go away so he could arrange everything, and she could come to the party when the other guests did. He was going to be his own bartender and serve drinks until we returned. He wanted her to be surprised by how well he had planned and organized everything."

"Did she leave?"

"She said she was going birding and headed up to the house. Later, when I was taking a load of things to the tent, I saw her carrying a canoe down the hill from the back of the house. She carried it like a pro, above her head. When we left, she was paddling away past the dock. She was wearing binoculars and didn't look back."

"I met her later, when she came back from canoeing. I think she was his girlfriend."

Cat raised a finger in the air. "Maybe she killed him."

"Maybe." I couldn't help a little shudder. A display case of cakes and pies was on the counter near me. I asked her, "Do you sell desserts retail? Could I order a pie to pick up tomorrow evening about five forty-five?"

"Sure. We have pumpkin, apple, cherry, pecan—"

I held a hand up. Pecan was one of my favorites. "Pecan."

"What size?"

"Enough for six people who love pecan pie and don't think it's too rich to have big slices."

That wide smile reappeared. "Ours is rich, but I get what you're saying. I'm the same way."

I paid for the pie. She gave me a receipt.

I went out and turned around to make certain that the door latched behind me. Cat was hurrying back into the kitchen.

Walking through the park, I thought about how Cat had emphasized that Rich had been alive when she left his place after setting out the preliminary batch of party food. Was that true? She'd said "we" as if she'd worked with one or more of her employees at Rich's. I wondered who had been with her and whether they had arrived and left together.

During other investigations Brent had sometimes visited Dep and me, and he had tolerated listening to my theories. Sometimes our brainstorming had, I thought, been useful. It had certainly helped me organize my thoughts and guesses. I didn't know when I would next see him, though. Had Cat told the investigators about Rich's change in catering companies for his bank's Christmas party?

At home, I told Dep that I hadn't learned a lot about Rich's murder that I could share with Brent. She gave me a look as if to ask, *What did you expect?*

"I'll tell him about the catering switch the next time I see him. I did accomplish something," I informed my cat. "I noticed that I'm falling behind in making our house festive for Halloween."

I took baskets of decorations outside to the front porch. With Dep supervising from inside on the living room windowsill, I added a scarecrow, some totally unscared crows, and an extended family of goblins to the pumpkins that were already on the porch. Inside again, I strung up a crocheted spiderweb, complete with spider, in the middle of the center pane of the front window. I'd bought the scarecrow, the crows, and the spider and its web at The Craft Croft.

"There," I told Dep. "And in case you were planning some mischief, that spider and its web in the front window are not toys."

She jumped down from the windowsill. "Meow."

"Promise you'll leave them alone?"

Her lack of response did not bode well for the spider and its web.

I cautioned her, "You'd get all tangled up."

Tail up, she dashed to the back of the house.

In the kitchen, I sat at the island and ate a spinach, dried cranberry, and walnut salad and a bowl of homemade tomato soup with parmesan croutons. Dep watched me through half-closed eyes as if she thought that the foods humans ate were so strange that she couldn't force herself to take a good look. When I bit into a crunchy and juicy apple, she left the kitchen and went to the sunroom, which was separated from the kitchen by a half-height wall sort of like the one between the kitchen and the dining area in Deputy Donut. Dep perched on one of the room's wide windowsills. Watching a squirrel race up and down the trunk of the oak tree, she made strange little utterances and swished her tail back and forth.

I put my lunch dishes into the dishwasher. Yesterday when he first arrived at Lake Fleekom, Brent had mentioned that he'd rather be kayaking. He couldn't go kayaking today, either.

I could.

Unlike streams and rivers, Lake Fleekom would have no dangerous currents or rapids. Even the strongest winds wouldn't churn up much in the way of waves on such a small lake. Exploring Lake Fleekom by myself would be safe.

Right—it was also close to where a murderer had been the day before. He or she might still be hanging around in the woods.

But I'd be out on the lake. I wouldn't stay long, and I had no plans to interfere with the investigation. Besides, maybe the lake would be misty again, and I'd be out there marveling at being inside those clouds on the water. How many more opportunities would I have to do that before winter?

Although the day was warm, I changed into wool socks

and pants, a turtleneck, and a warm wool sweater. I put on sneakers, a weather-resistant jacket, and a sunhat. I rubbed sunscreen onto my face and the backs of my hands.

Feeling almost carefree, I ran downstairs. Dep was perched on the wing chair in the living room. She stared at me with her pupils at their widest. "I'm going kayaking without him," I admitted.

Dep licked a paw. Vigorously.

Chapter 12

✼

Driving toward Lake Fleekom, I daydreamed that Brent had driven his own car, with his kayak on top, to Rich's house or cottage, and we would end up exploring Lake Fleekom together in the mist.

I crested the hill above Rich's mansion. Disappointment was like a punch in the ribs.

There was no mist.

And Brent's car was not in Rich's driveway. A couple of unmarked cruisers like the ones that he and visiting DCI agents often drove were among the investigators' vehicles in both the circular and the straight sections of Rich's driveway.

I would be safe out on the lake. With so many investigators nearby, Rich's murderer, even if he'd stolen Rich's aluminum canoe from his dock, was probably not prowling around looking for more victims.

Rich's party tent was still near the beach and inside the perimeter of crime scene tape. The blue lake sparkled in the sunshine. I didn't see any boats on it.

I followed the road as it turned to the right. With a noisy leaf blower, Rich's neighbor was corralling leaves in his own driveway. He didn't look up. I kept going, around the left curve, through the woods, past the end of the pavement, and onto the uneven gravel. I pulled into the parking lot at Lake Fleekom County Park.

One of the advantages of carrying a kayak on a sports car was the car's low roof. I didn't have to move the kayak far either up or down. I unfastened it and set in on the ground.

I put on my life jacket and made it snug enough to keep my head above water if I fell in. Brent had bought us each waterproof cases for our phones. The cases would stay afloat if they tumbled out of our kayaks. So far, that hadn't happened, and I hadn't fallen into water that was more than ankle deep. I inserted my phone into the case, latched it, and zipped the case inside one of the life jacket's mesh pockets. Finally, I carried my kayak and paddle to the edge of the water and set the kayak down parallel to the beach, far enough out in the water that it would float even with me in it, but not too far out to step into it from the shore.

Once that summer I had put one foot into the kayak and accidentally started the kayak on its journey while my other foot was still on the shore. I'd ended up sitting in six inches of water. Remembering how the work-related tension in Brent's shoulders relaxed and how hard we both laughed after he was sure I was all right, I couldn't help smiling.

Since then, I'd more or less gotten the hang of getting into my kayak without entertaining onlookers. I rested my paddle across the coaming at the front of the cockpit, used both hands to grip the paddle and the sides of the coaming, put most of my weight on my hands, and carefully stepped in. The second foot didn't get very wet. With no one watching or anticipating hapless comedy, I was fairly graceful as gravity plunked me down onto the seat. I pushed away from the sandy beach.

Launching my kayak was always both freeing and exhilarating, almost like I imagined flying would be. I felt nearly weightless.

I tightened the straps to the footrests and braced my feet. Dipping first one end of the paddle and then the other into the lake in a comfortable rhythm of left, right, left, right, I slipped through the water almost silently. Steering had become automatic. I decided that exploring the entire shoreline, even slowly, couldn't take more than an hour or two, depending on how much I stopped to admire my surroundings.

I turned right, toward the end of the lake where the cottages were. Small birds twittered in almost leafless shrubs. Even though there was no magical mist hovering over the water, I felt sorry for Brent. The sun was warm, the sky was cloudless, and he was missing what might be the last kayak excursion until spring.

Between trees, I caught glimpses of a log cabin near the water. It appeared to be shuttered tight for the coming winter. Farther ahead, I recognized Rich's dock. Picturing Brent and Detective Gartborg reexamining footprints on the muddy beach, and not certain I wanted them to see me close to Rich's cottage and conclude that I was snooping, I angled away from shore. Not that Brent, if he saw a wide-brimmed straw hat and an orange life jacket in a red kayak, would fail to recognize me.

Although I was not, of course, snooping, I didn't see anyone around Rich's cottage. I passed it and eased closer to land. Cottages were on large properties with boulder-strewn woods between them. Some of the cottages must have been behind trees. I could only guess they were there because of pathways leading up into the woods from the water or docks jutting into the lake.

I counted eight docks or canoe launches on that side of the lake, and then the road that serviced the cottages must have ended. Across from the county park and its public beach, a long stretch of undeveloped shoreline undulated in and out between coves, leaning trees, and rocks. The forest on this shore seemed tangled and wild.

I came to an inlet where a stream emptied into the lake. The stream was deep enough that my kayak was not going to beach itself, and the current was sluggish. I started up the stream. It widened into a small pond. I went through the pond and up the stream until it narrowed and became too twisty to navigate. Ahead, I heard water tumbling over rocks and caught a glimpse of a miniature waterfall. I backed downstream, turned around in the pond, and drifted to a stop. A pair of mallards ducked their heads underneath the water. The kayak rocked gently.

I was close to Rich's house, but except for the smell of wood smoke and the sound of Rich's neighbor's leaf blower, I could have been the only person on earth. A turtle slid off a log and swam out of sight. The ducks took off, gaining altitude over Lake Fleekom.

This hidden little pond was the perfect place for someone to lurk in a boat on a morning when mist covered the lake, on a morning when the boater had just swung a cast-iron skillet at a man celebrating his seventieth birthday. It was a perfect place for an attacker to plan the next move.

Becoming chilled and needing to exercise, I paddled down the stream and into the lake. The leaf blower became louder. The door of a vehicle clunked. I paddled around junipers leaning over the water at the end of a stony point. I could again see Rich's house, the party tent, and beyond that, his neighbor blowing leaves off his dock into the lake.

I didn't mind if Brent saw me, even if he thought I was snooping. He would know I wouldn't interfere, at least not on purpose. However, I did not want Gartborg to think I was chasing Brent. I cut across the lake as far as I could from the two large homes. The neighbor looked up and waved. Did he recognize me, or did he wave at all boaters? I returned the greeting.

From what I'd seen while driving past his house, the front was wood with normal-sized windows. Except for their sturdy timber framing, the walls facing the lake were glass. Smoke drifted from a chimney.

I poked along the shore that was closest to the unpaved section of the road. What creatures had made the round holes in the dirt of the steeper banks? I watched, hoping a mink or an otter would peek out.

I toured every cove. One was slightly larger than the others, with a muddy beach that sloped down to the water. Grooves in the mud showed where a canoe or rowboat, something with a keel, had been dragged across the little beach since Monday night's rain. Brent's and my kayaks didn't have noticeable keels.

The cove wasn't a perfect place to pull a boat onto shore, but many people must have done it. Avoiding scraping against rocks sticking up out of the mud must have been impossible. There were red, green, and blue smudges on the rocks, plus silvery streaks that could have been scratched-off aluminum.

Dawdling, enjoying the warmth of the sun, the scenery, and the lightness of floating, I paddled back to the public beach. My car was still the only vehicle in the lot, which wasn't surprising on a Wednesday afternoon in late October.

I managed to disembark without completely resoaking my damp foot, and I didn't fall into the wavelets lapping the shore, either. I lifted my kayak onto my car, fastened it, and stowed my hat, life jacket, paddle, and my phone's waterproof case in the trunk.

Rather than head straight home, I drove slowly up the dirt road toward Rich's cottage. Yellow crime scene tape surrounded it, but no vehicles were parked outside. I passed it and about ten cottages and cabins with names like Dewdrop Inn and Dunrovin. The road ended.

I got out but could find no pathway that might lead around that side of the lake to the burbling stream, the duck pond, and eventually to Rich's house and the road back to Fallingbrook. Dense underbrush would make cutting through, even on foot, slow and difficult.

Lulled by my lazy tour of Lake Fleekom, I drove back at a turtle's pace, past the Bide-a-Wees and Hideaways, past

Rich's cottage and the two-track driveway that I now knew led to a shuttered log cabin. I slowed even more on the forested stretch beyond the county park beach. If people dragged their boats ashore in the cove with the grooves in the mud and the colored streaks on the rocks, did they bring them to and from the road? If so, there might be a place where they pulled off. . . .

And there it was, on the shoulder nearest the lake—a dried-up mud puddle with tire prints crossing it. The rain on Monday night and yesterday morning had ended yesterday before I left for work. That mud had probably been damp in the hours before Rich was killed.

I stopped my car, blocking anyone from driving through that dried mud.

Those prints might mean nothing.

It wouldn't hurt to check.

A narrow pathway disappeared into woods sloping toward the lake. I walked carefully down the path. As I'd hoped, it ended at the cove with the paint-smudged rocks. I crossed the small muddy beach to the water's edge, but could see no buildings, not Rich's or his neighbor's house, not even the party tent, and none of the recreational cottages across the lake from the homes. This cove was completely hidden from anyone who wasn't actually nearby on the water.

Could Rich's murderer have fled through the fog across the lake and dragged his or her boat ashore at this spot? Could some of the red streaks on the rocks have come from Terri's canoe? I started up the path toward the road.

I hadn't gone far when, to my left, I noticed that plants had been knocked over as if something heavy had been dragged through them. I hadn't noticed the line of broken saplings and bushes before because of the way it angled back from the more established pathway, but it was easy to spot when I was climbing toward the road.

The trail of bent and broken twigs went around a grove of

cedars next to a boulder. Between the green, scaly leaves of the cedars, I saw dull silvery metal.

I pushed the branches aside.

Someone had dragged an aluminum canoe behind the boulder and had left it there, upside down and almost completely hidden.

Chapter 13

※

Could the canoe behind the boulder and cedars be the one that Nina and I had seen on the dock of Rich's cottage the night before he was murdered? Accidentally pinching the cedar's needle-like leaves too tightly, I released their pungent fragrance.

A paddle was sticking out from underneath the canoe. I could read some of the dark brown letters on the shaft: R-O-Y.

This paddle resembled the ones we had seen at Rich's cottage. We'd been certain that one paddle had gone missing from that cabinet between Monday night, when Nina and I had first visited the cottage, and last night, when we'd been there with Brent and Detective Gartborg.

I wanted to rescue that wooden paddle from the damp ground and future rain and snow, but in case this almost-concealed canoe and paddle could be evidence in Rich's murder, I let the cedar branches snap back into place, left the canoe and paddle where they were, and called Brent's personal number.

He answered immediately. "How's the kayaking on Lake Fleekom?"

"Perfect except for the lack of mist."

"I'm in Royalson's driveway. I can't see you. Are you still on the water?"

I twisted back toward the lake as if expecting to see myself out there. Or a murderer. "I'm on the shore. I might have found the canoe that was on Rich's cottage dock Tuesday evening."

"Where?" The question was like a shot.

"In the woods between the county park and Rich's mansion."

"Are you near the canoe now?"

"Yes."

"Can you be seen from the road?"

"No."

"Is anyone else nearby?"

"Not that I know of." Shivering, although I wasn't really cold, I glanced over my shoulder again.

"We're on our way." Over the phone, I heard a car door slam, then another. Someone started the car's engine. Brent asked me, "Are you close to your car?"

"About a one-minute walk. It's partially on the road, blocking tire prints in a dried-up mud puddle. The way I'm parked, you can't drive through the prints, but be careful not to walk in them."

"Got it." I heard a smile in his voice.

Shaking my head at myself for warning a detective not to mess up possible evidence, I pocketed my phone.

And what damage might I have done by walking down the narrow pathway?

Risking compromising the evidence even more—and super-alert for cookware-wielding murderers to come crashing out of the bushes—I walked carefully and quietly up the slope toward my car.

All I heard besides breezes rattling the season's last leaves was the purr of a powerful engine and the crunch of tires on gravel.

While still mostly behind pine trees, I cautiously peeked at the road. A black unmarked cruiser drove past, turned around, and stopped beside my car. I emerged into the sunlight and waited near the dried-up mud puddle.

Detective Gartborg got out of the driver's seat. She was wearing low-heeled boots, black slacks that showed off her long legs, and a short fleece-trimmed black jacket with lots of pockets. Brent was in a suit that didn't look warm enough for the shadowy woods. He shook my hand. That was more formal than the quick hugs we sometimes gave each other when he wasn't on duty.

I pointed toward the pathway leading down into the woods. "The canoe's down there, about halfway to the shore." Then I pointed at the dried-up mud puddle. "Here are the tire prints."

Brent asked me, "Mind backing your car about thirty feet?" He tapped his phone's screen.

"Don't drive through the tire prints," Gartborg reminded me. I gave her a thumbs-up, moved my car, and walked back to her.

Brent moved the cruiser close to where my car had been, blocking the tire prints and more of the road. He removed a roll of crime scene tape from the cruiser's trunk. While Gartborg photographed the tire prints, Brent tied one end of the tape to a tree, strung the tape around the cruiser, tore the tape off the roll, and tied the end of it to another tree.

Gartborg slid her small camera into one of her jacket's many pockets and glanced from the woods to me. "Can you show us this canoe you found? Bring the crime scene tape, Brent."

Starting down the barely distinguishable trail, I admitted something that was probably obvious to both detectives. "The canoe might not be the one that I saw on Rich's dock on Monday night."

Gartborg reminded me, "The canoe you saw on the dock might not have been Mr. Royalson's."

I shuddered. "I hope it was. If it belonged to the murderer, he could have been lurking nearby when Nina and I were at Rich's cottage."

As if my caution about possibly compromising the scene taxed Gartborg's patience, she stayed right behind me, and it was easy to hear her quiet question. "Did you see, hear, or smell evidence of anyone else in these woods?"

Smell? Ewwww. "No, but I didn't expect to."

I took them past the canoe's hiding spot to where it had been dragged off the trail and into the woods. "It's up there, behind the boulder and beyond those cedars."

"I'll go look." Gartborg stepped carefully between snapped-off plants and eased around the cedars.

Brent stayed with me. He snapped pictures with his phone, opened his notebook, and drew a diagram of the paths and the location of the boulder. "Did you notice any marks or labels on the canoe on Royalson's dock Monday evening, Em?"

"No, and I didn't go closer to this one than this side of those cedars, so I couldn't see all of this canoe. or touch it."

Gartborg returned to us. "I took pictures. There are traces of mud on the bottom and a twig is caught on the inside where the yoke is attached. No one's underneath it."

I restrained a shudder. I hadn't thought about the possibility that anyone—dead, alive, or somewhere between—could be underneath the canoe.

"But," she added, "the ground under it is trampled as if someone or something might have been sleeping there." She agreed with me that the paddle resembled the ones we'd seen at Royalson's cottage. She and Brent strung crime scene tape around the boulder and the trees surrounding the canoe.

While Brent was on his phone arranging for forensics investigators to investigate the scene, I told Gartborg about the cove I'd noticed while kayaking. "The canoe could have been brought from the road, but the way it appears to have been dragged uphill and into the woods at an angle from the trail, I suspect it was pulled out of the lake onto a stony little beach down there." Trees screened the view of the lake and the cove.

Gartborg pointed out, "So those tire tracks beside the road might mean nothing."

"Getaway car?" I suggested.

Brent had finished his call and had his own theory. "Or the canoe was brought here on a vehicle, launched into the lake down there, brought back to the same spot, dragged into the woods, and abandoned."

Gartborg asked me, "Can you show us where you think the canoe might have been pulled ashore?"

I led both detectives down to the small beach with the grooves in the mud and the colorful streaks on the rocks.

Gartborg's phone rang. She answered it, listened for a moment, and asked into it, "Have you checked her home and the bank where she works? Not at either place? Keep looking."

Chapter 14

✹

Gartborg disconnected and turned to Brent. "They still haven't found Estable."

Terri was missing? Remembering Derek and his rage, I shivered in something like horror.

No wonder Gartborg had checked underneath the canoe.

"I need to use the computer in the cruiser," she said. "Meet you back there, Brent? Can you tape this off?"

"No problem. And if you need to drive somewhere, I'll hitch a ride back with Emily."

Gartborg gave him a funny look as if to say I couldn't be trusted, but she only said, "Okay." She strode away, up the pathway and out of sight into the woods.

I held the roll while Brent strung the yellow police tape around trees. No trees were right next to the water, so we weren't going to be able to completely tape off the beach from the lake. I offered, "You can borrow my kayak and position yourself offshore to keep people away from this little beach."

He squinted at the lake. "Your kayak would be a tight fit for me. Fortunately, the crowds of possible gawkers are small."

I grinned at his dry humor. As far as I could see, no one was on Lake Fleekom. "You should have come kayaking with me. Lake Fleekom isn't huge or wavy, but it's wild in places and interesting."

"And kayaking would have been more fun than what I was doing. Plus I might have learned more out here with you than we did inside Royalson's house. I might have discovered the canoe before you did. Thanks for calling about it."

"You're welcome." I unspooled more tape for him. "You didn't find clues about who might want him out of their way? No angry e-mails or letters, no lawsuits or disputes?"

"We're nearly done searching his house and cottage. We've taken his computer, phone, and other devices plus the files from his filing cabinet, and will thoroughly check them, but so far we have no answers."

"Do you have any guesses how the canoe could be connected with his death?"

"Do you?"

"What if the murderer decided to take advantage of the mist on the lake that morning? What if he knew about Rich's canoe, drove to about where my car was when you got here, parked, and walked or jogged to Rich's cottage? It's kind of far."

Brent reached for the reel of tape. "It's probably less than a half mile. It's about a quarter mile from here to the county beach, and Rich's cottage is about a quarter mile from there. It's not far for someone who is fit, and there was probably no one else around to see him or her. Visibility on the road might not have been great at the time. The fog could have been denser and higher than it was when you arrived. Also, we don't know when that canoe was taken off the dock. It could have been while it was still dark, anytime after you and Nina saw it, if it's the same one." He cut the tape and knotted the end around a tree. "We'll have to ask if anyone saw a vehicle parked out there where you found the tire prints." Holding the roll of tape at his side, he gazed toward the water.

I eased into the familiarity of brainstorming with him.

"Whether it was dark or light, the murderer could have gotten himself to Rich's cottage without being seen. He probably intended to adjust his plans if he thought anyone noticed him. He threw stones until he broke the powder room window, then he crawled inside and grabbed the skillet. He ran out the back door without bothering to close it. After that, I'm guessing that he took a paddle from Rich's cabinet and put the skillet into Rich's canoe. Maybe he spent extra time at the cottage or in the canoe on the lake, waiting until he thought Rich was alone."

Brent tilted his head in question.

"I found a place on the lake behind leaning junipers where he could have hidden himself and the canoe close enough to Rich's house that he could have seen and heard people, despite the mist."

Brent gave me one of those slow smiles that warmed me to my toes. "We'll have to bring our kayaks out here and you can show me."

"As soon as we're both free."

"It's a deal."

Thinking aloud, I developed more of my theory. "If things happened when they were supposed to according to Rich's to-do list, the murderer could have seen Terri paddle away and heard the catering truck leave. Then he could have guessed correctly, or maybe he had seen the to-do list and knew, that no one was with Rich. He paddled the rest of the way to Rich's house and attacked Rich. Then he fled into the mist in the canoe. He must have known about this cove before he parked his car, and he had to have driven through that puddle after it had dried enough for the mud to hold a print. After he paddled back to this cove, he pulled the canoe ashore." I pointed toward our feet. "He left grooves in the mud and aluminum on at least one rock." I turned and stared up the pathway. "He dragged the canoe up into the woods and hid it where no one would be likely to notice it soon. Then he got back into his vehicle and drove away."

"You keep saying 'he.'"

"I'm picturing two different men. Terri's ex-boyfriend, Derek, and Rich's neighbor. I don't know his name."

Brent supplied it. "Hank. Why do you suspect those two?"

"Derek stayed in Rich's cottage for five days. Hank lives on the lake and has a dock, so I assume he owns at least one boat. Both Derek and Hank could have paddled around this lake enough to know where they could drag a canoe ashore and hide it." *And now Terri is missing.* I didn't say it.

Brent looked surprisingly relaxed, standing with his feet apart, holding the roll of crime scene tape, and watching a couple of ducks slant down out of the sky and land on the water near where I'd seen the mallards earlier. He suggested, "If Derek murdered Rich, wouldn't it have been simpler to drive to Rich's, attack him, and drive away? Why bother with a canoe, especially to transport a heavy skillet?"

"I think Derek was riding a motorcycle yesterday. A canoe in the mist is stealthier. And bringing that skillet in a canoe might not have been as awkward as hanging on to it on a motorcycle."

"Good point."

I looked up into a pine tree, but couldn't see the bird crying like a scaled-down crow with a stuffed-up nose. "Could the tire prints in the mud near the road be from a motorcycle? I thought they were from one side of a four-wheeled vehicle, the back wheels following the front wheels, but not covering the prints completely because of the way the vehicle angled away from the shoulder and onto the road."

"They could be from a motorcycle, from a car, or from a small SUV or pickup. The prints might have nothing to do with the canoe that went missing from Rich's cottage dock or the canoe that you found up there behind that boulder."

Glancing up the hill as if I could see the canoe from the beach, I sighed. "And the canoe might never have gone anywhere near Rich's house on Tuesday morning. But if it did, the person who left the canoe in the woods would have needed a vehicle to get away."

Brent made a walking motion with his fingers. "Everything on this lake is within hiking distance of everything else. In addition to Rich's and Hank's houses, there are eleven recreational cottages, plus the county park and beach. He could have left his vehicle at any of those places, or even stayed for a while in one of the cottages."

"Did you check?"

"Yes. There were no signs of occupants at any of them, and the only one that had been broken into was Royalson's." His lips thinned. "You said that Terri Estable showed up in a canoe shortly after you found the deceased."

"I saw her put the red canoe underneath the deck as if she knew that was where it belonged, or as if she knew it didn't matter whether it belonged there or not. She could have known that Rich was never going to complain about it. If the red canoe originally came from that spot underneath the deck, Terri could have paddled it to his cottage and taken the skillet. Then she could have put that skillet into the aluminum canoe. One of her boots could have made the print I saw in the mud near the dock at Rich's cottage. She could have paddled the aluminum canoe to his house and attacked him. That skillet's heavy, but she's athletic."

"Why would she switch canoes?"

Watching water lap onto the beach, I imagined what Terri might have thought and done. "Maybe she didn't want to risk harming the fiberglass canoe with that heavy skillet, or maybe she thought the grayish aluminum canoe would be less noticeable in the mist, or she didn't want anyone to recognize the red canoe. Or she was hoping that someone would see and recognize the aluminum canoe and would blame someone else, particularly if that canoe did not belong to Rich. After she killed Rich, she could have hidden the aluminum canoe up there in the woods behind us and run back to Rich's cottage and gotten into the red canoe. She could have paddled back to Rich's house and acted surprised when I told her the party was canceled. She seemed upset when she heard sirens and realized that something bad could have happened, but she could have been acting. According to his list, Rich sent her away at ten twenty-eight, around the time the caterers arrived. The caterers left at eleven. Rich's skin was cool but not cold when I found him at about noon. Whoever killed him must have done it almost as soon as the caterers left."

Brent looked directly into my eyes. "How do you know when the caterers left?"

Fighting a blush was probably impossible, but I tried, anyway. "I went to their office this morning and talked to Cat." I wanted to put my hand on his sleeve and assure him that it was okay, but I restrained myself. "I'd picked up one of their cards before I found Rich's body. I wanted to order dessert for tomorrow night."

"Not donuts?"

"We get a break from them once in a while. Also, I wanted to talk about possibly working together if Cat ever needed a birthday cake made of donuts or something like that. Or gourmet coffee." I told him about the grudge Cat could have had against Rich. "But it hardly seems worth murdering over."

"Except to the murderer." He looked toward the yellow tape tied between trees. It rippled in a breeze I couldn't feel. "If the caterers committed the murder, they probably didn't arrive and leave by canoe. And if the murderer was Terri or Hank, they could have simply done the deed, retreated into a house, and waited for someone to find Rich. They didn't have to bother with canoes."

"But Derek might have found a canoe useful. Or maybe Terri or Hank knew they wanted the skillet from Rich's cottage. Besides, the mist that morning gave them a handy way to disappear without risking being seen going from Rich's tent into one of the houses. And there were those noises I heard like a paddle hitting an aluminum gunwale, which makes me believe that the aluminum canoe up there in the woods left the beach behind Rich's house shortly before I arrived. Sounds seem to carry strangely over water and even more strangely in the mist, though, so I can't be sure how far away the canoe was or what direction it was going. I thought it was being paddled farther away." Glad that Brent was willing to listen to me instead of returning immediately to Gartborg after he finished taping off the beach, I added, "If Terri had anything to do with Rich's murder, she could have worked with either Derek or Hank. Derek is quick to anger, as everyone in Deputy Donut noticed when he came in that time. Maybe Derek took Rich's canoe and did the actual murder while Terri acted as a lookout. Also, Terri and Hank seemed to know each other well considering that Terri had just reconnected with Rich. Maybe Terri and Derek got Rich to will her everything, and now she's working on getting Hank to fall for her and will her everything he owns. Terri and Derek will find another victim, and another, and . . ."

Brent conceded, "Royalson's will, especially his having signed it hours before he was murdered, makes Terri a prime suspect."

Folding my arms and hoping that Brent wouldn't guess that I was chilly and he wouldn't end our conversation, I asked, "What about the fact that she willed everything to him?"

"That doesn't make her look any less guilty, don't you think? She must have known that Royalson made her his beneficiary. Besides, her net worth doesn't compare to his. She owns a town house and a car and has some money in the bank, but not huge investments like he had."

"Wait. One other person knew about those wills. I didn't pay much attention to the witness's name when Detective Gartborg showed me the signed wills. Was it Henry somebody? As in 'Hank' can be a nickname for 'Henry'?"

"You got it. Royalson's neighbor, Henry Ferrinder, witnessed both wills." Brent was not dressed as warmly as I was, but he didn't look cold. His feet were probably dry, though.

In hopes of warming my toes, I wiggled them inside my sneakers. "The back of Hank's house is nearly all windows. He could have kept a lookout while Terri murdered Rich."

"How do you know how the back of Hank's house is constructed? Because of kayaking this afternoon?"

"Yes." I stared in that direction, but at least one treed point was between us and Rich's and Hank's houses. "The lake is small, so Hank can probably see most of it from his house or dock, but there are lots of places like this where someone in a boat can pull up onto or near the shore and hide."

Brent grinned down at me. "This is a great lake for kayakers and canoers, not so great for detectives."

Was Terri camping in the woods? Did she move to a closed-up cottage after they were checked for break-ins? Maybe she had found a key for one of them. Was she hurt, or worse? Hiding because she had murdered Rich? I asked, "Do you have enough evidence to arrest Terri? Her fingerprints must be everywhere, she was nearby, she had a motive, and one of her boots might have made that partial footprint in the mud near Rich's cottage dock."

"We do have more questions to ask her. After I took her initial statement, I told her not to leave town. Maybe she did, or maybe she's another victim. I hope that's not it. But to answer your question, no, we don't have enough evidence to arrest her."

"Yet."

He echoed, "Yet."

"When did you or anyone last see her?"

I thought he might not answer, but he did. "After I took her statement, she said she was going home. But as far as we know, she never made it."

"How did she get to Rich's house? Did she drive her own car, or did Rich bring her?"

"She drove there Monday afternoon. She said she wanted to make room for party guests, so early Tuesday morning, she parked her car on the road, around the curve beyond Hank's place."

"Maybe she meant much farther beyond, like in that dried-up mud puddle up there beside the road."

"Could be." He shot a piercing glance down at me. "You're shivering, Em, and as nice as these woods and this lake are, I should get back to work. Unless we can wrap this case up quickly, I probably won't make it to Samantha's party tomorrow night."

"I'm sorry."

"You should be. If you hadn't found that canoe, maybe we wouldn't have as many variables to discuss, and I'd be able to take tomorrow evening off."

"But, but . . . the canoe was here, and it could be important, and maybe one of you would have found it, but later, making the investigation last even longer."

He squeezed my shoulder with one large, warm hand. "I'll do everything possible to make it to your Halloween party on Saturday night."

"There will be donuts. And cider. And apple-cider donuts."

"I might have to dress up like a detective ducking out of work for an hour or so."

"I think you mean a detective taking a break so he can approach the crime with a fresh mind."

"I think I've been insulted." Carrying the roll of yellow tape, he followed me up the pathway. I took my time and watched where I stepped, but I knew it would be easy to trample clues without knowing I was doing it.

At the road, a marked cruiser was now supporting the crime scene tape where the unmarked cruiser had been, and the unmarked cruiser was in front of the dried-up mud puddle. Gartborg was in the driver's seat. She appeared to be focusing on the car's computer screen.

A rookie female police officer I'd seen at Deputy Donut only a few times was leaning against the marked cruiser.

Brent waved at her, put the tape into the trunk of Gartborg's cruiser, and got into the passenger seat. Beside his open door, I heard him ask, "Any luck?"

I couldn't catch what she said, but I thought she mentioned a BOLO.

Brent closed the car door.

I was not a police officer, but I would also be on the lookout for Terri Estable.

Chapter 15

❧

Speeding away, Gartborg sprayed gravel behind the unmarked cruiser. A small stone landed beside one of my damp sneakers. I couldn't help a startled exclamation.

The police officer guarding the scene asked, "Are you okay?"

"Sure. I was surprised that she did that so close to us."

"Maybe she didn't mean to."

"Is that how they teach you to drive in the police academy?"

She must have noticed that I was teasing. "Yes, and watch out unless you're bringing me donuts and coffee. I was an A student."

I laughed. "I'm getting out of here." I walked to my car and drove past her at about three miles per hour. She smiled. Warmed by the camaraderie that our donut shop had spread through our community, I waved.

I hoped that the police would find Terri Estable quickly, and that they would also find sufficient evidence to charge someone with Rich's murder. If they did, maybe Brent could make it to Samantha's potluck dinner the next night and to my party on Halloween. Social gatherings that included any of the six of us—Samantha and Hooligan, Misty and Scott, and Brent and me—were always fun, even though the other four had paired off in couples and Brent and I were not attached like the others were, no matter what Misty and Samantha liked to pretend.

Investigators' vehicles, including one like the unmarked cruiser that Gartborg had been driving only minutes before, were in Rich's driveway, but I didn't see either Gartborg or Brent as I drove past.

At home, I left the kayak on the car and went inside. Dep sniffed my mud-splashed pant legs. Despite the mud, which undoubtedly had its own odors, she could probably tell that I'd spent time around Brent without her. "He says he's coming to the Halloween party, Dep. How would you like to dress as a cat for the party?"

"Meow."

"I know, you wear that costume all the time, and it's perfect."

With a sniff, she turned away.

I won her over with a nicely fishy dinner and an invitation to cuddle on my lap while I read until bedtime.

Upstairs later, I crawled underneath the covers. Dep landed purring on my feet. I carefully did not mention Brent's name aloud, and Dep stayed with me. The next thing I knew, she and my alarm were both announcing that it was morning.

I dressed in my black pants and white shirt and made a spinach and Havarti omelette for my breakfast. Dep pushed kibble around her bowl, selected a piece, and nibbled at it.

The air outside was crisp. Walking to work, Dep showed her enthusiasm by holding her tail straight up and leading the way.

Thanks to Nina or Tom, the gas fireplace in our office had already made Dep's playroom toasty. I hung up my jacket and stowed the backpack I carried as a purse next to Nina's tote in a large, lockable desk drawer that Tom and I had designed especially for valuables in case our guard cat wasn't ferocious enough.

Nina and Tom were in the kitchen. I teased, "Did you two miss me yesterday?"

Nina moaned. "Terribly." She was smiling.

"What?" Tom demanded, straight-faced. "Were you gone?"

"I think so." I told them about finding a canoe that could have been the one that Nina and I had seen on Rich's cottage dock on Monday evening, the canoe that had been gone on Tuesday evening.

Tom commented, "It sounds like you were going places you shouldn't have been."

I pulled on my donut-decorated hat. "Brent didn't seem concerned."

Tom turned on an exaggerated glower. "Don't go getting yourself into trouble, Emily Westhill."

Nina stepped between us. "While you were gone, a police officer dropped off the coffee urn you left at the crime scene and thanked us for the coffee and donuts. Also, we dreamed up more kinds of Halloween donuts." The creations she showed me included fritter critters with googly sugar eyes; cat donuts with ears, whiskers, and bright green eyes; and witch-hat donuts with large licorice gumdrops on top. I particularly liked the ghost-shaped donuts with their chocolate chip eyes. Because they were the kind of donuts with holes cut out of them, some of their mouths gaped as if the ghosts were about to yell *Boo!* Other ghosts' mouths were puckered and nearly closed, as if those ghosts were on the verge of moaning piteously.

I gave Nina a new title. "You're our artistic director. Show me how you made these."

She muttered that Tom, Jocelyn, and I had made artistic triumphs before she came to work with us, but I could tell she was pleased. "This is more about taste than appearance, but I think Rich was wrong about the fudge frosting. When we double it, the chocolate almost overwhelms the delicate vanilla in the custard. What do you two think?"

Tom suggested, "Let's try putting about one and a half times as much fudge frosting on one."

I did that. Without bothering to etch the Boston scream face on the donut, we divided it and tasted it.

I held my hand up with the tips of my forefinger and thumb touching. "Perfect."

The other two agreed, and the three of us turned out scary-cute donuts and fritters at a rapid rate.

None of us expected many takers for the licorice gumdrop–topped witch's hats, but we had several among the Knitpickers and the retired men.

Apparently, they had discussed Rich and his death the day before when I hadn't been there and were happy to switch to a less somber topic and tease Cheryl. They told her to bring Steve to their morning meetings and teach him to knit.

Virginia, one of the Knitpickers, had qualms. "Bad idea. Cheryl's knitting basket is full of UFOs. She could teach him to knit, but then he would never finish objects, either."

Cheryl teased them right back. "If I finished mine, I wouldn't know what to do next."

"Choose another one to finish," Virginia suggested.

A Knitpicker waved a knitting needle, showing off the red-and-green-striped Christmas bell ornament she was knitting. "I can make these in silver and white or whatever color combination you'd like for wedding bells, you know."

Cheryl nearly choked on her coffee. "I like my single life just fine, thank you. I'm having fun and meeting new people while I'm at it, that's all."

The bell knitter raised her eyebrows. "People?"

Cheryl blushed. "Well, only one, so far, not including the late Rich Royalson." She frowned, but being Cheryl, she couldn't maintain a sad look for long. "I like Steve, but I can't see it ever going further than that. For one thing, he's a freelance writer, and he's here doing research, then he'll probably go back to Ohio and we'll both date other people. Or maybe not, in my case. A permanent man would mess up my life." She attempted a stern face, a nearly impossible feat for her. "Stop laughing!"

The Knitpickers and retired men continued their teasing

chatter, and I went back to helping make imaginatively decorated and tasty donuts. We had extra orders to fill for Halloween parties. I had already invited Tom and Cindy to mine.
I invited Nina, who was almost speechless with excitement
about meeting Cindy Westhill, but she quickly recovered and
started talking about which cute Halloween donuts I should
serve at the party. "Besides the ones we've been serving here,
let's decorate Long John donuts as zombies and make carrot-
cake donuts, but we'll call the carrot-cake donuts scare-it
cake donuts. I can't wait to help you make them."

"Why wait?" I asked. "Let's make some for here, but I
think you'd better decorate the zombies, Nina."

She laughed. "They don't have to be pretty!"

I countered, "They need to be recognizable as zombies and
not be mistaken for people with bad cases of seasickness."

Tom asked me, "Is Brent coming to your party?"

"I hope so. I promised him apple-cider donuts. It depends
on how the investigation is going."

Tom's attentive look reminded me that he had been a detective before he was police chief, and he still had a lively interest
and lots of friends in the Fallingbrook Police Department and in
other police services. "Who's the DCI agent directing this one?"

"Her last name's Gartborg. Brent called her Kim."

"I've never heard of her," Tom said.

Grinning diabolically at me, Nina opened her eyes wide
and flexed her fingers in a clawing motion.

I pursed my lips and wrinkled my forehead in an attempt
to look disapproving.

Nina laughed.

Still teasing each other, the Knitpickers and the retired men
left at noon as usual. With a sly grin, Tom suggested, "Maybe
we should order a table big enough for all of them to sit together instead of leaning out of their chairs until they almost
fall over trying to give one another a hard time."

I guessed, "If they sat together, they'd probably clam up."

"Besides," Nina pointed out, "they want to sit next to the front windows, and one large table would block the entryway more than they do when they're leaning out into the aisle."

After our lunch crowd left, a big, gray-haired man came in by himself. It took me a few seconds to recognize Rich's neighbor, Hank, the man who had witnessed Terri's and Rich's wills, the man who had been particularly solicitous of Terri when I was guarding the party tent and waiting for the police to arrive. Hank was old enough to be Terri's father, but Rich had been, also. Maybe, if Terri was interested only in men's money and possessions and killed them after she was certain she was their heir, their ages didn't matter to her.

Sighing, Hank sat down heavily on one of the stools at the counter between the dining area and the kitchen. He was wearing a suit and tie.

I asked what he'd like.

He flexed his fingers. "A nice hot mug of coffee. I see you have daily specials from different parts of the world. I don't care for strong, dark coffee, but I do like to try new things."

"Today's is from Brazil. It's a light medium roast with hints of chocolate and fruit."

"I'll try that, and I'd also like a pumpkin spice donut with cream cheese icing."

I brought them to him. He picked up the mug in both hands. "Ah, that's better."

I glanced toward our front windows. "Is it still cool outside?" The temperature had been predicted to rise.

"No, but these old fingers don't hit the piano keys as easily as they used to unless I warm them up. I'm giving a concert at Happy Times Retirement Home in an hour."

"Then I wish we had a piano here. You could warm up playing for us."

Hank's sudden smile seemed genuine. "That would be great."

I asked him, "Don't you live next to Rich Royalson's house?"

His face cloudy, he nodded. "I didn't get to talk to you there, much, I'm afraid. That poor man. He was happy again, but hardly had any time to enjoy it."

I thought I knew what Hank meant, but I asked, "Happy?"

"With that woman, Terri, who you prevented from going into the tent, not that I blame you. That was the right call under the circumstances."

"Thanks," I said drily. "Rich and Terri were in here the day before the party. Rich said that Terri was the love of his life, and they'd recently reconnected."

"That's how I understand it, although I didn't know about Rich's relationship with Terri until after Rich's wife, Patty, died. Your donut is delicious, by the way."

I thanked him and pretended ignorance. "Rich was married to someone besides the love of his life?" I hadn't meant to sound catty but was afraid that I had.

"Yes." He gulped at the coffee. "Thank you for giving me a new coffee to try. I like it very much. I gather there's love, and then there's love. I wouldn't know, never having been married or even tempted." He looked at his watch. "I'd better go. Can you put the coffee in a paper cup with a lid, and the rest of the donut in a box?"

Saying that I could, I turned around. Tom was watching donuts in the fryer, but Nina was staring at me. I went into the storeroom, grabbed a take-out box and a cup and lid, and took them back to Hank.

He was studying his phone, and he'd left money beside his plate. I boxed the donut and transferred the coffee from the mug to the paper cup. "Thanks," he said. "I was sure I'd spill half the coffee if I tried to do that. Keep the change." He picked up the box and the cup and hurried out of Deputy Donut.

I watched him go. Happy Times Retirement Home was probably less than a five-minute drive away. Hank had given himself about forty minutes to get there. Maybe he needed to arrive early to warm his fingers. Maybe the paper cup of coffee would help.

Chapter 16

I returned to the kitchen and told Tom and Nina about the conversation I'd had with Hank. "When we started talking about Terri, Rich, and Rich's late wife, he realized he had to leave."

Tom said, "One of the things I remember about Royalson's wife's death is that no one witnessed her canoe capsizing. Also, there were rumors that when his wife died, Royalson was having an affair with an employee at the bank where he worked."

Nina groaned. "Terri, I guess."

Tom nodded.

I asked, "Why did Rich wait twenty years to get back together with Terri?"

Nina guessed, "So he wouldn't look guilty."

"Here's what I heard," Tom said. "Terri quit her job at Fallingbrook Mercantile right after Royalson's wife died. Terri ended up with a lower salary, reduced benefits, and shorter vacations at Gooseleg State Bank. As far as I know, she stopped seeing Royalson after his wife's death."

I arranged Long John donuts on a tray. "I heard the DCI agent say Terri works at a bank. Maybe it's still Gooseleg State Bank. Maybe Terri was afraid that Rich had killed his wife, and she changed banks to keep him from doing her in, too."

Nina piped ragged purple shirts onto the Long Johns. "But

she came back and got her boyfriend to rent Royalson's cottage so she could, as the boyfriend yelled at her on Monday afternoon, seduce Royalson."

I stirred orange food coloring into cream cheese frosting. "Maybe Terri killed Patty Royalson but dropped Rich because she wanted to appear innocent. She's adept in a canoe. She could have gone out after Patty on that icy day and somehow managed to tip over Patty's canoe without harming herself. Or she didn't have to do that if she had already punched a hole in the canoe."

Tom squelched that idea. "The Royalsons' canoe was intact when it was found."

"Still," I said, "maybe Terri stayed away from Rich for twenty years until, she hoped, most people forgot her possible role in the murder." Gooseleg State Bank was the one that had hired Cat's Catering at the last minute for their Christmas party after Rich had hijacked the Gooseleg bank's caterer for his own bank's party. Did Terri have anything to do with that peculiar last-minute swapping of caterers, and if so, could her involvement have been connected to Rich's murder?

I asked Tom, "What about the man who was just in here, Hank, who is now Rich's neighbor? He talked like he knew Rich's late wife. He called her Patty. Do you know if he lived beside Rich and Patty when Patty died?"

Tom shook a basket of fried donuts to drain the oil. "No idea, but anyone who lived or was staying out at Lake Fleekom at the time would have been questioned about what they saw and heard. As I recall, no one admitted being anywhere near the lake when Patty Royalson overturned her canoe. Her husband reported her missing about seven that evening when he got home for dinner and discovered that she and a canoe were gone. It was already dark, but he and the investigators believed it was still light out when she launched her canoe."

I turned to Nina. "I wonder if the canoe Patty overturned

was the one we saw on Rich's cottage dock on Monday night, and maybe the one I found yesterday."

Nina added vanilla frosting pants to the Long John zombies. "The canoe we saw could have been at least twenty years old."

I spread orange icing on baked scare-it cake donuts. "Hank said he didn't know about Terri twenty years ago, so he might not have known that Rich was having an affair."

Nina laughed. "It's not necessarily something that people tell their neighbors."

"You might be surprised," Tom said. "The things I've heard . . ."

"Tell us!" Nina exclaimed.

Tom only smiled, shook his head, and handed me a wire basket of mostly cooled donuts.

Unlike Tom, I had gossip that I was willing to share. "I overheard the DCI agent say that they haven't been able to locate Terri, either at the bank where she works or at her home."

Tom's frown was grim. "That's not a good sign."

"Ooooh," Nina said. "Do you think someone did something to her? My bet is on that horrid ex-boyfriend."

Tom lowered a basket of cut-out ghosts into the hot oil. "Let me know if he comes in here again. If he does, one of you will take over the frying, please, and let me be his server."

We promised we would, but I had thought of another reason why Terri might have killed Rich. I suggested to the other two, "What if Terri killed Rich's wife? Maybe after she was cozying up to him again, she guessed that he figured out she had murdered his wife, so she killed Rich, not only for his money but also to prevent him from turning her in."

Nina added green faces, hands, and feet to the zombies. Their green ankles showed beneath their torn-off pantlegs. "I like your theory."

Tom shook a finger at Nina. "Don't encourage Emily to do anything more about the case than maybe discussing it with the detectives."

I blushed. I knew that Tom and Cindy wanted me to be happy. Although they never said so, I was sure that one of the things they thought would make me happiest would be pairing off with their son's, my late husband's, best friend. I was also certain that they didn't think that if Brent and I fell for each other we would be disloyal to their son's memory.

The idea made me uneasy, though. Brent was a wonderful person, and I liked being with him and talking to him. Maybe, someday, I would be able to untangle my feelings about him. *Maybe in the meantime,* a voice inside my head reminded me, *he'll find someone else. Like Detective Gartborg.* I mentally told the voice in my head to be quiet, and that if it refused to, I was going to ignore it.

Sometimes I thought Tom was almost as keen on matchmaking as I was. There was a difference, however, between being a matchmaker and a matchmakee. Maybe, if being the target of a matchmaker was making me uncomfortable, I had overdone my matchmaking. But I had succeeded with my two best friends. Both Samantha and Misty were happily dating men I'd chosen for them, although I had decided that Hooligan was right for Samantha after the thought must have already occurred to both of them. Remembering their momentous first encounter, I smiled. The sparks between those two had been almost visible. They still were.

With black icing, Nina piped dreadful-looking faces on the zombies and outlined the creatures and their outfits. She placed blood-red sprinkles on their shirts and slid the tray into the display case.

Cheryl returned with Steve but without any knitting projects, either finished or unfinished. I went out to the dining area to take their orders.

"I recommend the witch's hat donuts," Cheryl told Steve.

I added, "If you like licorice gumdrops."

Steve put his hands up to his throat like he was being strangled.

Cheryl defended her choice. "They're really good licorice gumdrops."

He pointed a finger at her. "You must be a middle child."

Cheryl quirked an eyebrow and tilted her head. "How did you know?"

"Middle children are the ones who eat pretend candies like licorice, candy corn, and molasses kisses. They can't fight the older kids for the chocolate, and the littlest kids get whatever they want."

"You're not a middle child?" she asked him.

"I'm an only child."

I said firmly, "So am I, and I like all of the candies you mentioned. How about a Boston scream donut then, Steve? They have lots of chocolate on them."

"That sounds perfect. And some hot chocolate to go with it."

"Cheryl?" I asked.

"A witch's hat donut for sure. And do you have any of that licorice-and-lemon tea?"

"Ugh," Steve said.

Cheryl asked, "Will it be too much, boiling water for tea?"

"Not at all. We have water that's close to boiling all the time. And if that's not working, we could quickly boil some on one of our gas burners."

"Cooking with gas is great, isn't it?" she asked. "That's what I have at home, for the burners, at least. The oven's electric."

"Me, too," I said, picturing the kitchen that Alec and I had designed and wondering how difficult it would be to connect a gas line to Rich's cottage, not that I was going to have anything to do with renovating it, now. "I'll be right back." When I returned, Steve was making Cheryl laugh with disparaging remarks about so-called pretend candies.

She leaned toward him. "Have you tried Wisconsin Limburger?"

He stared at her for a second. "Don't even mention that."

After everyone left and we closed, the walk home with Dep was lovely. It had been an amazingly warm October so far. Dep arched her back when she saw the goblins on our front porch. I opened the front door. She skittered sideways into the house.

Rich had commented that he didn't want anything resembling Halloween upstaging his birthday, but I didn't think that Samantha would mind someone wearing Halloween colors to her pre-Halloween potluck dinner. I put on a short orange denim skirt, black tights, a black sweater, and black flats.

Dep stalked to the sunroom and jumped onto one of her padded windowsills. I packed a small bag of medium-roast but flavorful coffee beans from the Dominican Republic into my backpack, called a goodbye to Dep, and drove to Cat's Catering.

Cat came out of the kitchen and handed me the pecan pie in a heavy-duty plastic container with a clear lid. She reminded me that she was interested in the possibility of jointly catering events.

In my car again, I wondered if the detectives had yet contacted Terri.

Her town house was near Samantha's. . . .

Chapter 17

Streetlights were on in the development where Samantha's, Derek's, and Terri's town houses were. Hoping, probably in vain, that no one would notice or recognize my red car with the red kayak on top, I drove slowly past Terri's town house. No lights were on inside, but I could see pumpkins beside her front door and mums blooming along the path between her porch and the sidewalk. Everything looked tidy, but she hadn't been missing long. Impossible as it seemed, Rich's death had been only two days before.

I sped up and parked around the corner.

Was Terri hiding from the police inside her house? Maybe she would open the door if she saw me on her porch among her pumpkins. However, I couldn't go barging to Terri's door with no explanation. Northern Wisconsin women took food to the bereaved, usually a hot dish in which cream of mushroom soup served as both the liquid and most of the flavoring. I didn't have one with me. I should have brought donuts. I sighed. If I had to, I would sacrifice that delicious-looking pecan pie. I wasn't sure how I, maker of donuts and other delicious desserts, would explain to Samantha and the others, including two sharp-eyed police officers, how I had managed to show up at a potluck dinner without the promised dessert. If necessary, I could speed back to Cat's Catering or to Cookies and Bakies in downtown Fallingbrook for a replacement.

I slid out of the car, put on my backpack, and picked up the pie in its container.

No one else seemed to be around. I rang Terri's doorbell. She didn't answer. I waited and rang it again. And again. After five minutes, I still didn't know where she was.

Or where she wasn't.

She could have been sick, injured, or worse inside her house. I was disappointed that I hadn't found her, but glad that I didn't have to give up the pie.

I turned around.

Derek Bengsen stood at the end of the short path, blocking the sidewalk. The streetlight above him turned his blond hair almost silvery. His hands on his hips, he glared at me. He was wearing scuffed boots, torn jeans, and a black tank top that showed off substantial biceps and did not look warm enough for the cooling evening.

I thought, *Pies work as weapons only in comedies.* Smiling with faked confidence and walking toward him, I mentally prepared to leap over a row of chrysanthemums and bolt across Terri's neighbor's yard.

Derek demanded in an unpleasantly hoarse and raspy voice, "Do you know where she is?"

Since I'd been ringing her doorbell, I couldn't pretend I didn't know who he was talking about. "No. She doesn't seem to be home."

He scrubbed a hand through his hair in a distraught manner. "Her boss called me and wanted to know why she didn't show up at work yesterday or today. And she hasn't been here, either. I keep checking back." He was either a good actor or he didn't know where his ex-girlfriend was. "Aren't you the chick who told me that her new boyfriend's party was canceled?"

"Yes." Was he connected to Terri's disappearance? I could probably edge around him without jumping over flowers. Maybe potentially helpful witnesses were peeking between curtains in nearby town houses.

"Terri took that day off, and that was the last time I saw her. The bank where she works hasn't seen her since Monday."

"I thought maybe she'd be here. . . ." I let my voice trail off and hoped the container of pie in my hands would complete my explanation.

"And I was in your donut shop, too. I followed her in."

Pinching my lips together, I nodded. If he came after me, I would scream.

The corners of his mouth turned down in apparent contrition. "I'm sorry I lost control. I was just so"—he seemed to search for words—"so mad at the way she treated me that I wasn't thinking. I mean, she has a right to date whoever she wants, right, even if he's old enough to be her grandfather?"

That was stretching the age difference. "He's dead." That was also how my voice sounded.

"I heard about that. After I left his place, the police asked me questions for hours. I suppose I did look guilty, coming into your shop and yelling at him, so I understand why you sent them."

"I didn't send them. The police are interviewing everyone who might know anything about Rich Royalson. Your connection to Terri would be enough—"

He waved my comments aside. "I didn't know him. I didn't kill him. And don't go blaming my friends who were at his cottage. They thought he was funny. They laughed at him. We all did. And right after Royalson kicked us out, my friends went home to Gary. I've known them forever. They got into some trouble when we were kids, but they're good guys. We all have jobs. I deliver furniture and appliances." He flexed one of those impressive biceps. "I can lift and carry nearly anything."

I didn't doubt that. I barely managed to restrain myself from backing farther from him. Maybe he didn't realize that what he'd said could be interpreted as a threat. He went on defending the men that Rich had referred to as Derek's drunken buddies. "You can check with the police. They know for a fact that my friends were in Gary when Royalson died. I was just angry when I came into your shop. It didn't mean anything. I bet you say things when you're mad that you don't mean, but you can't take them back, can you?"

"No, you can't." I let him interpret that however he pleased. "You were angry at Rich Royalson on Monday. Why did you come to his birthday party on Tuesday?"

He eyed me like he was about to challenge my right to question him, which was fair enough, but he answered. "After he yelled at me in your shop, he called and invited me." I doubted that, but unless I could see Rich's or Derek's phone records, I had no way of proving that Derek was lying. "He said he was sorry for the way he treated me, both in your shop and at his cottage." I doubted that, too. "He said Terri told him I was not responsible for the way my friends acted when I rented his cottage. They got a little carried away." His shrug rippled more muscles. "What can I say? I told Royalson I was sorry and that they were just having a little fun and things got out of hand. You know how that goes, right?"

"I've heard." *And things getting out of hand sometimes ends up with someone dead. . . .* I didn't say it.

Derek laced his fingers together and stretched them, his palms toward me. It was too dark to see dirt on his hands, if there was any. His knuckles popped. "How can I make it up to you for how I acted in your shop?" Shoving his hands into the back pockets of his jeans, he rolled his shoulders forward slightly in a pose that could have looked humble if he hadn't widened his stance at the same time.

I wanted to race away from this man who would undoubtedly catch me in about three strides. I attempted a courteous smile. "Come in sometime and try our donuts and coffee."

With what could have been a sheepish grin, he stepped aside. "Okay." He eyed the clear top of the container in my hands. "Were you going to give that to Terri? I can keep looking for her. I'll see that she gets it."

"That's okay. I'd like to give her my condolences in person."

"Condolences," he repeated with a hint of sarcasm. And maybe a flash of anger.

I felt like I was teetering on the edge of a blade. Saying, "And this is for a potluck dinner," I strode toward Samantha's.

Where was Terri, and was Derek only pretending that he didn't know? And where was his motorcycle? I hadn't heard or seen one before he appeared on the sidewalk in front of Terri's house.

I turned around and scanned the sidewalk behind me. Derek was not in sight. I tried not to run the rest of the way.

Samantha's outdoor decorations did not include skeletons or ghosts, which wasn't too surprising for an emergency medical technician dating a policeman. Instead, she had witches and black cats. It looked like she had tried to carve a scary face on her pumpkin, but her innate kindness must have prevented her from creating anything that might frighten young trick-or-treaters. The pumpkin looked surprised and slightly goofy.

Carrying my pie up to her porch, I wondered if I should have worn a costume.

Samantha opened the door. She wasn't in costume unless the orange and black streaks in her dark brown curls counted. She often tinted her hair to go with the season and to cheer her patients. She saw me grinning at her hair and joked that she'd been trying to copy Hooligan's hair color and had failed. Her smile was huge. I gave her a one-armed hug.

Hooligan showed up behind her in the narrow entryway. I handed him the pie. His hair might have been orange when he was a kid, but now it was auburn, which didn't keep him from looking charmingly boyish, especially in his jeans and tweedy gray sweater. "Misty and Scott are already here," he said. "Come join us in the living room."

Neither of our two tall blond friends were in costume, either, or in uniform. They'd been holding hands on the couch, but they let go of each other and stood up. Misty's black slacks and turtleneck set off her fair skin. She wore a necklace made of strands of multicolored beads. Scott was wearing black slacks and an orange shirt.

"Brent probably can't make it," I said.

Misty hugged me. "Gartborg is keeping him busy." She grinned. "With work. Hooligan and I were lucky to get away. But never fear, we'll make it to your party Saturday night, no matter what, and we'll drag Brent along, too."

I whined, "I need friends who aren't first responders, friends who work normal hours."

"Like you," Misty said, "always having to go into work early and never able to stay out late."

"I do, sometimes."

"When you can't help it." I could tell she was teasing, but she was undoubtedly remembering nights when emergencies had kept both of us out later than we'd intended.

Hooligan brought in a bottle of champagne, opened it, and divided it between five glasses. "We'll start with this and work our way to sparkling water for those of you who have to drive tonight."

I eyed him suspiciously. Champagne? And Samantha's super-brilliant smile? I caught Misty's eye and raised an eyebrow. She winked as if she also had a good guess about what might be about to happen.

When we all had our glasses, Hooligan raised his and began a toast. "To my . . ." Grinning, he turned to Samantha. She pulled her left hand out of her pocket, where, I realized, it had been the entire time I'd been there, and displayed a diamond ring on her engagement finger. Hooligan was glowing as much as Samantha was. "To my wonderful fiancée," he said.

Misty and I squealed and managed to drink to Hooligan's toast before setting our glasses down haphazardly and running to Samantha to hug her. And we didn't leave Hooligan out of our hugging frenzy, either.

"When did you ask her?" I demanded.

Hooligan squeezed Samantha next to him. "Last night."

Misty asked, "Have you set a date?"

Samantha gazed adoringly up at Hooligan. "Probably next summer, definitely in Fallingbrook, but we haven't decided where. I'm going to want you two, Misty and Emily, to be my attendants."

I asked, "Wouldn't you rather have me cater and stock a donut wall?"

"No way! You are both going to take that evening off and party." She patted her head. "I haven't decided what color my hair will be."

Misty suggested, "You can dye it to match Emily's and my dresses."

"Or powder it to match mine. Ooooh, I like it!" Samantha spoke in an exaggeratedly dreamlike voice. "Maybe we should have a winter wedding. I'll wear white velvet and snowy hair." Although I'd known her since the beginning of junior high, I couldn't always tell when she was joking.

"What about your honeymoon?" Scott asked. "Where will you go?"

"We haven't decided that yet, either," Hooligan said. "We're open to suggestions."

Samantha raised her chin and made a small-mouthed and patently fake haughty face. "Or keeping it secret so that the rest of you won't come along."

Placing one hand over my heart, I staggered backward. "I feel wounded." I carefully did not back into anything.

"Ha," my unfeeling bride-to-be friend said.

Our appetizers were the charcuterie plate that Scott had brought and the veggie plate that Misty had brought.

Samantha and Hooligan had made delicious coq au vin. By the time we finished that, Scott, Hooligan, and I were drinking sparkling water because we were all driving. Scott offered to take me home, but I wasn't leaving my car and kayak on the street overnight, plus I had to work early the next morning, and I wasn't sure when or how I would retrieve my car.

Because of my early hours, I didn't have any of the coffee I'd brought, although those who did said it was delicious. "I know," I said. "I get lots of it."

Scott smiled. "Braggart."

I did eat a nicely large portion of the pecan pie. Everyone agreed that they would buy pies from Cat's Catering in the future.

"Unless Cat turns out to be a killer," Misty added ominously. She apparently wasn't afraid of Cat's pie, though. She had seconds.

I didn't stay long after dessert. We all gave one another goodbye hugs.

Watching for Derek or his motorcycle, I walked to my car. With its doors securely locked, I drove past Terri's town house. It was still dark inside, and the porch light hadn't been turned on.

I almost didn't notice the white slip of paper sticking out between her storm door and the jamb.

It had not been there earlier. Was it a note from Derek, perhaps threatening? The police wouldn't leave a message where anyone could read it.

Anyone could read it. . . .

I stopped, checked my mirrors, and craned my neck around. Hoping there were no security cameras focused on me, I got out and walked casually to Terri's door as if I had every right to be there.

The white thing was a folded piece of paper. I pulled it out and peered at it in the dim light. It was an advertisement for a snow removal service.

Certain that Terri or Derek was about to fling the door open and ask what I was doing there at ten o'clock at night, I clumsily refolded the flyer and stuck it between the storm door and the jamb. I walked as normally as possible to my car. Driving away, I saw similar flyers at other doors and scolded myself for not having paid attention to the other houses before going up to Terri's porch. For sure, someone in the neighborhood had a security camera, or the witnesses I'd hoped were peeking between their curtains when Derek confronted me were now calling the police to report a prowler in an orange denim skirt.

If Terri had opened her front door since I was last there, she probably would have taken the flyer inside, or it would have dropped to her porch. She either hadn't gotten home yet, or she'd been inside when the flyer was delivered.

I wondered if she'd been located. I wondered what Brent was doing, and how he and Detective Gartborg were trying to solve Rich's murder.

I would be glad when they arrested someone. Gartborg could move on to her next DCI assignment, and Brent might again be free to join the rest of us at parties and dinners.

I didn't mind that he hadn't been there to see Misty's and my excitement over Samantha and Hooligan's engagement. Brent and I weren't dating each other, but he might have thought we were pressuring him to change our comfy and supportive relationship. I didn't mind if Scott and Misty felt pressured to consider becoming engaged, but I understood why Brent should be cautious about dating his late partner's widow.

I hadn't been cautious with Alec, and I had never regretted saying yes to him.

Meanwhile, if I could do anything non-dangerous and non-interfering to help Alec's best friend solve this latest murder, I would.

Where could Terri be? If Derek had done something to her, I didn't want to be the one to find out. The police could do that.

But what if she was all right, and merely scared of someone—Derek, for instance? Rich might have given her the keys to his house and cottage. Could she be hiding at either of those places when police investigators weren't there?

She'd seemed very friendly with Rich's neighbor, Hank, but shortly after he mentioned her at Deputy Donut, he'd realized he had to rush off to his performance at Happy Times Retirement Home.

Maybe Terri was hiding from Derek and the police in Hank's house.

Maybe Hank had killed Rich, and fearing that Terri might suspect him, Hank had killed her, too.

I could drive past Rich's and Hank's houses and Rich's cottage. Maybe I would figure out if Terri was staying in any of those places, either on purpose or against her will.

Lake Fleekom wasn't far out of the way home.

Chapter 18

❧

Staring at Rich's mansion, I drove slowly down the hill. If I saw any sign of investigators or murderers, I would turn around and go home.

The moon would be full on Halloween, which would be perfect for my party that night. This was only the twenty-ninth, but the moon was high, almost round, and very bright. Rich's mansion was dark. No vehicles were in his driveway, the tent was still on the lower part of his side yard, and his gates were closed. Yellow crime scene tape surrounded the property. Watching his house for signs of life, I followed the road as it curved right and passed Hank's house.

I couldn't see anyone in or around Hank's house, either, but lights in back illuminated trees near the shore. As usual, no vehicles were in his driveway. A man fastidious enough to blow leaves off his dock probably kept his cars or trucks tidily in the two-car garage attached to his house.

At the unpaved part of the road, I slowed down. I couldn't see crime scene tape near the pathway leading into the woods where I'd found the canoe. I guessed that the canoe and paddle had been taken to the forensics lab and a mold of the tire prints had been made so they could be compared to the tires of suspects' vehicles.

No one was at the public beach.

I tucked my car close to trees on one side of the parking

area, shut off the engine, made certain that the dome light wouldn't come on, opened the door, and listened. All I heard were wavelets washing onto the beach and a late-falling leaf floating down, touching branches, and settling almost soundlessly on the ground.

I slipped out of the car. Leaving the door ajar and navigating by the light of the moon, I walked quietly to the water's edge.

I couldn't see Rich's and Hank's houses from this secluded beach, and I couldn't see Rich's cottage. I could barely make out the cottage's dock. I stood listening and watching.

I could get back into the car, drive to Rich's cottage, check it visually as I drove past, and take another look at his and Hank's houses on the way home.

If I drove past Rich's cottage and Rich's and Hank's houses, my car's engine and headlights would be noticeable.

Kayaking near the backs of the buildings would be nearly inaudible and wouldn't involve bright lights. From my kayak, I would be able to check the lake sides of all three buildings. I would be able to kayak quite safely on that lonely, moonlit lake. Hank had told me that he had never been married. I had the impression that he lived alone. Unless Terri or someone else was in Hank's or Rich's house, or some of the cottages were occupied this late in the season, Hank might be the only person who could look out and see a kayak on the lake.

Maybe he wouldn't think it was unusual for people to kayak at night.

No other boaters would bash into me unless the fingers of mist curling up from the lake thickened into an impenetrable blanket and we couldn't help a collision. But no one else was likely to go out in a boat in the semidarkness at this time of year, no one in their right mind, anyway.

When it came to kayaking, was I ever in my right mind? Maybe I was addicted to the freedom of skimming across the water. Maybe I also associated kayaking with Brent.

I could imagine Alec telling me not to go out on this lake

by myself at night before the murderer was caught and to call Brent instead.

There was no reason to call Brent. I didn't know where Terri was. I merely had a guess, lots of guesses, and maybe I could rule out some of them.

Besides, the investigation was keeping Brent too busy to answer calls about unsupported hunches.

Even if I didn't find a clue to Terri's whereabouts, I could simply enjoy the moonlit magic of this lake, with mist swirling around me.

How could I resist?

I muttered, "I'll be careful."

Thanks to the moon and a flashlight, I quickly removed my kayak from the top of the car. I carried the kayak to the edge of the water and retrieved my paddle, life jacket, and my phone's flotation case from the trunk. I stowed my backpack in the trunk, closed the lid as quietly as I could, and locked the car.

A short skirt, a sweater, tights, and flats weren't the best outfit for kayaking on a chilly October night, or any other time. Maybe my life jacket would provide extra warmth. I fastened it on and tucked my phone in its case into a pocket. After hitching my skirt up around my hips, I managed to clamber into the kayak without getting my feet—or anything else—completely soaked.

And then, there it was, the euphoria of effortless floating. Sitting among the growing wisps of mist was spectacular. I wished Brent could have been enjoying it with me.

I paddled across the lake without going close to the cottages. Seeing no lights around Rich's cottage or any of the Bide-a-Wees, I kept going and steered the easily maneuverable little craft through shallow water beside the wild and undeveloped shore.

Hank's and Rich's houses were still far away, and the white party tent was ghostly in the moonlight. I could have stayed warmer by paddling faster, but I didn't want my movement or splashing to be noticeable to anyone on the shore or the lake if anyone else was out here.

Besides, floating on this calm water and absorbing all this moonlit beauty was worth a little shivering. Listening, watching, and occasionally merely drifting, I stayed close to the wooded shore. I eased past the stream flowing out of the duck and turtle pond. Slowly, I paddled into shadows behind junipers leaning out over the last point of land between the pond and Rich's property. The shadows, the high bank, and the trees should shelter all but my head from potential watchers in Rich's or Hank's houses.

I peeked between juniper branches. Rich's house was as dark in back as it had been in front. No one seemed to be around, but I kept watching until my wet feet reminded me that I had a nice warm cat waiting for me at home. Sitting up straighter, I dipped my paddle toward the water.

A light moved behind one of the upper windows of Rich's house.

I stilled the paddle and grabbed a branch to prevent my kayak from drifting away from the treed point.

The light went out.

I watched. The light did not reappear. I was about to turn around and go back the way I'd come, as far as possible from Rich's house and the person who might be inside it, when someone appeared on Hank's lawn at the end of the hedge between Hank's and Rich's houses.

I didn't move.

Seemingly unconcerned about watchers, he—I was sure it was a he by his size and the way he walked—strode across Hank's beach, slipped into a canoe near Hank's dock, and paddled toward the middle of the lake. He paddled quickly, without splashing or banging against gunwales.

Unless I wanted to confront him or be confronted by him, I didn't dare return to the public beach via the end of the lake where Rich's cottage was. Similarly, if I paddled straight across the lake and the person in that canoe turned around, he might see past the curling mist and notice me. Plus, although I would try to paddle quietly, I might end up close enough for him to hear one end of my paddle splash as it went into the water and the other end drip as it came out.

The best and perhaps safest choice was to stay close to the shore near Rich's mansion where trees and the party tent would partially shield me from the view of anyone who might be looking out one of the windows near where I'd seen the light. And maybe by the time I was skulking along that shore, the person in the canoe would be at the other end of the lake, too far away to see or hear me in the rising mist.

Hoping that if anyone did see me they'd mistake me for some sort of kayaking fiend, which wasn't too far from the truth, I paddled cautiously around the point and past the party tent.

I stayed close to Rich's dock and rounded the end of it, and then I was in open water between his dock and Hank's. I passed the hedge that divided their properties.

Lights were on in Hank's house, flooding the glass-walled back room with a warm glow. Maybe Terri was in there, enjoying a nice warm mug of something delicious by the fireplace.

Or screaming for help.

No one was screaming that I could hear, but that didn't prevent me from imagining it.

I stilled my paddle again and held my breath.

"Meow." It sounded like Dep.

Chapter 19

A catlike form sat near the shore on Hank's side of the thick cedar hedge. "Meow."

My heart thundered. I managed to call in a strangled whisper, "Dep?"

"Mew."

How could Dep have gotten here? All the time I was telling myself that the cat meowing beside the hedge could not possibly be Dep, I was picturing someone breaking into my house, grabbing my darling kitty, and bringing her to this isolated lake where a man had been murdered two and a half days before.

Staying underneath cedar branches, the cat slunk up the hill and away from where I sat in my gently rocking kayak.

Carefully, I turned and scanned what I could see of the lake. If the man and his canoe were on the water, they were out of sight in the moonlit mist.

I paddled to Hank's beach. Listening for noises from the houses and watching the lake, I thrust myself out of my kayak and pulled it higher on the sand to keep it from floating away. Bent over, knowing that Brent wouldn't approve, I darted to the hedge. "Dep?"

"Mew." This time, the plaintive cry came from close to Hank's house. I ran up the hill beside the hedge until I was near one corner of the windowed back room.

"Mew." There was a click and a rattle.

A large, gray, long-haired cat let himself into Hank's back room through one of those cat doors that unlocked when a cat wearing a transmitter came near it.

I called Dep again. No answer.

Exhaling, I relaxed my shoulders. Dep was undoubtedly still safe at home, and Hank had a talkative cat who probably smelled like cedar at the moment.

I could not see Terri or anyone else in the room. It was an enviable retreat, with warm shades of wood paneling on the walls, gorgeous rugs on the floors, and comfy chairs and couches underneath lamps placed just right for reading. A fire burned low in a massive stone fireplace. The gray cat curled up in a kitty bed in front of the hearth and settled his chin on his front legs. I could almost hear him purr.

Next to the wall of windows, a shiny black grand piano displayed only one photo on its closed top. I crept to the window nearest the piano.

The photo was a cute one, obviously vintage, of two teenagers dressed for prom. The boy was wearing a white dinner jacket with a red carnation in the lapel, and the girl was wearing a shimmery silver dress with a white orchid pinned to the bodice. Both about seventeen, their smiles were somewhere between proudly overjoyed and painfully shy.

They looked familiar.

It didn't take me long to figure out that the boy had to be a much younger Hank.

I'd seen many photos of the girl, taken other years, in Rich's cottage.

Hank had dated Patty, the girl who had later married Rich.

Hank had left Deputy Donut abruptly after he'd mentioned Patty Royalson.

And now a man I thought might be Hank was out on the lake where Rich's wife had drowned. Did Hank have anything to do with her death or with her husband's, twenty years later?

And there I was, trespassing on Hank's lawn and peeking into his windows while my kayak was on his beach. And the night was lighter than ever, with the nearly full moon shining on the growing mist.

Hoping that the mist would envelop me and my kayak, I scuttled back to the beach and paddled away from the two houses and toward the cove where someone had dragged a canoe onto the beach and into the woods. I was shivering.

Hoping that the person who had canoed away from Hank's house was not already in that cove, I listened. If the man was out here on the lake, he was silent.

For once, I hadn't felt that thrill of floating free when I launched my kayak at Hank's beach. I paddled as quickly and quietly as I could past the cove.

I swung farther out into the lake to survey the county park's beach before I attempted to land. I wasn't sure how I would get to my car if someone was prowling around on the beach. Encountering police investigators would be embarrassing, but better than coping with a murderer. My kayak paddle, a hollow aluminum shaft with plastic blades, would not be a particularly good weapon.

Gliding past the beach, I peered over the mist. The only vehicle I saw was mine. The moon's reflection was like an ethereal white ball on the windshield. I paddled quickly, accidentally splashing my paddle too loudly, to the beach.

I had stopped shivering. I disembarked. And plunged both feet into the shallows.

I carried the kayak and paddle to my car and stowed my paddle, phone case, and life jacket in the trunk. I let the trunk lid drop into place. The sound was loud enough to echo from the other side of the lake. Sliding the kayak into its carrier on the roof was not much quieter. Not knowing where the canoer was, I didn't turn on a flashlight, which made fastening the kayak to the straps on my car more difficult than usual.

I had snapped the latches in back and was going around to the front when I heard an engine and the rattling of a vehicle traveling on bumps and potholes in the gravel road. It was coming from the direction of Hank's and Rich's houses. Could it be the person who'd moved a light on Rich's mansion's third floor? Or was someone heading for one of the Bide-a-Wees, perhaps arriving Thursday night for a long weekend?

Maybe someone was planning to investigate this public beach. . . .

I slipped into the driver's seat and quietly shut and locked the door.

Headlights lit the road. A small, dark pickup truck bumped past and continued toward the cottages.

As soon as it was out of sight, I jumped out of the car and latched the kayak's front tie-down straps. Because of moonlight reflecting off the misty lake, they were easier than the back ones. The rattles from the pickup truck dwindled.

I quickly got into the car again and was about to close the door when a light, blurred by mist, wobbled near Rich's dock or one near it. The light disappeared.

Had it been the person from the canoe or someone else? I didn't think it could have been the driver of the pickup truck. I could still hear faint rattling as if the pickup was almost at Rich's cottage.

Hugging myself for warmth, I stared through the windshield.

I'd hoped that when I was kayaking, I'd been hidden in the mist, and maybe I had been. I was short, and people in kayaks could be lower than people in canoes.

Above the mist, I saw the dark silhouette of a head, shoulders, and, occasionally, a hand at the top of the paddle. It was eerie. Without coming close to the beach where I sat uneasily peering over my steering wheel, the canoer headed down the middle of the lake toward Hank's and Rich's houses.

Had he seen the moon reflecting off my windshield either

of the times he'd canoed past? Had he noticed that a kayak had appeared on top of the car between his trips across the lake?

I could no longer hear the rattling pickup truck. I didn't want to get out of my car, but I needed to see where that canoe went. Leaving the door open, I ran lightly through the stony sand to the water's edge.

The beach was lower than my car, and all I could see of the person piloting the canoe was a stocking cap. I guessed he was Hank, returning home.

Where was Terri? Had she or an investigator been inside Rich's house with a light? Maybe all I'd seen was the reflection of an unusually bright star or of an airplane flying too high for me to hear.

I couldn't see Hank's or Rich's homes or docks. When the person in the canoe went out of sight, I returned to my car and this time I closed the door. Quietly. The entire time that person had been canoeing, he hadn't banged his paddle against a gunwale. Not once.

I was almost certain that the canoer had gone from Hank's beach to Rich's little Cape Cod cottage and was probably returning to Hank's beach. Had the canoer visited Terri in Rich's cottage? If she was still in his cottage after he left, was she all right, or had the canoer done something to her? She was short. Maybe she'd been paddling in the bow of the canoe.

Or lying in the bottom of it.

It was nearly eleven thirty, but between adrenaline and the chilly insides of my car, I wasn't sleepy.

Besides, the sooner Rich's murder was solved, the sooner Detective Gartborg might leave town. Brent and I might be able to kayak together on the moonlit, misty lake.

I eased my car away from the beach and bumped it along the gravel road. Toward Rich's cottage.

A battered, rusting dark gray pickup truck was parked outside Rich's cottage. Hairs on the back of my neck prickled as if my skin could warn that someone was watching me. I didn't see anyone in or near the truck or the cottage, and yellow crime scene tape still surrounded the property.

Regretting coming to this lonely spot late at night in a memorable car with a kayak on top, I turned around after the next curve in the road and headed back. I wanted to speed, but racing down that dirt road would be noisy, plus I needed to keep my eyes open for any clue about where Terri was, and if she was a murderer or being held captive—or worse—by one.

The pickup truck was still parked near Rich's cottage. I remembered to glance at its tires. The truck wasn't a big one, and its tires did not appear to be much wider than a car's or an SUV's. Although I needed to be home with Dep, who might be missing me as much as I was missing her, I forced myself to drive slowly down the unpaved section of the road. I passed the driveway to the old log cabin, the public beach, and the narrow trail that led to the tiny cove.

I drove a little more quickly after I reached the pavement, but I scanned Hank's and Rich's houses.

As if the only light in Hank's piano room came from the dying embers in his fireplace, barely any light shone from the back of his house to the trees near his beach.

I saw no lights or other signs of life around Rich's house, either.

Chapter 20

❧

I tried not to accelerate around the curve that would take me to the road running up the hill and away from Lake Fleekom. At the top of the hill, I exhaled. I also turned up the heater.

Kayaking on that lake had been beautiful, but now I was mainly aware of the sinister creepiness of being alone on a foggy lake when the only other people nearby could have been murderers desperate to keep their secrets.

I was almost certain that Hank had been the person I'd seen paddle across the lake and back.

I wasn't positive that I'd seen a light moving inside Rich's house, but if I had, who had been there?

Meanwhile, someone had driven an old pickup truck to Rich's cottage and parked it there. If Hank was the canoer, he couldn't have been the driver of the truck. Who else would visit Rich's taped-off cottage in the foggy, moonlit dark, and why? I couldn't help picturing Derek. And Terri. Maybe looking for the kayaker they'd spotted out on the lake at night.

Meanwhile, I hadn't learned anything that made me think I needed to tell Brent I'd again gone kayaking on Lake Fleekom without him. The detectives were probably already looking into any connections that Hank might have had with Rich, Terri, and Rich's late wife.

Maybe the pickup driver was an undercover cop. If so,

Brent probably already knew that I had driven past Rich's cottage. He might also know that my car had been parked at the public beach and that I'd been out on a kayak. I half expected my phone to ring.

At home, Dep greeted me as soon as I opened the front door. I picked her up and hugged her. "Am I ever glad to see you! Sorry for being out so late." I told her about my fright when another cat had meowed with a voice that had sounded like hers. "I didn't know how you could have gotten all the way to Lake Fleekom, Dep, but I was scared."

She purred.

Although I had to work the next morning, I set my alarm for a half hour later than usual. Warmed by my cat and my happiness for Samantha and Hooligan, I fell asleep.

Around three, I heard Dep puttering with squeaky and jingly toys. She returned to bed, and I drifted off again. She let me sleep until my alarm went off. Even though it was still dark, I had mostly forgotten the menacing chill of Lake Fleekom at night, and once again I smiled, thinking about the way Samantha and Hooligan had glowed at the party.

I made a quick roasted-pepper and Gouda omelette. After my late night, I was going to need lots of coffee, but I could drink it at work, so I didn't brew any at home. I put on my backpack, fastened Dep's halter around her, and attached her leash.

I thought I might need to carry her if the morning was chilly, but the brisk air seemed to make her frisky enough to dash, quickly switching directions and nearly tripping me, most of the way to work. We arrived on time.

Again, Tom had turned on the gas fireplace in our kitty playground and office combination. I waved at him through the window from the office into the kitchen, removed Dep's halter and leash, and went into the kitchen. A few minutes later, Nina was in the office talking to Dep. Wearing our donut-festooned hats and our logo-embroidered aprons, Tom, Nina, and I prepared our shop for another day of serving fun

Halloween treats and warm, fragrant drinks to our customers.

Cheryl showed up about five minutes earlier than the Knitpickers and the retired men usually arrived. I took her a mug
of coffee. She cradled it in both hands as if they were cold.
"Can I ask you something, Emily?"

"Sure."

"Do you think I could be in trouble with the police for
being one of the first people to arrive at Rich's party?"

"What makes you think you're in trouble?" I reminded
myself of Brent, asking a question instead of answering.

"I told them about meeting Rich here and that Rich had
brought a different date to Deputy Donut that same afternoon. Rich's behavior didn't hurt me, far from it. I thought it
was funny, especially considering that I was also with another date, but the detective from that Wisconsin bureau,
whatever you call it—"

"The Division of Criminal Investigation."

"Right. That glamorous woman with the smooth silver hair
kept asking me how I felt when Rich came in with another
woman. I forget how many ways she tried to get me to say I
was so hurt and angry that I wanted revenge. But I wasn't hurt
or angry. I was amused. And why would I have wanted revenge? After that one hour of Rich going on and on about himself and about Boston, I had already decided not to meet him
for more dates."

I patted Cheryl's hand. "You told me that at the time. Don't
worry. They have to talk to everyone who was at Rich's on
Tuesday morning. Sometimes the questioning can feel harsh,
even though it's not meant to be. Did Brent Fyne also talk to
you?"

"No, but I saw him, and I'd much rather talk to him."

I couldn't help smiling. "Me, too."

She didn't want a donut. "I'm meeting Steve here this afternoon. One a day is probably enough. One donut, that is."

Grinning, I went to the kitchen. Cheryl could pretend all

she wanted that she wasn't interested in a permanent man in her life, but she was certainly taking care of her appearance and concerned about her weight. From the kitchen, I glanced back at her as she greeted the other Knitpickers assembling around their usual table. Her jeans looked new, and she must have bought an entire wardrobe of sweaters. This one was butter yellow. Maybe she was completing her UFOs and wearing the new sweaters to Deputy Donut.

That afternoon, she and Steve both ordered jack-o'-lantern donuts. They laughed when they saw the funny faces that Nina had given them. "Wait until you see the zombie Long John donuts she decorated," I told them.

"I'll have one," Steve said promptly.

I took him the most disreputable-looking one that Nina had made that day. Cheryl said it was too much of an artwork to eat. Steve promptly broke it, exposing its vanilla cream filling, and gave her half. She blushed and protested. "But I can eat it now that you've ruined it." She took a bite. "Yum!" Steve set the other half on his plate.

I told him, "I hear you're a writer. What do you write?"

He gave a self-deprecatory shrug. "I'm freelance. At the moment, I'm doing research for an article about Wisconsin cheese for a trade journal."

Cheryl looked down at the jack-o'-lantern donut still intact on her plate. "You could write an article about donuts, or donut shops, or coffee. They make the best of everything here."

Steve said, "That could be better than sampling Wisconsin Limburger."

There was a commotion at the door, and Misty came in with Hooligan and a couple of other cops.

I left Cheryl and Steve to discuss smelly cheeses while I took orders from the police officers.

"You can't keep calling yourself Hooligan!" one of the officers said. "And get married. Imagine the ceremony. 'Do you take this Hooligan to be your *awfully* wedded husband?' "

"You can call me Hoo," Hooligan said, "Like 'Hoo's on first.'"

"Do you take this Hoo to be your *waffle-y* wedded husband?" the man intoned.

"Hoo who?" the other man asked.

Ignoring them, Misty and I tried to guess when the wedding would be and if Samantha would powder her hair.

I suggested, "She could heap artificial snow on it."

Misty rolled her eyes. "There's also theatrical dye. It comes out when you wash your hair, but I don't know how quickly. Maybe she'll be able to go into the ocean with white hair during their honeymoon and come out a brunette."

I raised an index finger. "Maybe we should tag along and wear temporary hair dyes. She and Hooligan won't recognize us until we come out of the ocean."

Misty turned her mouth down at the corners, giving herself a nearly tragic expression. "No wonder they're not telling us where they're going."

Hooligan must have heard her. "We haven't decided yet."

I asked him, "And when you do, will you tell us?"

"Probably not." Already thinking about his and Samantha's wedding reception, Hooligan wanted to try our daily special coffee, a medium roast from Panama, which was intensely flavorful with the tiniest hints of fruits and spices.

The other two male officers wanted our regular medium-dark Colombian roast, and Misty opted for green tea. They let me choose their donuts, so I brought them each a cat donut. The cat faces were all different and not terribly scary. The police officers laughed and apologized to Dep through the office window before biting into the donuts.

At Cheryl's insistence, she and Steve split their bill. Cheryl paid with cash while Steve used a credit card. They were discussing touring donut and coffee shops in northern Wisconsin to research the article he would write after he submitted the cheese article. He warned Cheryl that he'd have to find a different trade journal because a cheese magazine probably wouldn't be interested in donut and coffee shops. Cheryl winked at me. "Unless they're cheesy," she said. Waving, she went out of Deputy Donut ahead of Steve. He had eaten his half of the zombie donut, and his jack-o'-lantern donut was gone, but once again, he had slid the candy corn that had been the jack-o'-lantern donut's eyes underneath the rim of his plate.

The police officers left soon afterward. The rest of the afternoon, when we weren't waiting on customers and making coffee, tea, and hot chocolate, we concentrated on preparing for the next day's Halloween rush, plus my party and our orders for takeout. We made extra batches of both yeast dough and dough leavened with baking powder and baking soda.

The last customers left a little past four thirty. We tidied the kitchen and the dining room, and then Tom left. Nina and I joined Dep in the office.

"I'm thinking of taking a dozen donuts to Terri," I told Nina. "I know they won't be much of a consolation for a grieving person."

"Especially if you take her any Boston scream donuts, skulls, zombies, or ghosts."

"Maybe I should take six of the most cheerful jack-o'-lanterns and six of the cutest cats. I'm not sure she's grieving, but it might be one way of trying to figure that out."

She slanted a perceptive look down at me. "You're trying to solve Rich's murder, aren't you?"

"I know better than to interfere, but it doesn't hurt to learn as much as I can while maybe doing something nice for Terri."

"And helping your handsome detective."

I wasn't going to give her more ammunition by again denying my ownership of Brent. "And his temporary boss," I added.

"Want me to come along?"

"If you have time and want to."

She crossed her arms. "Want to? I'll sulk all day tomorrow if I don't."

"That wouldn't be a good plan," I teased. "Jocelyn's working here tomorrow. You wouldn't want her showing you up, would you?"

"Ooooh. I see what you're doing. Forcing us to compete with each other so we'll work harder to show you that we're both perfect." The two women had worked together at Deputy Donut during the week before Jocelyn went to college. Both in their early twenties and each possessing a great work ethic and a lively sense of humor, they had hit it off.

I admitted, "Both of you are perfect, and you'll be even more perfect if you come along with me to try to talk to Terri. I'm never sure what to say to the bereaved."

"Or to people pretending to be bereaved. I'll pack the donuts while you get Dep ready."

The two of us walked to my house with Dep, left her inside, and got into my car. Nina joked, "Too bad you don't have something more subtle to drive while sleuthing."

"We're not sleuthing. We're on a mission of mercy. But just to be safe, I won't park close to her town house. We'll walk the rest of the way."

"Suits me," said my assistant, who as far as I knew, walked nearly everywhere.

This time, I didn't drive past Terri's first. I parked around the corner.

Nina carried the box of donuts and adjusted her strides to my shorter ones. Above us, the setting sun painted rosy edges around lavender clouds.

Even from several houses away, we saw Terri. She was standing in her front yard beside a heap of what looked like clothing.

Chapter 21

✣

We turned off the sidewalk onto the path leading to Terri's house. She looked up at us. Her blue blouse and khaki slacks were wrinkled and her eyelids were puffy. "I don't know what to do." She seemed to swallow a sob.

I couldn't tell whether she was crying about Rich's death or about the pile of clothing, shoes, magazines, makeup, and jewelry in her front yard, but I took the opportunity to offer condolences. Nina did, too. I added, "I know it won't help or change anything, but we brought you some donuts, in case company drops in."

Terri wiped her eyes. "Rich and I finally got together after years of being apart, and now he's gone. We hardly had any time together. I don't think I can take it."

Nina looked down at the pile of belongings on the ground. "Are you moving out?" She was holding the donut box awkwardly as if she didn't know what to do if Terri refused it.

"No. My old boyfriend must have come here when I was . . ." Her mouth twisted. "While I was gone. He dumped everything I'd been keeping at his place. He could have asked me to come get the stuff. He didn't have to make such a big deal. It's like he wanted to hurt me by making certain that all of the neighbors see how angry he is."

I offered, "Would you like us to help you take everything inside?"

"Would you?" She raised a tearful face and examined our expressions. "We can, I don't know, maybe dump them on the living room floor. That would be better than here, and I can wash everything he touched."

Nina asked, "Do you have a laundry basket or something like that for us to carry the stuff in?"

"Good idea." Terri sounded less devastated. "I have three. I'll go get them." She held out her hands, palms up, toward Nina. "I'll take those inside while I'm going." Nina handed her the box of donuts.

Nina and I waited outside. Terri returned with three wicker baskets. We helped her put the discarded belongings into them.

Terri gasped and pulled a clamshell bowl like the one we'd seen at Rich's cottage out from underneath a down-filled jacket.

Trying to keep a neutral expression on my face, I glanced at Nina. Staring back at me, she opened her eyes wider for a second. She was probably as amazed as I was, and neither of us was terribly good at hiding it.

I was trying to word a question, but Terri explained, "Rich meant to give this to me twenty years ago, but . . . things happened, and he didn't. Derek could have broken it, carrying it in that old pickup truck of his."

I put an innocent expression on my face. "I thought he rode a motorcycle."

"He has a truck, too, for winter and whenever he wants to carry something big. Like my stuff, which is probably all rusty and dirty from being in the back of his pickup truck."

I bent and took a better look at the coat that had been on top of the clamshell bowl. The sun had set only minutes ago, and I thought I saw a thumbnail-sized chip of peeled-off rusty paint. It was dark gray. I commented, "And with flecks of paint, too, unless his truck isn't gray."

"It was gray before it got so rusty."

Had Derek driven to Rich's cottage the night before when I was fastening my kayak on the car? What had he been doing there—looking for Terri with plans to harm her? Looking for something valuable to steal?

Terri gazed at the clamshell bowl in her hands. "I don't know how Derek got hold of this."

I thought I did. Derek could have broken into Rich's cottage and stolen the bowl when he stole the skillet.

But I wouldn't have been surprised if Terri was lying. She could have helped Derek break into Rich's cottage and take the bowl and the skillet. She could have left the bowl at Derek's place or in the back of his truck.

She could have taken the bowl after she and Rich signed the wills, but if she had, how had Derek ended up with it?

Maybe she had staged the entire dumped-my-things drama, but I wasn't sure why she would have. For sympathy? Had she been expecting someone else to come along when we did? Maybe she'd wanted to impress Hank with a tale of woe.

However, I held my tongue and didn't dare exchange another glance with Nina. As far as we knew, Terri had no idea that we'd ever seen the bowl or its twin before.

"That bowl is beautiful." Nina sounded choked up. "Want me to carry it? I'll be careful."

"Sure," Terri answered. "I'll just take this basket inside."

She started toward the door. Nina turned the bowl over and studied its underside in the fading sunset. "It's a Cindy Westhill. Number one out of ten."

I gave Nina a little nod to show that I understood. It was definitely the bowl we'd admired inside Rich's cottage.

Terri didn't turn around. "What does that mean?"

Following her to the door, Nina answered, "Cindy Westhill is a famous potter. She made only ten like that, and that one was the first."

Her basket on one hip, Terri opened the storm door. "Is it worth a lot?"

Nina answered. "Yes. People collect Cindy Westhill pottery, and it's in museums like MoMA, the Museum of Modern Art in New York City."

Terri pushed the inner door open with her rear end. "Oh." She wailed, "And Rich meant for me to have it!"

Carrying a full laundry basket on one hip, I grabbed the storm door to keep it from bumping into Nina and the bowl that my mother-in-law had crafted twenty or so years before.

Terri emptied her basket on the avocado-green carpeting of her living and dining room combination. The box of donuts was on a shiny mahogany dining table beside a stack of mail. The flyer I'd placed between her storm door and the jamb the night before was on top. Nina carefully set the clamshell bowl beside the box of donuts.

Brightly colored little fish darted in and out of a mermaid's castle in an aquarium bubbling on a stand near the front window. Terri explained, "This was my grandmother's place, fish tank and all. That's why the furniture is so old-fashioned."

"It's lovely," I said. "My couch and a matching chair are from my grandmother. But I didn't inherit any fish." I wondered if Dep would enjoy watching an aquarium. Probably, and she'd also be frustrated because I would make it impossible for her to get at the fish.

Terri hiccupped something between a laugh and a sob. "I like the fish, but I don't care for the décor. Avocado, gold, and orange aren't my favorite color combination."

Nina gave her a gentle smile. "I get that. You can change the carpeting and upholstery when you decide what colors you'd like. Or sell everything—not the fish—and start fresh."

"I suppose," Terri said. "I'm taking this basket outside for more. You two don't have to help."

Nina followed her, but I hung back for a better look at an envelope that Terri had dumped on the floor along with the rest of the things from her basket. The envelope was addressed to Derek, and the return address was the address of the house I was standing in, complete with Terri's full name,

Terri Estable. Both the address and the return address were written in feminine writing that, to my inexpert eye, matched Terri's signature, complete with the *T*'s long, curlicued top, on the will Gartborg had shown me in Rich's cottage. I aimed my phone at the envelope and snapped a picture.

Halfway out the door, Nina turned around and stared at me.

"I'm coming," I said. I was almost certain that the writing on the envelope also matched the writing on the guest list that Cat had seen a woman—probably Terri—tape to a tablecloth in Rich's birthday party tent.

I joined the other two women outside and helped gather the last of Terri's things from the lawn. Trying to sound like I was merely trying to make conversation, I told Terri that I'd seen Rich's guest list at his party and wondered why there were fewer names on it than there were chairs for the guests. "And judging by the number of vehicles, there were fewer names than the number of people who showed up."

Obviously trying to suppress a grin, Nina turned her face away from Terri.

Terri threw a half-empty shampoo bottle into the basket nearest her. "I have no idea. Rich made all the preparations. He must have left people off his list." She studied my face. I hoped I wasn't showing my skepticism.

As if feeling she had to cover for my unsubtle sleuthing, Nina faced Terri again and suggested, "If you're looking for a new color scheme for your living room, you could use the colors in your Cindy Westhill clamshell bowl as an inspiration."

I turned a laugh into an almost believable cough. Nina was apparently determined that someone's interior decorating should be based on that bowl.

Nina shot me a quelling frown. "And display the bowl prominently. Unless you sell it."

Terri tossed a pair of pink cowboy boots into the basket. "I'm keeping it forever to remind me of Rich. Anyway, Rich left me his house. I'll probably sell this place and move there."

I rested my hands against my cheeks, reminding myself of our Boston scream donuts. "Rich's house looks big for one person."

"It wasn't too big for Rich. Besides, it hasn't been too big for me, though I've only been staying in part of it, and only at night."

I must have succeeded in looking perplexed. She explained, "I've been barricading myself into a cozy guest room overlooking the lake on the top floor. It's, like, the second floor in front, but the third floor in back." Had Terri looked out last night, seen me, and snuffed her light to get a better look at the person kayaking near Rich's house?

Nina carefully placed a bottle of cologne into a basket. "Why did you barricade yourself in?"

Terri sniffled and wiped the back of her hand across her eyes. "I was afraid of Derek and of what he might do to me."

Trying to sound as empathetic as I probably looked because of whiffs of the cologne making my eyes water, I asked. "What about his friends? The ones who came to a party and damaged Rich's cottage?"

"I suppose they might come back. They're his high school buddies. They were mad about having to cut their cottage vacation short. They said they were going back to Gary. I don't know if they did."

I wondered if they had returned to Lake Fleekom and murdered Rich, either because he enraged them by kicking them out or because they wanted to get Derek and Terri into trouble. I prompted, "You said you've been staying in Rich's house at night. Only at night?"

"Yeah." The one-syllable answer was barely a breath.

I added a bag of cosmetics to a basket. "You poor thing. Being so scared must feel terrible. How did you hide from Derek in the daytime when you weren't in Rich's house?"

Terri waved a hand toward the south. "There are stores down on Packers Road. Derek would never have looked for me parked behind the post office or sitting in a tearoom. He drives a furniture company truck. Most of his deliveries are to people's houses, not to stores."

Although I thought I knew the answer, I asked, "Haven't you been going to work?"

"I didn't dare. Derek was so mad that I was afraid he'd come into the bank and do something terrible."

Nina gazed around at neighboring houses, still bright in the sunset's afterglow. "This has all been horrid for you. How did you work up enough courage to come back here this evening?"

"I needed to feed the fish, and Derek usually goes out on Friday nights, so I figured it was safe. Good thing I did. If I hadn't, my stuff might have been out here for a long time." She wiped her nose with her hand again. "Or stolen." She dropped earrings into a basket.

Still trying to talk like a friend might, but feeling guilty for my deceit, I asked, "How did you get into Rich's house?"

Terri looked down at the sneakers on her feet. "Rich gave me remotes that open his gates, his garage doors, and his other doors, so all I had to do was push buttons, drive into the garage, shut the gates and the garage door, and let myself into the kitchen. I like that house. It's big, but I'll be able to go birding in my canoe anytime I want except when there's ice, and maybe then, I can skate. And the next-door neighbor is nice. If I get lonely, I can go over and talk to him. Or if I'm scared. I haven't figured out what to do. It's all so sudden and . . . and horrible. I could sell Rich's house, but keep this place and his cottage so I can spend weekends at the lake and go canoeing or skating. His cottage is insulated for winter and has a furnace." She sniffled again and picked up the basket. "I can't think. I can't believe he's gone, and that we're not making these plans together."

After we removed her belongings from her front yard, we carried the baskets into the house and set them on the living room floor. Nina and I said we had to go.

Terri asked, "Would you like to stay for tea and donuts?"

I held my palms up toward her. "We didn't bring donuts in case we stopped in. They're in case someone else stops in."

"Okay, thanks, but I don't know who that might be."

Nina added, "And you need to get out of here in case Derek comes back and sees that the stuff he dumped outside is gone. He'll guess you're home."

Concerned for Terri, I asked her, "Does Derek have a key to your place?"

She stared at the aquarium. "I never gave him one, but . . . maybe I should have the locks changed before I stay here longer than a few minutes." Sighing, she turned a pinched and hurting face toward us.

"You definitely should," Nina said.

Chapter 22

✺

As soon as Nina and I locked ourselves into my car, I excused myself and called Brent's personal number.

"Hi, Em." That man could pack a lot of warmth into two syllables. "Misty told me."

Thinking about the murder case, I was confused. Did Misty somehow know that I'd gone kayaking alone the night before or that Nina and I had been visiting Terri? "Told you what?"

"About Samantha and Hooligan." I could tell he was smiling.

"Yes, it was quite a celebration. But that's not why I called. Maybe you already know where Terri Estable is—"

He interrupted. "No. Do you?"

"She was in her town house a few minutes ago."

"Safe and well?"

"Yes. I think she's planning to leave there soon, though, and go stay at Rich's tonight."

"Rich's?" He sounded amazed.

"His house."

I heard him blow air out between his lips.

I added, "I should be home in about ten minutes. Do you have time for a quick dinner?"

There was a pause as if he was trying to figure out how to

rearrange his schedule. Beside me in the car, Nina was grinning and holding both thumbs up. I shot her a pretend glare.

"Don't wait for me," Brent answered, "but I might call you
after I talk to Ms. Estable. Thanks for telling me where she is.
I'll grab Kim and go over there now, but no matter what, I am
coming to your party tomorrow night."

I hoped he could. If an investigation prevented him from
joining the rest of us, it wouldn't be the first time. I understood. Alec had also been dedicated. "Okay. See you then." I
disconnected.

Nina teased, "If that's the kind of conversation you always
have with your detective, it's no wonder you claim he's not
your detective."

I started the car. "You got it. That's the kind of conversation
we always have."

"Always?"

"Usually."

"You're usually helping him with investigations?"

"Okay, sometimes. And I did invite him to dinner. You
can't pretend you didn't hear that."

She laughed. "I got the impression that the police didn't
know that Terri was staying in Rich's house."

"So did I. She said she was hiding from Derek. Maybe she
was truly afraid of him, but not going to work and hiding in
a parking lot and a tearoom could also mean that she was
hiding from the police."

"Plus, if she was truly afraid of Derek, wouldn't she have
gone to the police instead of hiding from them?"

"I would," I said, "but I know and trust the Fallingbrook
police, and the Gooseleg police, too. Maybe she doesn't. But
hiding in Rich's house when it was still a crime scene is probably not a good way to avoid the police. It could have been
an excellent way of getting them to notice her."

"Maybe she was hoping they would, but why?"

I turned toward the part of Wisconsin Street where Nina's
loft was. "I don't know. Maybe so she'd be forced to tell

them her fears about Derek? Maybe she doesn't want to believe he's a danger to her, despite how he acted in Deputy Donut."

"I'm not sure any of that makes sense."

"Neither am I. Maybe it has something to do with Derek's buddies who supposedly went home to Gary."

When I stopped in front of Klassy Kitchens, Nina said seriously, "Lock your doors tonight."

"I always do. See you in the morning!"

Lights were on inside Klassy Kitchens, and Harry and Larry were polishing brushed nickel fixtures with apparently identical cloths. Nina waved at them. Even their huge smiles were identical. I wasn't surprised that they liked her.

I drove home, fed Dep, and took hamburger patties and homemade buns out of the freezer.

Purring, Dep rubbed against my ankles. "Meow?"

"Maybe he's coming tonight. Meanwhile, let's put up some more indoor decorations where you can't reach them or take them down." Dep scampered to the living room and sat in front of the door. "Even if he is coming," I informed her, "it will be after he talks to Terri." Dep stared at the door.

Orange didn't go well with the ruby, emerald, sapphire, and topaz hues of my living room, so I stuck to a mostly black color palette and strung up streamers, witches, cats, more spiders and their webs, and gray, goofy, loose-jointed skeletons that would dance in the slightest movement of air.

Dep left the front door when she heard me opening packages in the kitchen, but when she discovered that I was only getting out chocolate bars and putting them into cute orange wicker baskets with jack-o'-lantern faces, she ran into the sunroom and stared at the window. She couldn't see much besides her reflection, but I didn't blame her for admiring that. "Pretty kitty," I said. She stretched out a front leg and made certain that all of the fur on it was lying in the correct direction.

I set the baskets of candy in the china cabinet in the dining room where I could easily find them the next evening when the doorbell began ringing, and where Dep wouldn't be able to fish for chocolate bars and bat them all over shiny wood floors in the dining room and living room.

Brent phoned about eight thirty. "Can I come over for a few minutes? I won't stay long."

"Sure, and stay as long as you need to." Blushing at what I'd said, which might have sounded like an invitation I didn't mean to make, I disconnected.

Brent arrived almost immediately. I opened the door, and he enveloped me in a bear hug that lifted me off the floor.

Dep objected. "Meow!"

Laughing, Brent set me down, carefully. I didn't land on Dep. I was a little out of breath.

Brent picked up Dep and rubbed noses with her. "Did you miss me, Dep?"

Purr, purr . . .

I asked Brent, "Have you eaten?"

"No, but I didn't come here to be fed. I have questions, I'm afraid, related to Rich Royalson's murder."

I started toward the dining room. "It's only cheeseburgers."

"Only? I don't know when I last had a home-cooked meal. Probably here, about two weeks ago."

"It was cheeseburgers then, too. Come on back to the kitchen."

"There's nothing wrong with cheeseburgers." Carrying Dep, he followed me through the dining room and into my bright, warm kitchen. I poured potato chips into a bowl for both of us and added smoked paprika to sour cream for a dip. I cooked the hamburger patties and topped them with lovely aged Wisconsin cheddar. Brent was returning to work, so he asked for tomato juice instead of beer. He sat at one of the stools at my granite-topped counter.

I poured tomato juice into a pebbly handblown glass goblet and gave it to him. "Did you talk to Terri?"

"We did."

"Did she tell you where she's been staying?" I put our cheeseburgers on chocolate-brown plates that Cindy had made and set them at our places at the counter.

"In her car and a tearoom. But you said she told you she'd been staying at Rich's house." He tilted his head in question.

"She claimed he gave her remotes to open his gates, garage doors, and doors into the house. She was barricading herself into a guest room on the top floor because she was afraid of Derek Bengsen." The dip was subtle, but tasty.

"I didn't guess that. We'd thought maybe she was staying with Bengsen, though he had said he didn't know where she was, or maybe with a colleague from the bank in Gooseleg. None of her friends admitted to knowing where she was."

I took carrot sticks from the fridge and put them onto a plate for us to share. "Didn't you have someone posted at Rich's mansion at night?"

"She must have slipped in while our officer was on another part of the property. If we had caught her there during the investigation, she would have been in trouble." He gave me one of his assessing detective looks. "I'm afraid to ask how you discovered where Terri was this evening."

"Nina and I took donuts to her, you know, like people do when someone's bereaved."

"You knew where she lived?"

"I'd noticed Derek's address in Rich's rental book because it was near Samantha's. On the internet, I found a T. Estable listed in the same town house complex. This evening when Nina and I arrived there, Terri was standing on her front lawn with a pile of her things that she said Derek Bengsen had dumped when she wasn't home."

"She told us about that."

"The clamshell bowl that went missing from Rich's cottage was in that heap. When we left, it was on her dining table along with the box of donuts. A bunch of her belongings were piled on the living room floor."

"She must have put it all away between the time you left and the time we got there. Did you pick up on any new clues that add to your suspicion that she could have murdered her newly rediscovered boyfriend?"

I pulled a Cindy Westhill bowl overflowing with fruit closer. "She implied that Rich wrote that guest list, but in my unscientific opinion, the handwriting on that list was similar to her signature on her will and to the writing on an envelope that I saw at her place with her name and address as the return address. The addressee was Derek. That guest list noticeably left people off, including Derek, who had threatened Rich. Derek told me that after his quarrel with Rich in Deputy Donut, Rich invited Derek to the party. I didn't believe him, but what if Derek was right? Maybe Terri was using the quarrel to make Derek appear to be both a party crasher and a murderer, and he might not have been either one."

Brent took out his notebook and wrote in it.

I continued with my theories. "I suspect he was both. He and Terri could have been conspiring to get older people to will them everything. For instance, it might be nice to know if the grandmother who left everything including a fish tank to Terri really was Terri's grandparent, and it would also be nice to know how that person died."

He looked up from his notebook, and something like amusement sparked from those gray eyes. "You think of everything, don't you? We'll check on all of it, including the grandmother with the fondness for sixties and seventies décor. We won't let either Derek or Terri escape our grasp if we discover that we do have enough evidence."

"And I wonder about Derek's friends, the ones who supposedly damaged Rich's cottage."

"You don't have to worry about them. They were friends of Derek's from high school. They all get together occasionally for road trips on their motorcycles. We checked. All three of Derek's friends were at their jobs in Gary on Mon-

day and Tuesday. Three different jobs, three different companies. Their alibis are about as solid as alibis can be."

"Which brings us back to Derek and Terri. And possibly
Hank. He came into Deputy Donut yesterday and said he
was going to play the piano at Happy Times Retirement
Home. He mentioned Rich's wife, then he asked to take his
partly finished coffee and donut with him. He hurried away
to Happy Times. It takes about five minutes to drive there
from Deputy Donut, but he gave himself almost forty minutes. It was like he didn't like the way the conversation was
going."

"Could he have needed to practice on that piano before
playing for the residents?"

"I suppose."

"Was he walking or driving?"

"I don't know, but I assumed he was driving because it's a
long walk from Lake Fleekom to Deputy Donut, and then to
Happy Times."

"That's a reasonable assumption. We haven't ruled him
out." Brent picked out a bunch of grapes. "So, tell me about
last night."

My face flamed. "I believe Terri about spending nights in a
room on the top floor of Rich's mansion. Last night, I
thought I saw a light move in one of the rooms up there."

"In the front?"

"In the back."

"How did you see that?"

"From my kayak. The moon was almost full, so after
Samantha's party, I drove to Lake Fleekom to see if it was
misty like it had been on Tuesday morning. Mist was forming, so I toured the lake. It was wonderful, even more magical than in daylight. You . . . you should have been there."

"You're obviously right about that. Where did you park?"

"The county beach. And I saw something else that might
be important. Hank canoed from near his own dock to some-

where near Rich's cottage and then back to his own house. At least, I think it was Hank. I don't think he saw me."

"Anything else?"

I pulled peel off an orange. "While I was fastening my kayak to the car, a pickup truck went toward the cottages. I was curious, so I drove past Rich's cottage. A pickup truck was parked in front of it. I'm not sure, but it could have been Derek Bengsen's. It was old, dark gray, rusty, and not a big one. I thought the tires could have made those prints I found in the mud." I explained that Terri had mentioned that Derek's truck was rusty, and that I'd seen a piece of rusted-off dark gray paint on some of the clothes dumped on Terri's front yard. "Derek might have gone to Rich's cottage to search for Terri." I couldn't help a shudder at the thought of what he might have done if he'd found her.

"Did you learn anything else?"

"That's about it." Knowing that Brent would worry about my safety, I was not going to admit to being fooled by the meowing of a cat or to chasing after the cat and spying through Hank's windows. I was sure the police had already discovered or would learn of Hank's earlier relationship with Rich's late wife. I had already hinted at it when I told Brent about Hank rushing out of Deputy Donut.

Brent leaned back and gave me a warm but slightly devilish smile. "When I asked you to tell me about last night, I meant Samantha's party."

"Oh." I blushed. I'd let my feelings of guilt fool me into thinking he was asking about my snooping. "There was a lot of squealing from Misty and me when Hooligan and Samantha told us they were engaged."

"I'm sorry I missed it. You know how police like squealing."

I crossed my arms and tried to look stern. "Very funny, especially since you tricked me in your best detective fashion into squealing on myself."

"You'd have told me anyway." He was probably right. He

stood up. "I should let you get some rest. You have to work early, right?"

"Yes, and you'll probably work all night."

"Only a couple more hours. I'll see you tomorrow night at your party."

At the front door, he picked up Dep in one arm and hugged me with the other. Between us, Dep rumbled with deep, contented purrs.

Brent leaned down and murmured near my ear, "You're not thinking of going kayaking again tonight, are you?"

"No."

"Because if you were, I'd come along."

I gave him a little push. "You have to work."

"Keep your kayak on your car in case we get a chance?"

"Okay."

"See you tomorrow night." He handed Dep to me and opened the door. On the porch, he looked down at my Halloween decorations. "And don't come out here by yourself. There are goblins."

I laughed, shut the door, and locked it. I heard Brent's feet on the porch steps, then nothing. Dep wasn't even purring. She wriggled. I put her down. She pressed her nose against the door.

"And you're not going out among the goblins tonight, either, Dep," I told her. "It would be different if you were a black cat, but you are a torbie, a tortoiseshell tabby, too cute for any self-respecting witch. Who can take those donut circles on your sides seriously?"

"Meow."

Chapter 23

❧

Finally, it was Halloween. Dep seemed as excited as I was to leave for work. With our fun donuts, chatty customers, and the costumed kids who would arrive late in the afternoon, Halloween was sure to be entertaining. "And today and to-morrow, you'll see Jocelyn," I told Dep.

"Meow!"

It was still dark outside when we stepped out onto our front porch. The goblins were where they'd been when Brent cautioned us about them the night before. Maybe because of Brent's warning, Dep arched her back, puffed herself up, and attempted to stare them down. I picked her up and carried her until we could no longer see our house and she was con-tent to walk. In the dark, she paid no attention to the decora-tions in everyone else's yards, including the inflatables, most of which were deflated, possibly so that the owners could sleep without fear of fires. Or of giant ghosts peering through second-floor windows.

Tom was already working in the kitchen when Dep and I arrived in the already toasty office. I unsnapped her leash and halter. She dashed up a ramp to a catwalk high above me. Eyes wide, she stared down as if challenging me to turn into a witch, fly my broom close to the ceiling, and chase her around ramps and kitty-sized staircases.

Laughing, I shut her into the office and went into the kitchen.

Tom lifted the day's first batch of apple fritters—to be made into fritter critters—out of the boiling oil. Nina also arrived early. "I can't wait to see Jocelyn again," she said.

She didn't have to wait long.

With her long dark hair tied back in a bun, Jocelyn bounced in, put on her Deputy Donut apron and hat, and gave us all pretend high fives. We didn't actually touch one another. Some of us had gooey hands, and Jocelyn had just washed hers.

"What are you making?" Jocelyn asked. "Fritter critters? Cute!" She pitched in with the decorating while I made dough and cut out donuts. Tom fried them. He never said so, but I suspected he was always concerned that one of us would splash hot oil on ourselves, and that was why he always wanted to tend the fryers. He was careful no matter what he was doing, which was probably why he'd been a good detective and a beloved police chief.

Jocelyn refused to attempt decorating the zombies or indenting screaming faces into the fudge frosting on the Boston scream donuts, leaving both artistic endeavors to Nina. However, Jocelyn was game to decorate the jack-o'-lanterns, ghosts, witch hats, scare-it cake donuts, and cat donuts. She also created spider donuts by stoppering the holes in donuts with fried donut bits and covering the spheres with chocolate frosting. Stripes of frosting served as legs, and she stuck googly sugar eyes on the chocolate-covered donut bits. She didn't stop there. She pressed more sugar eyes into a cruller and drizzled green icing into the valleys of the cruller to make legs, letting the icing pool to create little feet. She stood back and regarded her latest creation, which resembled a fat caterpillar chewing on its tail. "There! Shall I make more creepy crullers? Do we have enough sugar eyes?"

We told her that we had plenty of sugar eyes and that she should definitely make more creepy crullers.

As we worked, Tom, Nina, and I told Jocelyn that costumed kids were invited to come into Deputy Donut beginning at three thirty for free cider and donuts. Most stores in town were planning to shell out to trick-or-treaters after the Halloween parade.

Jocelyn asked how old the trick-or-treaters would be.

"Up to twelve," I answered, "but we won't be asking for ID."

Jocelyn made a worried face. "So, they're starting their sugar high early? Lucky parents."

"The parents can have donuts and a beverage, too," I told her. "They'll all be high on sugar."

Jocelyn tilted her head, causing her donut hat to slip. "What if we make smaller donuts, crullers, and fritters for the kids? I don't want us to look stingy, but I think we'll have less waste and happier customers if we don't overfeed the kids."

Tom and I looked at each other and nodded. "Good idea," I said. "Should we give their parents full-sized donuts?"

Nina burst out laughing. "The kids would complain."

"And we'll give the kids small cups of cider or juice," Jocelyn informed us.

Tom and I smiled at each other. "Jocelyn's back," he said.

The first customers of the morning came in. The Knitpickers and retired men seldom met at Deputy Donut on Saturdays, but other regulars were excited to talk to Jocelyn.

Two female firefighters were surprised when she told them she didn't plan to continue in gymnastics, not even coaching. "I like little kids," Jocelyn explained. "I hope to teach kindergarten. I'll continue gymnastics as a hobby and to stay fit, but I don't want to participate competitively anymore."

She had almost made it to the summer Olympics. She hadn't complained, but merely coming close had probably been both thrilling and disappointing. With her energy, enthusiasm, and love of children, she'd be good at teaching, and she would probably love it, too.

I helped serve customers during the first rush of the morning, but I was in the kitchen drawing black features on white skull donuts when Jocelyn told me that someone wanted to talk to me.

I looked over the half wall. Wearing black slacks and an

orange sweater instead of her chef's whites, Cat from Cat's Catering waved from a table for two where she was sitting by herself. Her straight brown hair gleamed.

I washed my hands and went to talk to her. "What can I get you? It's on the house."

"Just a small coffee. Your special for the day, pumpkin spice latte, sounds delicious."

"Can I tempt you with a pumpkin spice donut with cream cheese frosting to go with it? Or a pumpkin jack-o'-lantern donut?"

She touched her perfectly flat stomach. "They sound wonderful, but I do too much tasting as it is."

I smiled back at her. "I know what you mean."

She joked, "We have to make certain that it's good enough for our clients, right?"

"For sure." I went to get her latte.

When I returned with it, she had propped her phone against a clever stand shaped like an adorable cat. "I made a video of what we do. Is this a good time?"

"Yes. We have extra help today, and although there are lots of people in here, they've all been served." I pulled the table's other chair close to her and sat down. "They like to hang around with their friends."

"You've made your place very welcoming. We could probably work well together. Here." She turned the phone toward me. "Have a look at this. It's not long."

The video showed plates of steak and salmon with potatoes and roasted vegetables being served at a wedding reception. Cat explained, "We provided everything—the linens, chair covers, dishes, cutlery, and food."

"It's a charming and romantic setting, and the food looks delicious. Did you make the video?"

"Yes. And now, this next part was taken at the family reunion I told you about, after Rich Royalson came along on his bicycle." The video showed an extended family picnicking at Lake Fleekom County Park. Cheerful people were eating fried chicken, potato salad, baked beans, and veggies. A couple of watermelons waited nearby. Cat paused the video. "You'll recognize this. I'm sorry that it will bring back sad memories, but try to see it as a video showing what we do."

She restarted the video. There was the party tent on Rich's lawn, with nothing on the tables inside it besides white table-cloths and a corner of the taped-up guest list. In front of the tent, Rich turned and looked at Terri, who was expertly backing the red canoe away from shore. She didn't seem to notice him and didn't look up when he waved. With no audio, I couldn't tell whether he had called to her or not.

The next scene showed everything inside the tent the way I remembered it, except there was no body and no skillet behind the bar. Then Cat must have backed up the hill for a wider view. Rich stood in the tent's entryway. He was waving at Cat.

Waving goodbye, possibly for the final time.

Again saddened, I checked all four corners of the screen. There was no date or time stamp, but a forensics investigator should be able to figure out the exact time.

I expected the video to end, but it didn't, and Cat continued sipping her latte and looking at her phone as if there was more she wanted me to see.

She had continued recording as she walked up the hill. She bobbed past the side of Rich's stone mansion, causing me to feel a little dizzy. The picture became less jumpy as she panned to the lake. Rich was standing inside the tent, gazing down at a table with some of the food on it and tented labels for the food that had been scheduled to arrive later, at twelve twenty-five that day.

Terri's canoe had disappeared into the mist, and no one else was in the picture. Threatening to make me woozy again, the phone's camera turned toward the driveway. It showed the Cat's Catering van. With the phone still recording, Cat climbed into the passenger seat. The video showed the front of Rich's house. No one was there. The van turned, filming both the circular driveway and the straight driveway leading to Rich's three-car garage. No other vehicles were nearby. The van pulled onto the road, and that segment ended.

The final scenes in the video were taken in the kitchen at Cat's Catering, a marvel in cleanliness and stainless steel. Two men and two women in white chef's coats and hats grinned and waved at the camera. I wondered if they'd all been purposely showing off kitchen gadgets that could be used as weapons. One held a butcher knife, one a cleaver, one a meat-tenderizing mallet, and one a rolling pin. No cast-iron skillets, long handled or otherwise.

"What do you think?" Cat asked.

I thought, *The people who work for you look slightly mischievous and perhaps dangerous, but possibly fun to be around.* I said, "I will definitely refer you to anyone wanting more than donuts and beverages at a catered event."

Even though I would not be helping with the catering at Samantha and Hooligan's wedding reception, I could tell them about Cat's Catering. First, though, I'd have to be certain that no one from Cat's Catering had bashed Rich over the head or would wield their other deadly kitchen tools around reception guests. I asked Cat, "Did you see Rich's cottage, too?"

"No. Where is it?"

"On the other side of the lake from his house. A mile or so by road, closer by water."

I couldn't tell if her laugh was amused or an attempt to cover guilty knowledge. "That's convenient!"

Yes, I thought. *Maybe too convenient for at least one person.* I told Cat that I'd fetch Tom to see her video.

Smiling, Cat thanked me.

She didn't look like a murderer.

Chapter 24

I was tending the fryers when Tom returned to the kitchen with Cat's empty coffee cup. "She's heading to work. They're catering three different parties this evening."

Cat looked back as she opened the front door. We exchanged friendly waves.

I asked Tom, "What did you think?"

"We could work with them." Tom could work with anyone. "She has a steady hand except when she's walking up a hill. She could have skipped that part."

"I noticed that, too. She might have taken that video so she could 'prove' to the police that she left the area before the murder. Then she could have stopped the recording, turned around, and gone back to Rich's place and killed him. She was in a perfect position to determine that Rich was alone. But why would a caterer do something that would end a party before it began? It hardly seems like the world's best marketing ploy."

"Hardly. And did the driver of the van participate in the murder? If so, what was his or her motive?" Some people would have made those questions sound sarcastic. Tom was sincere.

I told him Cat's story about losing money after the banks switched Christmas party caterers. "Maybe the driver of the van lost out on expected pay that night?"

Tom gently arranged donuts cut with zombie cookie cut-ters, complete with outstretched arms and unsure, staggering legs, in a frying basket, keeping them far enough from each other so that their arms and legs wouldn't attach themselves to other zombies in the hot bubbling oil. "People have killed for less, I suppose, but usually in the blind rage of the moment."

I held up a finger. "Maybe that's it. Rich constantly handed out insults and backhanded compliments. Maybe right before Cat and her driver left, he said something that enraged them. Rich was smiling and waving when they left, but that's how he was. He probably didn't realize he was insulting. It seemed to be part of his personality. Maybe he was congratulating himself for giving what he considered to be valuable advice."

"If Cat and the van's driver turned around and went back and killed him, wouldn't she have edited out the part of the video showing that she and the driver appeared to be the only people there besides the victim?"

"Maybe she left the empty driveway in the video because everyone would think that a killer would not have shown that Rich was the only other person around."

Tom guffawed. "You're like Alec, always coming up with devious motives for people."

"I take that as a compliment."

The grin Tom threw me was tinged with the grief we would always share. "It was meant to be. Why don't you call Brent and tell him about the video? Things have settled down in the dining room for the moment." The zombies in the oil were puffing up and beginning to look threatening. Tom turned his face toward Jocelyn and Nina and raised his voice slightly. "Jocelyn and Nina can handle nearly anything."

"I heard that," Jocelyn said.

Calling over my shoulder, "You can!" I went around the half wall and past the serving counter to the office.

As usual when Dep saw me tap my phone's screen, she tried to help. I thought she believed that my friends were inside the phone, and she might be able to help them escape. It often worked. She heard their voices, and they showed up at the door shortly afterward.

This time was no different. Brent said he could use a walk, and he'd be right over. "Meet me in the office," I told him.

Leaving Dep peering into her basket as if Brent might be in there among the toys and could be persuaded to come out and hug her, I returned to the dining room and refilled coffee mugs.

Brent passed the patio and headed up the driveway toward the parking lot and the rear of our building.

I unlocked the office door and let him in. Purring, Dep rubbed against the legs of his dark gray pants until he picked her up and let her spread cat hair over his suit jacket, too. I noticed his tie and burst out laughing. Grinning white skeletons danced with each other on the tie's black background. "Sophisticated," I managed.

"We can always use a little whimsy in a roomful of cops."

I teased, "A roomful of cops is already whimsical."

I was happy to see the twinkle in his gray eyes. "Thanks."

"Have you made any charges in Rich's murder?"

The twinkle disappeared. "No. And we don't seem about to. But maybe you found out something important this morning?"

I gazed out toward our nearly full parking lot. "Cat from Cat's Catering showed me a video she'd made. That skillet was nowhere in sight, and Rich was alive when she and whoever was driving their van were leaving."

"I've seen the video."

That slowed my rapid-fire commentary. "Oh. You probably figured out that she might have thought she could use that video as an alibi." Then I went back to talking fast. "She showed the van from the inside as it was leaving, but she and whoever was driving could have returned to the scene after she stopped recording. Maybe they went around the lake to Rich's cottage for the skillet—"

"Whoa." Brent gently plucked Dep, who looked about to climb to the top of his head, off his shoulders and cuddled her like a baby in his arms. "Other employees of Cat's Catering reported that Cat and her driver returned to their shop at ten after eleven, so even if Rich had brought that skillet to his party, they hardly had time to find it and kill him with it."

I suggested, "Maybe they went back."

"They couldn't have. They left immediately in another van that Cat's employees had loaded, and Cat and her driver arrived only a little late at their eleven-fifteen engagement, which, they admitted, they managed to do only by breaking a few speed limits. The client at their next job, an engagement party, corroborated their time of arrival."

That deflated me. "They didn't act on their grudge against Rich for breaking his contract for his Christmas party?"

"We've pretty much cleared them."

"I'm sorry for bringing you out on a wild-goose chase."

He held Dep up to his face. "Don't be. I appreciate your help. You never know what piece of information will be the one that ties the evidence together. Besides, I needed the walk." He nuzzled Dep. "And the cat." Dep purred.

She was still purring when he set her on the couch and I let him out the back way. "See you tonight." He walked down the driveway and disappeared north on Wisconsin Street.

Maybe he should have stayed a little longer.

Terri Estable came in.

Wearing tight jeans, a sleeveless pink top, and the cowboy boots I'd seen on her lawn the evening before, she sat at the table where Cheryl and Steve usually sat, near Nina's huge painting.

Pasting on a smile, I asked what she'd like to eat and drink. As Cat had, Terri wanted a pumpkin spice latte. She ordered a Boston cream—not scream—donut to go with it.

Back in the kitchen, I asked Nina to cover one of her Boston scream donuts with more fudge frosting and turn it into a Boston cream one for Terri. Grinning, she said she would. I prepared the latte and took it to Terri along with her donut with its reconfigured frosting.

She asked me, "Are you allowed to sit down on the job? I'd like to talk to you."

"I'm allowed." I sat in the chair across from her.

She stirred her latte. "I wanted to thank you and the tall girl with the cheekbones and big eyes over there in the kitchen. What you did last night, bringing me donuts and helping clean up the mess, was thoughtful. I'm sorry I was too upset to thank you properly."

"You thanked us. And besides, we weren't there for thanks. We were doing what people do, bringing food for when unexpected company drops in after a tragedy. We didn't know we were going to help clean up a mess, but we didn't mind. We'd have done it for anyone, and you probably would have, too."

The tears pooling on her lower eyelids looked real. "It's been terrible. And when I think of how Derek must have treated that beautiful bowl that Rich was going to give me twenty years ago, I just start shaking. It could have been broken. Now it's one of the best things I have to remind me of Rich."

I centered the cream pitcher and the sugar bowl on the table. "Why did you leave the bowl with Derek?"

"I never did."

That didn't surprise me, since Nina and I had first seen that bowl after Rich had supposedly "stolen" Terri from Derek.

However, Rich could have given Terri the bowl Monday evening or Tuesday morning. But if he did, why had she avoided telling us? If she and Derek had only pretended to break up and had conspired to kill Rich, I could believe she had taken the bowl she thought of as rightfully hers and left it at Derek's. But then, was dumping her things on her lawn merely part of an act? I asked, "Didn't you say that the things Derek dumped on your lawn were things you'd left at his place?"

"Yeah, but that was before I discovered the bowl in the pile. I don't know where Derek found that bowl. I guess it was in Rich's cottage when we rented it. I don't think Derek was ever in Rich's house. Not legitimately, anyway. I also don't know why he took that bowl. How would he have known it was expensive? He's not, like, into art, and he had supposedly stopped stealing things long ago. That just goes to show how you can think you know someone when you don't, and how you can think that someone is reformed when he isn't. Boy, was I ever wrong about Derek." Her shoulders slumped.

"Did you see that bowl when you were staying in the cottage with Derek and his friends?"

"No. But I didn't snoop around."

Based on her reaction when she spotted that bowl among her belongings on the lawn, she truly had not seen that bowl for twenty years. Either she hadn't looked inside the cabinet containing the platters when she was staying in the cottage, or Rich had put that bowl there after he kicked Derek and his friends out and before Nina's and my first tour of the place. But I only asked, "How did Derek get to and from the cottage for your shortened week there?"

"On his motorcycle. I rode on the back."

"Could he have carried that bowl on his motorcycle when you left the cottage after Rich put a stop to the party?" Nina and I had seen that bowl after that, so I knew that Derek hadn't taken the bowl then, but I wanted to know if carrying it—or a large skillet—on Derek's motorcycle was possible.

Terri's nod was almost too emphatic to be believable. "Sure. Derek's bike is big, with lots of those hard compartments on the sides and back like saddlebags and a trunk."

I didn't think any of those compartments could have been big enough to hold that skillet, but there might have been other ways to carry that skillet on a motorcycle. The skillet might have fit inside a cello case, but probably would have required one for a bass, which would have been difficult to balance on a motorcycle. And where would Derek have gotten the case, and if he had, what had he done with it afterward?

It still seemed unlikely that he had carried that skillet on his motorcycle. As I'd theorized before, he could have used another mode of transport, like the canoe that had been conveniently left on the dock at Rich's cottage.

I asked Terri, "How did you carry the things you needed for the week, like clothes and food?"

"Two of the other guys tow trailers behind their bikes. They brought the food. You know, chips, beer, cereal, cookies, and those little dried sausages."

I couldn't help making a slightly disgusted face. "Was that all you ate?"

"Yeah." It was no wonder that she hadn't opened kitchen cabinets. She explained, "Derek and his friends planned the menu."

After five days of that diet, they should have been thankful they were kicked out. I attempted a neutral expression. "Does Derek have one of those trailers?"

"No. He let me use one of his saddlebag thingies for my clothes, but he didn't open the other compartments when I was around. I wonder if he took other things from Rich's cottage that day, maybe to sell. And maybe he dumped that bowl with my things last night in hopes that the police would arrest me for stealing it. Ha. That would have backfired. Rich willed it to me along with the house and cottage and everything in them. They're mine."

Or they will be, I thought, *if you didn't kill Rich.* Murdering people for their belongings was frowned upon. However, Alec had believed that people got away with murder more often than anyone knew.

Terri added, "I can't help wondering if I made a lucky escape from Derek. I hate to even think it, but maybe he killed Rich. He probably didn't mean to kill him, but only to, like he said, make Rich sorry for taking me away from him, but something happened, and he accidentally killed Rich." She covered her eyes and sniffled.

Was she telling me what actually happened, except that she, not Derek, was the killer?

She stirred her latte, clanking the spoon against the mug. "I mean, why did he show up at the party? It wasn't like he was invited."

I hadn't believed Derek when he'd told me that Rich had invited him, but I asked her, "Could Rich have invited him when you weren't around?"

"Hardly. He didn't talk to Derek after Derek came in here and yelled at us. Rich was with me the entire time after that until he sent me out canoeing the next morning." She wiped her eyes. "If only I hadn't gone canoeing, if only I'd disobeyed Rich and stuck around, Rich would be alive right now. I wouldn't have sneaked peeks at the party preparations. I'm sure Derek meant to crash Rich's party. It was like Derek thought if he showed up after the party was supposed to start, people would believe he had come out to the lake that very minute when he'd really been there all along."

It was kind of close to what I thought about Terri returning from canoeing shortly before the party was scheduled to begin. I asked, "Did you see Derek anywhere near the lake before he showed up at Rich's?"

"No. I was out in my canoe, and it was too foggy to see anything."

I reminded her, "You said you heard at least one other boater."

"Yeah. Someone with an aluminum canoe who wasn't good at paddling, at least not paddling quietly."

"Did you hear a motorcycle while you were out there?"

She gazed across the room toward the wall between the dining area and the hallway leading to our restrooms. "I might have. I'm not sure what all I heard. When I listen for birds, I block out other sounds, you know?"

"I'm afraid I don't have those talents."

She must have realized she had contradicted herself by saying she heard a canoe and could tell by the sounds that the canoer wasn't an expert, but she hadn't heard a motorcycle. With her brows lowered in an earnest expression, she leaned toward me. "But maybe I don't block out sounds from other boats when it's foggy. You don't want to risk colliding with another canoe and maybe capsizing."

Had she seen me out on the lake the night before last in my kayak? I realized I was leaning back as if preparing to deny everything.

"You know," she said slowly, "I said I was out on the lake the entire time between when I left Rich and when you saw me come back, and that's what I told the police."

Exhaling, I nodded.

"I lied." The tears spilled over. "I wasn't out there the entire time."

Chapter 25

✻

Was Terri about to confess to killing Rich? I wished I was facing Deputy Donut's kitchen instead of sitting with my back to it. I could have signaled to Jocelyn or Nina to come closer and eavesdrop. Or to call Brent . . .

Diners talked and laughed. Cutlery and dishes rattled. As far as I knew, no one was paying attention to Terri and me. "What do you mean?" I asked softly.

She twisted her napkin around her fingers. "I wasn't canoeing that whole time. I went ashore for part of it. I saw Rich's neighbor, Hank, out on his lawn, and I wanted to talk to him." She set the napkin down.

Watching it slowly uncurl, I avoided looking into Terri's face in case she would feel freer to talk.

She poked at the napkin. "See, a long time ago, about ten years before Rich's wife died, Rich was in charge of loans at Fallingbrook Mercantile Bank. I was Rich's executive assistant. Hank came in and asked Rich for a second mortgage so he could buy a cottage across the lake. The cottage had just come on the market and was for sale for an amazingly low price, like the people who had inherited it were from out of state, you know? And they wanted to get rid of it. So, Hank wanted to buy it. He applied to Rich for a second mortgage on his house so he could afford the cottage." She took a deep breath. "What Rich did next wasn't very nice, but he was my boss, you know?"

I nodded, even though I was sure that none of my bosses had ever done anything even remotely as sleazy as what I suspected Terri was about to tell me Rich did.

"He went out to Hank's house. I went with him because, well, I often went on those appraisal trips. Rich was teaching me all about banking. I followed Rich around while he dictated notes. While we were there, Rich saw a photo on Hank's piano—did you know that Hank's a retired concert pianist?"

"No. He mentioned playing the piano, but he said his fingers didn't work as well as they used to."

"He wasn't, like, super-famous, but kind of."

"What was in the photo?" I thought I knew.

"It was Hank with Rich's wife. They were only teenagers, so Hank knew Patty long before Hank bought the house next door to Rich and Patty. I got the impression that Rich didn't like Hank displaying a picture of Rich's wife. He marked Hank's house down for every little fault and discounted the fact that the property was waterfront. Then, later, he called Hank in to the bank. I took notes in that meeting, too. Hank seemed to think he was there to sign the papers for the second mortgage, but Rich told Hank that the bank wouldn't grant one. He said it kindly."

I was having no trouble picturing this meeting, and Rich being the apologetic but superior—and powerful—bearer of bad news. I looked into her face. "What happened next?"

She was gazing down at the donut she had not yet touched. "Rich bought the cottage. He was proud of paying way below market for it. The value has gone up in the meantime, and he has been making money renting it out, besides. It was clever, but . . ."

I could hardly breathe. Terri had told me why Hank might have killed Rich. I asked, "Is that why you stopped to talk to Hank on Tuesday, Terri?"

"Yes, to, you know, clear the air and apologize. I could have done or said something at the time that could have helped Hank end up with the cottage. I didn't want to get Rich into trouble, so I didn't. But on Tuesday Rich and I were planning for me to move in with him. Since Hank lived next door, I thought Hank and I should start on the right footing as neighbors, so I reached out a friendly hand."

I couldn't help picturing our latest version of zombie donuts puffing up and reaching out not-so-friendly hands—and feet—toward one another in their bath of boiling oil. "What did you do after you talked to Hank on Tuesday morning?" She and her canoe had appeared on the beach, but I wasn't sure where she'd been before that. Hank had burst through the hedge between his and Rich's properties. I again saw Terri removing that spray of cedar from Hank's hair in a gesture that had appeared tender and familiar.

"I went back out and canoed around the lake, listening and watching for birds, and I stayed out there until about noon, the time Rich said I could return. I was going to run upstairs and change my clothes, but I could tell from the way you were acting that something was wrong. I heard the sirens and knew that something had happened. I never expected it to be as terrible as it was, though." She looked up at me. "You saw me canoeing out in the lake, didn't you?" She opened her eyes wide. "Say you did."

"I'm sorry, I didn't. I heard someone out there, though. I thought it was an aluminum canoe."

"That's what I thought I heard, too. Maybe someone saw me, maybe the person in the aluminum canoe. And I don't know what Hank was doing between the time I left him and the time you found Rich." She gave me a sidelong look as if that last statement was her entire reason for coming in. Was she hoping to spread a rumor that she'd been with Hank part of the time when Rich could have been murdered, but not all of it, and therefore Hank had time alone and could have murdered Rich? She leaned toward me. "If you were the first one to find Rich, how come the police aren't questioning you about his death? No offense, but you were, like, the only one with him. You could have . . . well, as I said, no offense."

Maybe this hinted allegation was her real reason for visiting Deputy Donut. "They did question me." I gestured toward the rest of the café. People were talking and laughing and enjoying the treats that Jocelyn and Nina were serving. Actual jack-o'-lanterns smiled from corners. "The police know from talking to people that I was still here when Rich died." The medical examiner couldn't pinpoint the time of death, but he could come close. I didn't tell Terri that three of the five officers who were first on the scene were close friends of mine, but I pointed out, "Anyone who was invited to Rich's party could have come early. Do you know who all was invited?"

"I'm not sure I remember, now, and the investigators took all of Rich's notes."

"Have you thought more about why people were left off the guest list, and who they were? It could be important."

She stared at me between half-closed eyelids for long and uncomfortable seconds. "I . . . that list was written before Rich invited some people, like other people he might have dated, you know? I put that list where those people would see it because as far as I was concerned, they weren't welcome, and I wanted them to figure that out. Rich was *my* boyfriend." She closed her mouth tightly with her lower lip sticking out on one side. "So, I left a couple of people off the list, like that woman and man that he invited when we were in here on Monday afternoon and I was trying to get him to leave after Derek scared me."

"Cheryl and Steve."

She lifted one shoulder. "Whatever their names were. I wasn't paying much attention."

She'd admitted leaving people off the guest list without quite admitting that she'd written it. Having seen her handwriting on the wills and on that envelope, I was sure she had.

Why had she pretended on Thursday evening outside her town house that she hadn't known why people were left off the list? Maybe her petty behavior embarrassed her, or maybe there was a more sinister reason, like a conspirator's name that she hadn't wanted anyone to see. Derek's name had not been on that list, and, I realized, neither had Hank's. I asked, "From where you were sitting, up on the hill near Rich's deck, you couldn't see everyone who was pulling into Rich's driveway on the other side of the house, but did you see or hear of any uninvited people coming to Rich's party?"

"Just Derek." Her lips puckered as if pronouncing his name was like sucking on a lemon.

"Did Rich invite Hank to the party?"

She stared toward the office. "Not as far as I know."

Wondering what Dep was doing in the office that seemed to be catching Terri's attention, I asked, "Why didn't you tell the police about coming in off the lake, talking to Hank, and going back out canoeing?"

"I guess I wasn't thinking. I was too stressed. I was gone from Rich's place the entire time, so that was sort of like being out on the lake."

Sort of, I thought, *but not exactly.*

As if she were going to carve faces in the fudge frosting of her Boston cream donut, Terri stabbed her coffee spoon onto it. "Besides, when I was talking to Hank, I swore him to secrecy. I had no idea that Rich was about to die, and I didn't want Rich to think I was playing around on him. And as far as I know, Hank didn't tell the police about our little meeting in the mist on his beach that morning, either, but what if he tells them, just to give himself an alibi? They'll think I lied to cover up something."

"Wouldn't admitting that the two of you were together give you an alibi, too?"

She drew squiggly lines in the frosting. "Maybe, for the time we were together, but we weren't together the entire time. It would have looked better for us if we'd told the truth at first, but I didn't, and he probably didn't, either. Besides, me being with Hank even for that short time would look suspicious if certain things came to light."

I wanted to be silent like Brent would have been in a situation like this, which often made the person he was talking to—me, for instance—explain everything. Instead, I asked, "What things?"

She spooned craters in the fudge. "Like Rich willing me everything shortly before he was murdered." She wiped the back of the hand holding the fudgy spoon across her eyes. "Monday night, we both signed new wills that made each other our beneficiaries. It was just a routine thing, you know, because of the change in our relationship. We were so happy to be back together." She exhaled loudly and shakily. "And neither of us had up-to-date wills. But wouldn't you know? The police found those wills. They only found me last night after the first time they talked to me, Tuesday afternoon, but they grilled me about those wills and about Rich's and my relationship, past and present, for hours last night and again this morning. As soon as they let me go, I came over here to thank you." She took a sip of her latte, which was probably almost cold. "And for some decent coffee and one of Rich's favorite donuts." She touched the pockmarked donut almost reverently. "Can you stay here while I eat it, if you're not too busy?"

I turned in my seat. I couldn't see Tom, so he was probably beyond the half wall, manning the fryers. Nina was at the serving counter talking to a firefighter on his break. Catching me looking at her, she tilted her head in question. The only thing I could do to show her that everything was fine was wink. She gave me a little nod and reached into the display counter for a staggering zombie donut.

Jocelyn was pouring coffee and chatting to people near the front of the shop, and no one seemed to be waiting for help from one of us.

"Sure," I answered, "unless someone needs me, then you'll have to excuse me."

Terri said in a small voice. "I don't want to be alone."

"Are you still afraid of Derek?"

"Not after I told the police about him and arranged to have my locks changed."

"Do you have family?"

"Not here."

"Tell me about your grandmother."

With a wistful smile and between bites, she made the grandmother sound real and like Terri had known her from the time she was a small child. But for all I knew, Terri was making it up. While she was talking, I again noticed how muscular her arms and shoulders were. Despite being short, she could lift a canoe above her head as if it weighed nothing, and she could probably have swung that skillet at Rich's head.

Rich must have been taken by surprise. It was likely that he didn't see his attacker or the skillet until it was too late if at all. Anyone might have sneaked up on him, including a stranger. Or the woman across from me.

Terri paid me, said goodbye, and left. Out on the patio, she tapped the screen of her phone. Holding her phone next to her ear, she walked north as if she might have left her car near the police station.

She'd said she'd visited Deputy Donut to thank Nina and me, but Nina hadn't come to Terri's table, and Terri hadn't gone to talk to Nina, either. Terri must have expected me to give Nina the message.

I wanted to tell Brent about Terri's allegations about Rich's crooked dealings with Hank, but I had been letting the other three do the running around while I talked to Terri.

I cleaned Terri's table and served smiling and appreciative customers. Finally, I told Nina that Terri had come in to thank us.

Nina's grin was impishly crooked. "It's not like we had an ulterior motive."

"Of course not."

Tom was frying donuts, and Jocelyn was greeting and serving customers. While Nina and I frosted and decorated donuts, fritters, and crullers, I told Nina what Terri had said.

Nina quipped, "Maybe we gave Rich the wrong nickname. Instead of calling him the Boston Screamer, we should have called him the Boston Schemer."

It wasn't nice to laugh at the dead, but I couldn't help it. "And now, thanks to Terri, we know that Rich's neighbor, Hank, must have had a grudge against Rich."

Nina looked toward the door. "Who's that man who just came in and seems to be looking for someone?"

I turned around. "What an amazing coincidence!" I made certain that my tone told Nina that I didn't think it was a coincidence at all. "That's Hank."

He spotted me, gave a little wave, and sat where Terri had.

"Oh, boy," Nina said. "This is getting good."

"I'll wait on him," I told her.

She laughed. "How did I guess? I'll watch your back."

Chapter 26

Hank ordered an espresso, a jack-o'-lantern donut, and a zombie donut. When I served them to him, he smiled. "You folks are great. These look like a professional artist decorated them."

"One did." I told him about Nina and pointed out her painting.

He whistled. "Is it for sale?"

"All of the art we display in here is, through The Craft Croft."

He fingered the glass top of the table. "Your tables, too?"

"No, but I suppose we could consider painting more and selling them."

"Did Nina paint this one?" It had pink frosting and multicolored sprinkles.

"I did."

His brown eyes were warm with admiration. Could he have killed his neighbor over a deal that had gone sour thirty years ago? "There's a lot of artistic talent in here."

"Thank you. My mother-in-law, Cindy Westhill, is an artist. She gave my father-in-law, Tom, who is also my business partner, and me pointers and helped us paint them. Tom and I hadn't hired Nina yet."

The Westhill name didn't seem to ring a bell with Hank. "Does Nina have art shows?"

"Some of her other works are at The Craft Croft."

"That's a great place to start, but her talent should spread beyond Fallingbrook."

"Rich Royalson said the same thing."

"He had good taste in art, even if his taste in architecture tended toward the ostentatious." I couldn't help comparing the simple elegance of Hank's timber frame home to Rich's stone mini-château. Hank's house fit into the landscape. Rich's dominated it. From what I'd seen of the cabins and cottages on that lake, Rich's cottage also stood out as being different. Hank flashed me a cheerless grin. "I'm surprised he didn't buy that painting as an investment plus everything else Nina has for sale at The Craft Croft."

If Terri's tale about Rich's sneaky purchase of the cottage was true, Hank knew firsthand about Rich's greedy investment practices. Trying not to show that I noticed the possible dig, I merely stated, "He didn't have time. He died the day after he saw that painting."

Hank thinned his lips and shook his head. If he was trying to look grief-stricken, he failed.

I returned my gaze to Nina's painting. "I hope Nina's on her way to a career in art. She's about twenty-five, so she has time for word to spread. The arts are difficult, though, as you probably know. Are you giving any more concerts soon?"

"Not this week, and 'concerts' is a grandiose word for what I do these days. Do you have time to talk?"

Did he, as Rich had, know people in the art world who could help Nina become noticed? I pulled out the chair across from him and sat in it. "Sure."

He asked, "How long did you know Rich?" Was he merely being friendly, or was he a murderer trying to figure out who the police might legitimately suspect?

I answered cordially and confidently, "I met Rich on Monday, the day before his birthday. He came here, tasted our Boston cream donuts, and ordered some for his party. And he saw and admired Nina's painting. How about you? Were you Rich's neighbor long?"

He answered as if we were two people making small talk, getting to know each other, not two people possibly suspecting each other of murdering a third person. "I met him about thirty-five years ago, when I moved into the house next door to his. Imagine my surprise to find a high school friend living next door." My attempt at looking bewildered must have succeeded. Hank explained, "Not Rich. His wife. I went to junior high and high school with Patty, back in Cleveland. She was Patty Brook, then. We were friends, but it was never boy-and-girl stuff. We both liked science and music, and we both were upset because our parents—both sets of them—had gotten divorced. That forged a bond between us, but not a romantic one. Because we were friends and didn't have dates for the senior prom, Patty and I went together. I still have our prom picture. I display it prominently because it's a great photo and I like looking at it. I like remembering the two innocent kids." All the time he was telling me about the photo, he was eyeing me as if watching for a reaction. It was as if he knew that I had trespassed and had studied the framed picture on his piano.

I was sure I was blushing, but I wasn't going to confess unless I had to. "Cute," I managed. "Had Patty changed much since graduation?"

"No. She was the same passionate biologist, dedicated to the environment and to wildlife. She loved living on the lake. She had intended to work as a biologist, but Rich prided himself on letting her be a lady of leisure."

"Did they have children?"

"No. Rich was fond of pointing out what terrible investments children were." His lips grim, Hank stirred sugar into his espresso. "By the time I moved next door, Patty and Rich didn't act like ecstatic young lovers, but they seemed comfortable enough together. They were good neighbors. I was traveling a lot and didn't do much with them. Rich and I got along with each other after she died, too, but we didn't socialize. Her death came as a shock. To everyone."

"I heard it was an accident."

"It was. Patty was always puttering around out on the lake, even in bad weather. People whispered that Rich killed her because he left the bank that day at lunchtime and didn't go back to work. What many people don't know, and that I didn't know for certain at the time, is that he was having an affair with his assistant, Terri, the woman who recently became his girlfriend. On the day that Patty drowned, Rich and Terri drove separately way up north to the Teddy Beddy Bye-Bye Motel. Terri went back to work after a long lunch hour, but Rich claimed that he fell asleep, and apparently it was true that he didn't check out of the motel until seven that night. The police were satisfied that neither he nor his assistant were anywhere near Lake Fleekom that afternoon." Hank drummed his fingertips on the table. "I knew Rich well enough to know that he would never have committed a serious crime. He was too conscious of his place in the community. He wasn't the bank manager, yet, but he was on his way up the ladder—loans manager, or something like that. About five years after I moved to the lake, I went to the bank for a second mortgage, and he was the one I talked to. And his assistant, Terri. She was at both meetings, plus she came out to my place with him to help him assess it. Terri adored her boss. And the way he looked at her, and said her name, well, I couldn't help feeling sorry for Patty."

"Did Patty know about Rich and Terri's relationship?"

"I don't think so. When I applied for the loan, I wasn't sure there was more to the relationship than, I don't know, the way people glance at each other when they're interested and don't know if the other one feels the same way. However, I learned after Patty's death that Rich had been having an affair. I don't think many people heard about that, or about Terri being gone for a long lunch hour the same day that

Rich didn't return from lunch at all, the same day that Patty capsized in the frigid water. I think Patty's death devastated Rich and ended his affair. Terri left the Fallingbrook Mercantile Bank almost immediately after Patty died, and I didn't see her for years except for a few times when I went up to Gooseleg. Whenever she saw me walk past the bank up there, she waved, so she remembered me from the two meetings I had with Rich and the time they came to my house." He bit into the jack-o'-lantern donut. "I like this combination of pumpkin, orange, and spices." With apparent concentration, he set the donut on his plate. "On Tuesday morning, Terri was at Rich's. She went out in one of his canoes."

"A red fiberglass one with wooden gunwales?"

"Yes. You probably saw it."

I nodded. "What other canoes did he have?"

"Only one other, an old aluminum one."

"The one that his wife took out the day she drowned?"

He squirmed uncomfortably on his chair. "I don't know if it was the same one, but it was similar to it."

"Sorry for interrupting." I tried to sound casually interested. "What did Terri do when she went out in the red canoe?"

"She saw me on my beach, landed her canoe, and got out to talk to me. She apologized for not having said or done anything when Rich turned me down for that mortgage and ended up buying the cottage himself. So that's why she always waved at me." He tore the remains of the donut in half. One of the candy corn eyes landed with a clink on his plate. "But you know what?"

"What?"

"I'd almost forgotten the details. I hadn't been sure what I was going to do with a cottage on the same lake as my house, anyway. It had been a spur-of-the-moment idea. Later I was glad that Rich tricked me out of that cottage. If I want to go canoeing, I can leave from my own dock, and I don't need the additional maintenance, upkeep, and taxes from another property." His fingers tapped out a rhythm on the glass covering the pink-frosted donut painted on the table. "Also, I could not have kept a piano in a poorly insulated cottage to be affected by heat and humidity, and I spend hours every day at the piano. I'd have had to canoe back across the lake to play the piano. I need to have it tuned often enough in a house where I can do a reasonable job of controlling the environment. After Rich bought the cottage, he had it properly insulated. It was probably a good investment for him, but I couldn't have afforded to do everything he had done to it."

"Let me guess. His cottage wasn't a Cape Cod when you looked at it."

A humorous glint in his eyes, he aimed an index finger at me. "You guessed right. It was a plain wood-sided cabin with a sloping roof and a chimney. He added white siding, shutters, and dormers, and as I said, insulation. I think he updated some of the plumbing, too. His not approving that second mortgage wasn't a big deal. It was actually a blessing." Frowning, he sipped at his espresso. He put the small cup down. "Patty loved that cottage. She preferred it to their house, which she found too cold and large, so that was another reason I was glad that Rich acquired the cottage. Patty could be, as she put it, 'out in nature.' She also loved canoeing, no matter what. She could have driven or walked to their cottage, but she preferred canoeing there. I always wondered if Patty's last canoe trip was to go enjoy the afternoon in that cottage. If I had bought it, I hope I would have known better than to go there by canoe when it wasn't safe."

"Do you canoe often on Lake Fleekom?" I was afraid I was going to get myself into dangerous territory and have to admit to my late-night kayaking, and worse, snooping near his house, but I wanted to hear what he'd say.

"I do, day or night, hot or cold, as long as there's no ice. Thursday night, I went out in the moonlight. The police had asked me if I knew where Terri was, and I was surprised to hear that she'd been missing since a few hours after you found Rich's body. You wisely kept her from seeing him and sent her up to sit near Rich's deck, and I went with her. She told me that she was afraid of her ex-boyfriend, that scruffy guy who tried to crash Rich's party. She said he had rented Rich's cottage and had flown into a rage when Rich kicked him and his friends out. On Thursday night it occurred to me that Terri might be hiding from the ex-boyfriend in the cottage, so I went out into the fog and canoed over there."

"Was she there?"

"I looked around with a flashlight and tried calling her name, but I didn't see evidence of anyone inside the building and no one answered when I knocked on the back door, the one that Rich and Patty always used. A rattletrap of a vehicle was coming up the road, and I went back to my canoe and paddled away. I didn't have my phone with me. I was planning, when I got home, to call the police and have them check the cottage, but when I arrived at my dock, Terri was there waiting for me. She'd noticed me out on the lake and wanted to talk to me because she was scared. She thought she'd seen and heard her ex's pickup truck go rattling toward the cottage."

I commented, "It sounds like it was a good thing you didn't hang around at Rich's cottage."

"I think so, too, but the ex was probably only looking for Terri. Still, I wouldn't want to tangle with him. We're about the same size, but he's younger. Plus"—he flexed his fingers—"I always have to consider my hands. Not because I still need to earn my living with them, but because I can't imagine not being able to play the piano. I don't know what I'd do." He had a nicely boyish grin. "Besides canoeing. When I heard that truck approach and slow down near Rich's cottage, slipping off in my canoe seemed like the best plan. I found Terri shivering on my dock and looking for reassurance, if not outright protection. I offered to let her spend the rest of the night at my place, but she turned me down. She'd been barricading herself in a room in Rich's house and planned to keep doing that. I told her to call me if her ex showed up at Rich's house, and she said she would. She ducked under the crime scene tape and ran back to his deck. I heard a car drive out along the road shortly afterward, and then I heard the noisy pickup truck speed past. About six in the morning, a car left Rich's. I figured that was Terri heading for work, and that she was fine."

"She was here a little while ago. She seemed okay, but grieving. Her ex hadn't found her."

"Good." The word had a solid, satisfied ring to it.

"It was nice of you to try to help her. Were you home when Patty drowned?"

"I was driving back from Madison after a concert." He shuddered. "I arrived home late that night and found spotlights shining on the lake and rescuers attempting to find her. It was horrible. I wish I had been home when she went out that last time in her canoe. I might have been at the piano. I might have seen her launching her canoe. I might have convinced her not to do such a foolhardy thing. They think she capsized because she was trying to save an animal, maybe a dog or a deer, which I could easily believe because it was the sort of thing she would have done, but whatever she might have been going after, it survived and she didn't." Pain crossed his face. "If I'd seen her struggling, maybe I could have gone out and rescued her. Or phoned for help."

Feeling Hank's pain about the loss of his high school friend, I repeated what Brent and I had told each other when talking about the night that Alec died. "There was probably nothing you could have done."

Pinching his lips together and shaking his head, he didn't look entirely convinced. I knew that feeling, too.

Did he also, at least partly, blame Rich for the loss of his old friend? Maybe that, combined with anger over the financial scam, had caused him to swing that skillet at Rich's head.

His hands were big with long, slender, strong-looking fingers. He was big, too. He had the size and strength to wield the skillet that had killed Rich. Maybe he knew about the skillet, either because he had seen it in the cottage as part of the furnishings when he was considering buying the cottage or because he had visited Rich and Patty there after Rich bought it. Was his comment about not harming his hands a way of trying to make me believe that he wouldn't pick up a heavy cast-iron skillet and swing it at someone?

Although Hank had seemed glad to hear that Terri was all right and had come to Deputy Donut that morning, I guessed that he already knew she was fine. I also guessed she had sent him to talk to me. He could have been the person she'd been phoning as she left.

Almost as if he'd read my thoughts, Hank leaned toward me. "I don't want you to think there was anything going on between Terri and me, but we were together Tuesday morning, quite innocently, from when she left Rich, who was alive and calling goodbye to her—I heard him—until she canoed back from my place to his."

I sat perfectly still and tried not to let doubt show on my face. Terri had told me that she'd been with Hank only part of that time, and that she'd gone birding in a canoe after talking to Hank.

Hank didn't seem to notice my suspicion-motivated stillness. He went on, "After I convinced her that I didn't care about Rich pulling that stunt with the cottage, we sat talking, mostly about the lake and about the birds she might see on it. She said it was time for her to go back to his place, and she canoed off in that direction. Moments later, she was yelling. She sounded upset, so I dashed over to see what was wrong, and you were there."

"When you and Terri were talking, did you hear or see anyone at or near Rich's?"

"I heard a truck that Terri said belonged to the caterers. It left, and then Terri and I went inside for coffee, so I didn't hear anything else until after she left. I went back outside, and she started yelling. It's a lucky thing Terri did come over to my place that morning, because she and I were together.

Otherwise, she might have been hurt, or the police might suspect one of us of killing Rich."

"Lucky," I agreed. Terri had told me she had sworn Hank to secrecy about their being together that morning, so why was he confessing all of this to a stranger? I didn't ask, and I refrained from telling him that if he and Terri were going to use each other as alibis, they should tell the same story. Their stories were close, but not close enough.

If they weren't together the entire time, either of them could have attacked Rich. They could have worked together whether she spent part of that time birding or not. The hedge between Hank's and Rich's properties was substantial, but Hank had been able to push through it when he heard Terri's raised voice. Hank and Terri could have been peeking through the hedge, with or without Terri's binoculars. Even if they hadn't seen the caterers leave, Terri had apparently heard their truck. Terri and Hank could have gone over to Rich's party tent. Terri could have distracted Rich, allowing Hank to hit him with the skillet. They could have fled and returned separately, seeming innocent, after I discovered Rich's body. And some of the stains on Hank's clothes might not have been paint.

I had already discussed with Brent how Terri could have switched the noticeable red canoe for the aluminum one that blended in with the mist. For all I knew, she could have covered her red hoodie with a gray camo jacket or something similar and joined Hank to attack Rich. After the attack, she could have taken off in the aluminum canoe, hidden it and her camo jacket in the woods, and retrieved the red canoe while Hank stayed in his yard and watched for partygoers, who could become potential suspects, to arrive.

I wanted to call Brent and let him know that Terri and Hank were telling me stories that might differ from the ones they had told him and Detective Gartborg. But I didn't want to leap out of my seat and cause Hank to guess that I was suspecting him and Terri of murder.

Hank tasted the zombie donut. "You folks really know how to make donuts."

I thanked him.

Nina, who had promised to watch my back, came by and asked if she could get Hank anything. I took the opportunity to introduce her to him. He stood, shook her hand, and praised her talent. "Keep following your dream, Nina." He sounded sincere. Nina and I went back to work.

Hank finished his donuts and coffee, put cash on the table, and left.

"I hope he's not a murderer," Nina murmured as we cleared tables, "or about to be killed."

"Killed?"

"Rich admired my painting, too, and look what happened to him."

I faked a punch at her for teasing me. "I need to call Brent. I'll be right back."

"Ooooh." Eyes wide, she watched me shut myself into the office with Dep.

Chapter 27

❁

In the office Dep was curled on the couch. She stretched, took one look at me, flattened her ears, and scrambled up a carpeted post. I reminded her, "You don't know how to back down."

She leaped to a ramp that took her closer to the ceiling. I picked up my phone and pressed Brent's speed dial. Dep trotted down one of her stairways, landed on the desk, and rubbed the side of her mouth against the phone.

I held it next to my ear, out of her reach unless she stood on her hind legs, which she must have decided was too undignified at the moment. Brent's personal line went to message. One hand on Dep's warm and furry back, I said into my phone, "Terri Estable, and Rich's neighbor, Hank, came into our shop today, separately. You might already know this, but they have conflicting stories about where they each were when Rich was killed." I ended the message with an optimistic, "See you tonight."

I looked up from my purring cat. Scott and a couple of his firefighters were coming into the dining room. Cooing goodbyes to Dep, I thrust my phone into my apron pocket and headed toward the front of the shop.

Scott waved at me and caught sight of Jocelyn. "Welcome back, Jocelyn."

She teased, "Why are you wearing your dress uniform, Chief Ritsorf? Is that your Halloween costume?"

He fingered the shiny brass buttons on his jacket. "I'm in the parade."

Looking up into his kind blue eyes, I thought again how perfect he was for Misty. "I thought the parade was for kids."

He winked. "Anyone who drives big red trucks counts as a kid." He ordered deep-fried mozzarella sticks, deep-fried mushrooms, a scare-it cake donut, and a coffee.

Jocelyn folded her arms. "We need to have a talk about proper nutrition, Chief Ritsorf."

Scott burst out laughing. "Watch how you talk to customers. You wouldn't want Emily and Tom to fire you."

"They won't." She was right. "You would put out any *fires* anyway. And it's my turn to rescue you—from poor nutritional choices."

"It's not your turn, Jocelyn. I never actually rescued you. Besides, I'm going to eat my vegetables. There are carrots in the scare-it cake donut, and I'm going to eat a full serving of mushrooms, too. And the way Tom fries things, they're never greasy."

Smiling, I retreated to the kitchen and helped Tom and Nina make more of the donuts, fritters, and crullers we had designed for Halloween. Graceful as ever, Jocelyn flitted around the dining room serving customers. After Scott and his colleagues left, she was still teasing regulars. They beamed at her.

She, Tom, Nina, and I made the smaller donuts, crullers, and fritters for the kids we expected later.

At three, we joined our customers out on the patio to watch little trick-or-treaters parade through Fallingbrook. One of our usual patrons, a grandfather who always sat with the other retired men weekday mornings, arrived and sat at a table close to the sidewalk.

At the head of the parade, a fleet of pint-sized firetrucks, police cars, and ambulances pedaled past. Some of the vehicles were being helped along by parents and by Scott, Samantha, and other first responders, all in uniform and on foot. A miniature nurse at the wheel of a firetruck headed for a collision with the curb, but Scott strode to her and nudged her back into the middle of the street. An inflated *Tyrannosaurus rex* huffed past wedged into a police car that was barely big enough for him—and was definitely not big enough for his tail. A fairy furiously pedaled a farm tractor hauling a trailer behind it. Superheroes, zombies, witches, and a surprisingly tall scarecrow rolled past in other toy cars and trucks. Many of the little vehicles looked vintage, but they were shiny and in apparently perfect condition despite the tendency of some of them to veer off course only to be straightened by attentive and smiling adults. Behind the vehicles, other kids marched, walked, straggled, dawdled, and in one case stood gaping at our colorful donut shop. We saw cheerleaders, lumberjacks, policemen, and a Bride of Frankenstein. A tiny boy wore a realistic firefighter's outfit, complete with reflective tape.

The grandfather on our patio pointed at a blue sparkly butterfly. "There's my granddaughter!" Beside the little butterfly, a smiling woman carried a furry turquoise narwhal. "There's my grandson!"

The narwhal wasn't the only one being carried. There was an infant Green Bay Packer, a sleeping bumblebee, several princesses, and at least two wriggly teddy bears.

Behind them was a marching band, kid-style. The motley group included Little Red Riding Hood, a long-fanged wolf wearing a bonnet, a sumo wrestler, and a doctor. With great enthusiasm, they beat on toy drums, rattled tambourines, clashed cymbals, tootled into kazoos, and banged sticks together. Three elegant witches wheeled a cauldron in front of them. Something like a kettle drum was apparently inside the cauldron. The witches chanted and boomed on the drum while obviously trying not to giggle.

Our hands became red from clapping, and our throats became hoarse from cheering.

In their police uniforms, Misty and Hooligan walked at the rear of the parade. The grandfather on the patio knew Misty and Hooligan from chatting with and teasing them in Deputy Donut. He called, "Nice costumes, guys!" Misty and Hooligan smiled and waved.

All of our customers except the grandfather moved back to their indoor tables. Tom, Nina, Jocelyn, and I decided that the afternoon was warm enough for Jocelyn and Nina to serve the trick-or-treaters outside.

We carried urns of coffee, hot chocolate, and mulled cider out to the patio and brought out trays of our small Halloween donuts, crullers, and fritters. We also took out paper napkins, plates, and cups. Tom returned to the kitchen. I stayed outside helping Jocelyn and Nina arrange everything.

The grandfather told us, "The grandchildren are coming here after they visit the fire department open house. When my granddaughter heard that she could sit in a firetruck, she insisted they had to go there right after the parade. Then I suppose they'll trick-or-treat all the way here. But no problem." He raised his mug of Colombian coffee high. "I'll be happy waiting here." He glanced down Wisconsin Street and called out, "What are you doing here on a Saturday afternoon?"

Wearing a hunter-green wool blazer and matching slacks, Cheryl walked toward us. "Same thing you're doing," she answered.

"Waiting for a granddaughter and grandson?" he demanded.

Smiling, she shook her head. "Coffee and donuts." She entered the patio enclosure and patted Jocelyn's arm. "It's good to see you, honey."

I opened the front door for Cheryl. She went toward the table she usually shared with Steve. I followed her and suggested that, instead of sitting back there, she might like to sit closer to the window where she could watch costumed kids come to the patio for their treats. She took a seat facing the window at the table where the Knitpickers usually met. I asked her what she'd like.

"Advice." Tom had everything under control in the kitchen, and Nina and Jocelyn were chatting to customers on the patio. I sat down beside Cheryl where I could also watch the trick-or-treaters. Cheryl folded her hands on the table. "You've helped solve murders, and you were at Rich Royalson's after he died. Do you know how the investigation is going?"

"The investigators don't tell me more than they tell the public. I haven't heard anything about them figuring out who did it."

"Has your detective friend said anything about suspecting me?" Her knuckles were white.

"How could he suspect you? I don't know who he suspects, but I doubt that it's you."

"That woman, then, Detective Garter Snake or whatever her name is, suspects me."

I tried not to laugh too loudly. "Detective Gartborg. And how could she suspect you? For one thing, you wouldn't hurt a flea, or a garter snake, and for another, you and Steve arrived at Rich's party together."

"That's the thing. We didn't. We came in separate cars. I left here early that day to get ready for the party, and I didn't see Steve until he drove into Rich's driveway. It was shortly after I did, and he immediately went to talk to you, so I can see why you thought we came together."

I ran a finger along the smooth glass covering the donut painted on the table. "Lots of us saw you here earlier that morning and can honestly say that between about eleven when you left here and shortly after noon when you arrived at the party, you couldn't have done anything except go home, change, and drive to Rich's. You didn't have time to attack anyone." *Especially considering that the murderer might have gone to Rich's cottage that morning and picked up a skillet on the way to murder Rich.* I could not imagine Cheryl lifting that skillet, let alone using any sort of force to hit someone with it. But I didn't tell her that. As far as I knew, the police were being closemouthed about how Rich had died.

Cheryl gave me one of her sweet, grandmotherly smiles. "Thanks, Emily. You always make people feel better. And Steve's staying up at Little Lake Lodge while he's researching Wisconsin cheese. Someone in the staff up there should be able to corroborate that he left there with only enough time to drive straight to Rich's."

She ordered a pumpkin spice latte. I told her about the spider donuts that Jocelyn had created, and she wanted one of those, too. As I delivered them to her, Steve came in wearing a bright orange shirt. "Do you like my Halloween costume?" he asked us.

"Very creative," I said.

Cheryl looked down at her pants suit. "It's better than mine."

I held my apron out to the sides. "Mine, too. Call me Deputy Donut. What can I get you, Steve?"

"Anything, as long as it's not black licorice."

"Try the spider donut," Cheryl suggested. "That cute girl out on the patio designed them. You get a donut and a donut bite, nice old-fashioned cake donuts, with chocolate frosting decorations."

"Sold," Steve said.

Cheryl touched her mug. "And I'm having a pumpkin spice latte."

"Dumping spices into perfectly good coffee must be some of your middle-child syndrome." I couldn't tell if he was joking. I didn't defend our pumpkin spice latte.

"We didn't drink coffee when we were children." She said it with a straight face, but her eyes glinted with their usual humor.

Steve turned to me. "Do you have coffee that's just coffee without added flavor?"

"Sure. Our regular Colombian. It's a medium-dark roast, with lots of flavor and no acidic taste."

"I'll have one of those."

I patted the back of the chair where I'd sat before I went to get Cheryl's donut and latte. "Sit here where you can see the patio and the kids in their costumes."

Steve hesitated for a second as if watching trick-or-treaters wasn't his first priority, but he sat in the chair I'd suggested.

A superhero with enormous padded biceps raced into the patio enclosure. A ghost was right behind him. Neither of them quite tripped over the cornstalks tied to the railing enclosing the patio.

Steve must have touched up his hair. Usually, his temples were gray flecked, but today the one I could see, the one on the left, was dark brown like the rest of his hair. Maybe his Halloween costume consisted of more than an orange shirt. Was he pretending to be a character from a movie or TV? I couldn't think of a brown-haired character who wore orange shirts.

"Aren't the kids adorable?" Cheryl asked him. "Look at that tiny pink elephant!"

Heading to the kitchen for Steve's coffee and spider donut, I heard him say, "Middle child."

When I returned to Cheryl and Steve's table, Misty and Hooligan were arriving on the patio. Smiling broadly, they each gave Jocelyn a quick hug and stayed to chat while Nina helped an ungainly turtle balance a tiny cup of apple cider and a small fritter critter.

"What's with the hugging police officers?" Steve asked. "Or are those just regular people impersonating police officers?"

"They're actual police officers," Cheryl told him. "You've probably seen them in here before."

"I think I have. But not hugging people. Who's the spider-donut-creating girl they were hugging?"

Cheryl beamed. "She works here summers, so we all know her. Is Jocelyn back for the weekend, Emily? She's still going to college, isn't she?"

"Yes, she's here for only the weekend. We figured today would be extra busy, so we forced her to give up her studies for the day and help us."

"She'll get straight As, anyway," Cheryl predicted.

I agreed.

A few minutes later, Misty and Hooligan were gone. They must have turned down mini-donuts and coffee. The patio was becoming crowded. I went outside to help Jocelyn and Nina hand out treats. Jocelyn told me, "Misty and Hooligan said to say hello. They're off work now and on their way home to give out treats, but they said they'd see you tonight at your party."

"You and your boyfriend are welcome, too. Nina's coming."

"That would be fun," Jocelyn said. "I'll ask him."

A goblin with a green-painted face stuffed part of a jack-o'-lantern donut into his mouth. "My favorite!"

Between handing out donuts to a skeleton and a lavender octopus, Nina asked me, "Did you notice how Misty couldn't stop smiling? She's crazy about Scott, and no wonder. You know all those restored vintage cars that kids were pedaling in the parade?"

I nodded.

Nina told me, "Scott finds those at garage sales and antique shops and makes them like new again. He gives them to needy kids."

"I didn't know he did that."

Jocelyn chimed in, "Misty just now found out. She thinks it's wonderful."

I handed a cup of hot chocolate to a kid wearing a cardboard sandwich painted to look like a phone. "I do, too."

Nina explained, "Other firefighters help him. Repainting the antiques can devalue them, but Scott and his guys don't care. They want kids to have fun playing with them. They sell the more valuable ones to museums and collectors and use the money to buy more toys and the materials for fixing them up."

Jocelyn beamed at two more trick-or-treaters. "Here's a fox and a lion."

Nina crowed, "And we have a new employee!"

A miniature chef smiled up at her, waved a wooden spoon, and piped in a high voice, "I make the best donuts in the universe!"

The numbers of trick-or-treaters thinned out as if it were time for the kids to rush home, eat supper, maybe, and plunder the neighborhoods where they lived.

Nina and Jocelyn were happy to stay out on the patio and wait for others. I went inside to start tidying the kitchen.

My phone rang. Brent. I answered.

Steve and Cheryl came to the counter to pay for their donuts and coffee.

"Just a sec," I said to Brent. I went to stand across the counter from Steve and Cheryl. She argued, "It's my turn, Steve."

Playfully, Steve elbowed her aside. He pulled a charge card out of his wallet, but had trouble inserting it in the card reader. I took it out, worked it in for him, and gave him the card reader. Steve seemed to have trouble typing in his PIN. After a couple of tries, the payment was accepted. Frowning, he pulled out his card and shoved it into a pocket. "Ready to go?" he asked Cheryl.

The charge card he had always used on his other visits to Deputy Donut gave his name as Steven Quail, which matched how he'd introduced himself to Rich and me on Monday afternoon. He'd said, "Steve Quail," but that was close enough. Although I hadn't paid a lot of attention when I jiggled this card, took it out, and repositioned it, I was certain that there had been two initials and a last name that started with *M* on it. The initials had been *S* and *Q*, and the last name had been something like "Meadow." No wonder he'd taken extra time to enter his PIN. He'd probably entered the wrong one first. Writers, I reminded myself, often had pen names. Steve guided Cheryl toward the front of the shop.

In my ear, Brent's voice asked, "Em? Are you still there?"

"Yes."

Maybe it was a trick of the light, but although I'd noticed earlier that the hair at Steve's left temple was dark brown, matching the rest of his hair, it seemed to me that his right temple was graying, the way it had always looked before.

"Em?"

"Right. Sorry. I wanted to tell you about Terri Estable and Rich's neighbor, Hank, and their differing stories about the morning Rich died."

Opening the door for Cheryl, Steve stared back toward me. He was probably disappointed that I hadn't asked him about his pen name. The names on his charge cards weren't familiar, but for all I knew, in addition to writing about food for trade journals, he could have been a famous author of children's books or maybe he owned a company that was a household name, and I hadn't recognized it. I wanted to apologize, but he was gone.

Brent asked, "What did Terri and Hank tell you?"

As Steve and Cheryl left the patio, the mystery man who had come to Deputy Donut a few hours after Rich's murder entered the patio enclosure.

Again neatly dressed in a tailored suit, he headed straight for Jocelyn and Nina.

Chapter 28

"Brent!" I hadn't meant my whisper into the phone to come out more like a screech. "Remember the mystery man I told you about, the man in a suit who came into Deputy Donut shortly after Rich was killed? He's out on the patio talking to Nina and Jocelyn."

"Keep an eye on him."

Tom was at the big mixer, watching as it kneaded a batch of the next day's dough. I caught his attention and pointed toward the patio. He stared toward our front windows. I knew he would shut off the mixer and run out to the patio if he had to.

Watching Nina, Jocelyn, and the mystery man, I told Brent about Terri stating that she'd been at Hank's during part of the time she'd originally claimed to be canoeing.

Brent already knew that Rich had made certain that he would be the one to buy the underpriced cottage, but Terri hadn't told him about delaying her canoeing on Tuesday morning to apologize to Hank for her role in the scheme. I told Brent that Hank had come into Deputy a short time after Terri left. "His story was similar, except he said that he and Terri had been together the entire time that Terri had originally claimed she'd been canoeing. So, Hank is giving himself and Terri alibis for the entire time, but Terri is leaving it open that Hank could have gone next door and killed Rich while she was supposedly canoeing, which destroys the alibis that Hank provided for himself and Terri. Maybe they'll get together and coordinate their stories before they talk to you again."

"Thanks. What you've told me might be helpful. We'll interview them again and get their latest versions."

"Before you go, I need to tell you one more thing. Remember the pickup truck I saw at Rich's cottage late Thursday night?"

"Yes."

Out on the patio, Jocelyn was cleaning tables. The mystery man was still talking to Nina. He handed her something like a business card. I looked over my shoulder. Tom was still gazing at them.

I told Brent, "Terri thought she heard Derek's truck rattle past Rich's house that night, and Hank said that when he was checking around Rich's cottage, looking for Terri, a rattletrap was approaching on the road. Hank got into his canoe and paddled away. When he arrived at his own dock, Terri was there, scared because of hearing Derek's truck. Hank said she didn't stay long, and after she went back to Rich's, Hank heard the rattling truck leave."

The mystery man left the patio and walked south on Wisconsin Street. I told Brent which direction the man was heading and went on with my story. "I don't know what Derek was doing around Rich's cottage after Rich was murdered, but I wonder if he, like Hank, was searching for Terri. And if she's still in danger from him."

"We haven't finished talking to him, either."

Smiling, Nina marched to the counter. Jocelyn was right behind her. Nina slapped a business card down where I could read it. I quickly said, "Don't go, Brent." I looked up into Nina's brightly smiling face. "The mystery man works at an art gallery?"

"Mr. Arthurs owns it," she said proudly. "It's a famous one."

Tom appeared beside me and read the card aloud. "The Arthur C. Arthurs Gallery, Madison, Wisconsin."

Flushed, Nina brushed at hair straying out from underneath her Deputy Donut hat. "Mr. Arthurs is coming to my studio on Monday to see my other work. He said if it's anything like what's here and at The Craft Croft, he'll offer me a one-woman show, maybe as soon as next August or September!" She cradled her face in her hands and made a face like the ones she'd been carving into Boston scream donuts. "Eeek!" She lowered her hands and went back to smiling broadly. "Rich Royalson called him about my work on Monday. Mr. Arthurs drove up here on Tuesday after a meeting that ended at ten in Madison." She held up an index finger. "Notice how deftly I discovered his alibi for the time of Rich's murder."

Jocelyn smiled at her. "Good detective work. Madison is four hours away. Four long hours every time I go."

I teased her, "You should have gone to a college that's closer."

Jocelyn shook her head. "Nuh-uh." I grinned. Her boyfriend also went to the University of Wisconsin in Madison.

Tom asked Nina, "Where was this Arthur C. Arthurs between Tuesday afternoon when he was here and just now?"

"He had to go home right after he visited The Craft Croft. Today was his first chance to come back. He brought his wife and they're making a weekend of it."

I congratulated Nina and then asked into the phone, "Did you hear any of that, Brent? The mystery man who worried me is an art gallery owner, Arthur C. Arthurs. Rich Royalson told him about Nina, so Arthurs knew Rich, but I don't think he came to Fallingbrook to murder Rich. He claims he was at a meeting in Madison until ten on Tuesday. He couldn't have been here when Rich was murdered."

"Thanks, Em. We'll follow up on that. Plus, you've given us those other leads. See you tonight."

We disconnected. I thought, *I hope you don't have to work, Brent.*

Tom, Jocelyn, and I congratulated Nina again.

"The Arthur C. Arthurs Gallery," she said reverently, but there was a telltale gleam in her eye that warned me she was about to make a joke or tease someone. "I wonder if he ever shortens his name to Art? Or shortens both his first and last name to Art? The Art Art Gallery! Or, you know, with the middle initial of C, he could have been Art C. Arthurs, and his friends called him Artsy"—she made air quotes—"Arthurs. So, he had to own an art gallery when he grew up."

Jocelyn and I laughed, but Tom stayed serious. "Are you sure he is who he says he is? He did show up here only a few hours after Rich Royalson was murdered."

"Nina knew who Cindy is," I reminded Tom. "She's familiar with the art world."

Nina stared off toward the back wall of the kitchen as if she could see through it. "I can't speak for him personally, but I know that the gallery is real." She flashed us a quick and happy grin. "And prestigious."

"Fine," Tom said. "But if he's meeting you at your studio, even if he's bringing his alleged wife, make certain someone else comes along."

"I'll come," I said.

Jocelyn made a sad face. "I'd go, too, but I'll be back at school."

"Don't worry, Jocelyn," Tom told her. "I'll go. I'll stand around and look dangerous."

Nina clapped her hands. "It will be like I hire my own security guard!"

The last customers left, and the four of us went out to the patio. We brought the urns, cups, plates, and napkins inside and then tidied the shop quickly so we could hurry home and hand out candy to trick-or-treaters.

I loaded the donuts I'd made for my party into the donut car. Less than thrilled about her cat carrier, Dep straightened all four of her legs and held them out to her sides. It was almost impossible to tuck her into the carrier, even though it had plenty of room if a kitty wasn't striving to shape-shift into an unbendable pancake with claws. Finally, she was in the carrier and we were on our way home in the fun donut car.

Carrying Dep, grumbling inside the carrier, up the steps, I grinned at the display on my porch. It was nicely Halloween-like without being too frightening for, I hoped, even the smallest kids. I unlocked the door, let Dep out of her carrier, and smiled as she bounced toward the kitchen.

I took the offensive cat carrier outside so it wouldn't be in our way during the party. Our donut car was always quirky, but now it looked almost like another Halloween decoration—an old-fashioned police car trying to disguise itself as a donut. I put the carrier into the trunk and carefully took my boxes of donuts to the kitchen.

I spooned some of Dep's favorite canned food into one of her bowls. Perhaps still in a snit about being unceremoniously carted home, she frolicked into the sunroom and sat on one of her warm, cushioned radiator covers next to a back window.

I pulled one of my individual servings of homemade chili out of the freezer. While the microwave oven heated it, I ran upstairs and changed into a floor-length, slinky black velvet gown. Silver reflective spangles and sequins decorated the lower third of the skirt. The black lace sleeves ended in points on the backs of my hands. Remembering the small witches who'd marched in the parade and pounded on a kettle drum inside a cauldron, I resigned myself to doing without a cauldron or a drum. But I did have the world's most perfect hat and wig combination. Like the dress, the hat was black velvet. Reflective silver spangles and sequins were sprinkled all over the floor-length black lace veil cascading from the point at the top of the hat. The attached hair was long, frizzy, and silver. I put the hat on and checked my reflection. The shoulder-length hair covered my short dark brown hair, including the curls that inevitably flopped onto my forehead.

It was a fun costume, and even without a mask, I didn't think I looked like myself. A mask or scary makeup would have added a nice touch, but I didn't want to scare little kids.

Downstairs again, I took the baskets of candy out of the china cabinet. I left them and the hat with its super-long veil and frizzy hair near the front door.

Finally, I went into the back of the house to enjoy the chili. It was hot, both heat hot and spicy hot, just the way I liked it.

I'd eaten about half of it when the doorbell rang. I ran to the living room, slapped the wig and hat combo on my head, brushed a puff of silvery fake hair away from one eye, and opened the door.

A toddler in a costume that resembled Dep took one look at me, burst into tears, and held his arms up toward his dad. Laughing, his dad picked him up. "Hold out your pumpkin," he told his son. The tearful child shook his head but held the orange plastic pumpkin where I could barely reach it. I slipped a chocolate bar into it. The child stopped crying and stared in awe at the candy in the bottom of the basket.

Grinning, his father thanked me and carried him to the sidewalk. A seahorse, a mermaid, and a dolphin toiled up the porch stairs. I gave them all candy.

I closed the door. My chili was becoming chilly chili, but it was still delicious.

The bell rang. I opened the door. Without a word, a two-year-old in a tiger costume that wrinkled around her ankles and wrists and would probably still fit her when she was six marched into the house and started climbing toward the second floor. Laughing, her mother ran inside and scooped her up. "We've been house hunting," the mother explained. "She likes touring houses." I gave the girl a chocolate bar.

Dep raced toward me, her eyes huge and her ears flat to

her head. "Sorry about the big cat invading your space," I told her. Instead of accepting the apology, she galloped past me and up the stairs.

The small tiger's mother asked me, "Have you seen the moon? It's full tonight, a harvest moon, and so near the horizon it's huge and orange."

I followed her out to the sidewalk and looked east. The moon was exactly as she'd described it. "Beautiful," I said. "Thank you."

The girl pointed at it. "Pumpkin!"

Her mother and I laughed, and I went back inside.

Between spoonfuls of chili, I doled out candy to the grim reaper, Alice in Wonderland, an astronaut, and several unidentified creatures. One of them might have been a surgeon in bloodstained scrubs.

I finished the chili and set out a platter of veggies and bowls of dips, chips, nuts, and pretzels for my party. Beer, white wine, soft drinks, and juices were in the fridge. I put two bottles of red wine on the counter, ready to be opened. I set out glasses and answered the door to a toothy animal that might have been an alligator and his baby sister in a charming bunny costume with a satin ruffle around her adorable, pink-cheeked face.

A werewolf grasped the leash of a real dog wearing a Dracula cape. A tarantula and a princess arrived together, followed by a baseball player and a bat, the kind that darts through the sky devouring mosquitoes.

Out on the street, a woman in a skeleton costume clip-clopped past on an actual horse, a black one with a horse skeleton painted in white on it.

I arranged the Halloween donuts on platters and set them on the coffee table. Around eight, the stream of kids dwindled. I left the wig and hat near the door, locked it, and went upstairs.

Dep was in the center of my bed with her legs tucked un-

derneath her and her tail coiled around her. She gave me a re-
proachful look.

"Sorry about all those kids coming and going, Dep. I
know their behavior didn't fit into our usually quiet evenings.
But Halloween happens only once a year, and your friends will
arrive in a half hour or so. But," I cautioned her, "they might
be dressed like big cats or other scary creatures."

She turned her head away.

I went into the guest room. Hampered by the tight velvet
skirt, I eased into the chair at my computer. I logged on and
searched for the Arthur C. Arthurs Gallery in Madison.

Chapter 29

✤

The Arthur C. Arthurs Gallery website showed a photo of the proprietor. He was the man who was no longer a mystery man.

Arthur C. Arthurs had an impressive history of discovering artists who later became well known. *Go, Nina!*

Brent would only need to verify that Arthur C. Arthurs had actually attended the meeting Tuesday and that it hadn't ended before seven or eight that morning.

In the back of my mind, I'd been wondering about Steve. Was there any significance to the graying hair on only one side of his head? When he had come into Deputy Donut that afternoon, he had asked how we liked his costume. I'd assumed he'd been talking about the orange shirt, but could the mismatched hair at his temples have been part of the costume? I couldn't think of any fictional characters who went around in orange shirts and had only one white-smudged temple.

Misty, Samantha, and I had joked about Samantha powdering her hair to make it white for her wedding, and Misty had pointed out that theatrical dye could wash out. Maybe Steve preferred to date older women but was afraid they wouldn't want to date a younger man, and he had been making his temples lighter in order to look closer to Cheryl's age. Maybe the article he was writing wasn't about cheese at all.

Maybe he was writing about dating sites for seniors, or he was doing research for an article about dating older women. And maybe he had accidentally brushed the powder out of one side of his hair today.

Perhaps the gray had been real, and he was now trying to look his own age, bit by bit. Eliminating the white and gray on only one side of his head hardly seemed subtle enough to be effective.

And then there were the charge cards with different names.

I supposed Steve could have been an undercover cop. That would explain his having valid charge cards with different names. However, I was fairly certain that a cop who was deeply undercover would not risk carrying identification that did not match his alias.

An even wilder guess was that Steve was an FBI agent, and he'd been following Terri and Derek from state to state while Terri conned men—and perhaps grandmothers—into willing her everything.

If the FBI was investigating crimes like that, wouldn't they have either taken over or informed the Fallingbrook Police and the Wisconsin Division of Investigation that they were also on the case? However, they could have told the other law enforcement agencies, and I wouldn't know about it. Brent didn't tell me everything.

Did Steve use two names because he was famous?

On the internet, I could find no photos of the Steve Quail I'd met. I did find one tiny mention of a Steven Quail who could have been Cheryl's date. He was fifty-five and licensed in Ohio as a private investigator. Cheryl's Steve could have been about that age.

That would explain a lot. He could have come to Fallingbrook to investigate something, possibly Terri and Derek, and he was using writing about cheese as a cover story.

Having found a possible reason for Steve's use of credit cards with different names, I decided to research Hank. He was still fairly well known as a pianist. I looked for connections between him and Rich's late wife, Patty Royalson. I found an obituary for Mary Patricia (Patty) Brook Royalson. She'd been survived by her husband, Richmond P. Royalson III, her mother, and her half brother.

The half brother's name was Stanley Quentin Meadows.

Staring at the name, I wheeled my chair back, placed my palms over my temples, and squeezed. Was S. Q. Meadows the name on the charge card that Steve had used that afternoon?

I told myself that Steve Quail couldn't be Patty's half brother, but even as I tried to convince myself, I stared at Patty's picture in the obituary and remembered the pictures I'd seen of her in Rich's cottage. The man I knew as Steve Quail had hazel eyes. Patty's had been blue. The shape of his squarish face was similar to her face in the photos. Although she had been a beauty, his face was attractive but less noticeable, as if the high cheekbones, patrician nose, and defined chin that contributed to her beauty had been airbrushed and smoothed from his face. Or he had schooled his face to show mostly neutral expressions. Patty had been vivacious and smiling.

Rich Royalson had asked Steve if they'd met before.

Steve had answered that they hadn't.

Could they have never met each other? If Steve was the Steven Quail who was a private investigator in Ohio he would have been thirty-five when Patty drowned. Perhaps he didn't make it to the funeral. The obituary said that Patty had been Rich's wife of thirty years when she died. That meant that if Steve was Patty's half brother, he had been a child, only about five years old, when Rich and Patty got married. Maybe he was too young to be invited to the wedding, and maybe he didn't spend time with Rich and Patty while he was growing up and after he was an adult.

Perhaps Steve, or Stanley, had looked familiar to Rich because of his resemblance to Rich's late wife.

Patty's maiden name was different from either of the sur-
names on Steve's credit cards. Following twisting paths
through obituaries, I discovered that Patty's father, who had,
as Hank had told me, been divorced from Patty's mother, had
remarried. He and his new wife had a son, Stanley Quentin
Brook. Stanley and Patty's father died when Stanley was only
five. Two years later, Stanley's mother married a man whose
last name was Meadows, and that man adopted Stanley and
changed the boy's last name from Brook to Meadows. He
had also moved the family to California, which could have
explained why Rich might not have seen Stanley since Stanley was about seven, if ever.

Was it a coincidence that Stanley showed up in Rich's
hometown shortly before Rich was murdered?

I checked my photo of the guest list for Rich's party. I already knew that Steve Quail wasn't on it. Stanley Quentin
Meadows wasn't, either, which didn't prove much, since Terri
had written the list and hadn't included people she didn't want
to feel welcome.

It was more likely that Rich hadn't invited his late wife's
half brother except by accident when he'd invited Cheryl and
the man I'd thought of as Steve. If Rich had written to the
man he might have known as Stanley and invited him,
Rich probably would have figured out on Monday afternoon
why the man looked familiar.

The doorbell startled me out of my theorizing. It was almost time for my party guests to arrive.

I trotted downstairs, plopped my hat and wig on, and
opened the door to three burly football players in Fallingbrook
High football uniforms. The three teens carried bulging pillow-
cases and thanked me politely for the chocolate bars. Luckily,
I had lots of them for any high school kids who were trick-or-
treating now that their littler sisters and brothers had returned home to sort their loot and go, probably reluctantly
and bouncing off walls, to bed.

I closed the door, grabbed my phone, and called Brent.

He answered right away. "Hi, Em, I'm going to clear away a few little things and come over."

"That's not why I called. A man who has been coming to Deputy Donut and dating one of our regular knitters is Rich Royalson's late wife's younger half brother." Dep must have recognized by my tone of voice that I was talking to a friend. She ran down from the second floor and rubbed hairs onto the skirt of my long velvet dress.

"Whoa, Em. Run that by me again?"

I told him about the dyed temples and the alias, Steve Quail, that Stanley Quentin Meadows apparently used as a private investigator and on dating sites. I also told Brent about the way the man had shoved his charge card into a pocket after having trouble typing in the PIN. I added, "I thought he had arrived at Rich's birthday party with Cheryl, which gave him an alibi, but today she told me they came in separate cars, and that he'd been staying up at Little Lake Lodge, at least at the time of the party."

"Thanks, Em. We haven't questioned him beyond a short interview right after the murder. Someone will go to Little Lake Lodge and have another talk with him if he hasn't already checked out. I'm not going up there tonight, though. I have a party to attend."

I smiled at the warmth in his voice. "See you soon."

I strode into the kitchen as quickly as I could in the constricting velvet dress. Dep followed me. I slid a tray of mini-quiches into the oven and set the timer.

The doorbell rang.

Expecting more teenagers or some of my friends, I flung the door open without remembering to put my hat and its attached wig on first.

And it was a friend. I hadn't invited the Knitpickers to my party, but Cheryl, dressed like Maria from *The Sound of Music*, was certainly welcome.

I wasn't sure about the tall ghost beside her, though. I

could barely catch a glimpse of his hazel eyes through the small eyeholes he'd cut in the sheet that served as his costume. A bulging pillowcase hung at his side. I could make out enough of the letters stamped on one corner of the sheet to know where the sheet had come from.

Little Lake Lodge.

The hand that wasn't holding the pillowcase snaked out from underneath the sheet. The glove on the hand didn't completely cover the cuff of the orange shirt.

The tall ghost was Steve Quail, also known as Stanley Quentin Meadows.

He grabbed Cheryl's wrist.

Cheryl complained, "Ow!" Staring at me, she gave her head a slight shake. Fear showed in her usually beaming blue eyes.

Brent would be here soon, I told myself.

Not wanting Steve to notice that I'd glimpsed an unspoken warning from Cheryl, I said as cordially as possible, "Come in." I turned around and gestured toward the rest of the living room. "Help yourselves to some of the goodies. I'll bring out mini-quiches in a few minutes. They're in the oven. The other guests will be here soon." I was babbling. "What can I get you to drink?"

Behind me, the front door closed, hard, as if someone had kicked it. I faced my guests again.

In one smooth motion, the ghost dropped the pillowcase while pulling a substantial cast-iron skillet out of it.

This skillet was a normal size, not a huge one, and it had a normal length handle.

It was probably easier to wield than the one that had killed Rich. Turning Cheryl away from him with his left hand, the orange-sleeved ghost lifted that skillet above her head with his right hand. He was wearing a glove on that hand, also. "Sorry, Cheryl, but you should not have told Emily that we went to Rich's party separately." With a loud exhalation, he swung the skillet toward her temple.

I screamed and tried to reach the skillet, but the ghost was tall and quick. I grabbed only a pinch of orange shirt sleeve. I couldn't hold on to it, but I hoped I disrupted Steve's possibly lethal aim.

The skillet crashed into the back of Cheryl's head. She slumped to the floor and didn't move or make a sound.

The ghost blocked the front door.

My phone was on the kitchen counter. Although knowing I was heading toward a dead end since there was no way out of my walled-in garden except through the house, I turned around and scrambled in that long skirt toward the back of the house. I would grab my phone, somehow dodge past the ghost, run out the front to a neighbor's, and call for help.

My dress would undoubtedly slow me down, but so would the corners of the sheet dangling around Steve's shoes.

Behind me, Dep hissed, a long and angry sound.

Steve was chasing me. He said, "Thanks for telling us you had a gas stove, Emily."

I made it into the kitchen and reached for my phone.

I heard another loud exhalation from Steve. Sheets rustled.

Pain sliced into the back of my head, and everything went bleary.

Chapter 30

✿

I was lying on the hard tiles of the kitchen floor. Hoping that playing dead would save me from a worse attack, I kept my eyes closed and tried not to move.

I couldn't see anything besides colors swooping around the insides of my eyelids.

I could hear.

Steve's voice. "Sorry, Emily. I don't know if you can hear me, but if you could, I'd tell you that you and Cheryl are nice people. I didn't want to hurt either one of you, but I was afraid that both of you saw my real name when I accidentally used the wrong charge card this afternoon. Cheryl mentioned that she'd told you we'd arrived at Rich's party separately, and then I went back to my room and discovered that I'd forgotten some of the white I'd been putting in my hair to make me look closer to Cheryl's age. It was only a matter of time before one of you would figure out that Patty was my big sister. My half sister, but she was like another mother to me until my stepfather moved me to California. I loved her, but I was only seven and she and I lost track of each other. I didn't know she married, and I didn't know she died until a few years afterward. She drowned, very conveniently, while that monster she married was having an affair. I bided my time until I could pay him back for what he did to Patty. I followed dating sites for this area, and he appeared on one recently. I guessed he would throw a seventieth birthday party for himself, so I connected with the only woman for miles around who was near his age and on the dating site he was on. I planned everything, even to sticking around afterward to continue pretending to research cheese. I was going to get away with murdering someone who deserved it. But you and Cheryl ruined my careful planning."

No, I thought, still playing dead, *you were wrong. Rich didn't kill her.*

I heard Steve's feet shuffle on the tile floor toward the range. "I can't let that happen," he said. I heard the *tick-tick-tick* of the gas stovetop's ignition, and the whoosh as the gas caught fire. Six times, one for each burner. And I heard him take six deep breaths, heard him blow six times.

One for each burner.

I was only stunned, but if he thought I was unconscious or dead, he might leave without noticing that, thanks to my late husband's caution, my top-of-the-line range automatically shut off the gas after the flames went out. If he realized that the gas wasn't likely to kill Cheryl and me, he might do something else drastic. Probably with that skillet.

What if I sneezed? Merely thinking it made my nose itch.

How was Cheryl?

And Dep?

I hoped that Steve would go outside by the back door and accidentally lock it. He'd be stuck between the house and the walls around the yard, making it easy for the police to catch him when they got here.

Between throbs of pain in my head, I realized that I had not called the police.

Brent was on his way, wasn't he?

I heard Steve walk, not toward the back door, but toward the dining room. Toward the living room.

There were sounds of a scuffle and an enraged howl from Dep, louder than any of the times I had put her into her carrier and taken her for a ride in a car.

Something crashed. Dishes clattered. Steve swore. Dep's little feet pounded toward me. Loud human footsteps pounded away from me. There was a semi-metallic thud like the skillet hitting the pine plank floor.

The front door slammed.

Silence.

Danger, I reminded myself. Steve must have left, but any stray spark might ignite lingering gas fumes. There was danger—for me, for Cheryl, and for Dep.

The sweet cat was urgently licking my face with her rough little tongue.

Cautiously, I opened my eyes. I was lying beside my kitchen island.

I smelled gas. Steve had lit all six burners and blown out the flames. By now, the gas should have shut off automatically, but what if it hadn't? *Move, Emily.*

The timer on the oven, which was electric, not gas, beeped.

I sneezed.

Dep patted my cheek with one soft paw. "Mew!"

I rolled over and rose onto my hands and knees. Looking perfectly fine, Dep rubbed against my arms. I clutched at a bar stool and pulled myself up until I was standing, leaning on the granite counter with both hands.

My phone was where I'd left it. "First things first," I mumbled.

Afraid that my velvet dress might rub against my tights and create a spark that would set off an explosion, I stumbled to the range. The gas seemed to have stopped flowing. Resting a hand on the counter beside the range, I turned off each burner, one by one.

I turned off the oven, too, and hoped it would keep the little quiches warm without drying them out.

In the hampering dress, I minced to the back door, opened it wide, and called, "Want to go outside, Dep?"

She streaked past me into the safety of the moonlit night. I left the door open to let in fresh air.

On the block behind mine, high voices hollered, "Trick or treat!"

Glad that Alec and I had replaced the old sunroom windows with new double-hung ones that opened easily, I shoved the lower halves upward and tugged the upper halves downward. Cool air streamed in through the lower sections.

"Stay out there, Dep," I muttered, "as far as possible from the house."

The lace-sleeved black velvet dress was elegant and sophisticated, but it was totally impractical and had no pockets. Carrying my phone in one hand and hoping that the fresh air coming in through the back of the house would replace the fumes before they could explode, I eased through the dining room and into the living room.

Cheryl was lying in a heap of Maria's skirts and petticoats next to the front door. The skillet's handle was sticking out below the wing chair.

I peeked through the peephole. I couldn't see anyone. I opened the door. Chilly air wafted inside. The goofy, loose-jointed skeletons I'd hung from the living room ceiling performed an almost silent and eerie dance.

Finally, I knelt beside Cheryl. The back of her head was bleeding, but she didn't seem to be in danger of bleeding to death, and I doubted that I was, either. I felt her pulse. To my relief, it was strong. And the fresh air was bracing.

I called 911, gave my address, and asked for an ambulance, police officers, and the fire department. "Two of us have been attacked. I'm okay, but the other woman is injured and seems to be unconscious. The attacker turned on the range and blew out the flames. The gas went out automatically. I opened doors and windows, but I need the fire department to make certain it's safe."

"Stay on the line," the dispatcher said. I heard the clicks of a computer keyboard. "Help is on the way. How bad are the other woman's injuries?"

I ran my hands down Cheryl's arms and legs. "No broken bones, as far as I can tell."

"Can you safely get yourself and the injured person outside?"

"Not knowing the extent of her injuries, I shouldn't move her."

"Are you dizzy or woozy?"

"No." It wasn't quite true. My head hurt, and I felt disoriented, probably due to shock and not to the fumes. I could no longer smell them. I didn't know if that meant they were gone or if I'd become used to them.

"I want you to go out into the fresh air. Leave the injured woman where she is. You have to keep a clear head for her sake."

I would have said the same thing when I was a 911 operator. "Okay," I agreed reluctantly. I could be outside but also close to Cheryl if I stayed on the porch.

Cheryl stretched her arms and legs and opened her eyes. "Emily? What happened?" She slurred her words.

"Steve knocked us out."

"*The Sound of Music.*" She squeezed her eyes shut. "I think I'm supposed to say I'm Maria, but I'm not, am I?"

"You're Cheryl, dressed like Maria for Halloween."

"That's a pretty dress you're wearing."

"I'm a witch."

"No, you're not. You're a lovely young woman."

I thought, *I Feel Pretty. No, that's a different Maria.*

I needed to get both of us outside. "Cheryl, do you think you can sit up?"

"*Climb Ev'ry mountain.*" She didn't sit up.

"What hurts?"

"Just my head, and it's not bad. I can't remember for sure, but I think Steve hit me. Only that's not his real name, is it?"

"I don't think so."

She sang, "*Steve, a name he calls himself.*"

"How about your arms and legs, your back, your hips, your neck? Do any of them hurt?"

"Not so much that I can't sit up. But I don't feel like knitting."

"You don't have to."

"I don't know where my knitting basket is."

"Did you leave it at home?"

Her smile was close to her usual grandmotherly one. "Yes, Emily, I think I did. Steve brought me trick-or-treating. He wanted to come here. Did you give him your address?"

"It's easy to find. And I think he's a private investigator, so it would have been easy for him, anyway." I touched the back of my head. It wasn't wet, and I didn't feel lumps or dents.

Cheryl managed to sit up. "Investigating Wisconsin cheese? There. I'm just about better."

"Can you move closer to the door, maybe sit on the doorstep?"

"That's a long way to run."

"You don't have to run."

"I was thinking of a song. But sure, I can."

I heard sirens coming closer. "Are you warm enough?"

"Almost, dear. You know, a doe is a deer. Really, I'm fine." Sitting, she scooted toward the porch.

I plopped my witch hat with its magnificent poufy wig onto my head and immediately felt warmer. Despite the 911 dispatcher's order, I went farther into the living room. Judging by how cold the living room felt, fresh air had almost replaced the air inside the house, at least downstairs.

Dep was sitting on the coffee table. She lifted one paw tentatively as if she were about to bat at a platter of donuts. "Mew?"

Another platter was on the floor. Most of the donuts from that platter were smashed, their fillings oozing out. A Boston scream donut was no longer screaming. Its fudge frosting was badly smeared.

That scuffle I'd heard, that loud kitty howl, that crash . . .

I looked down at Dep. "Did you trip that man in the ghost costume and make him fall into the donuts?"

A small voice in my ear said, "What?"

I told the 911 operator, "Sorry, I was talking to my cat."

"Are you sure you're okay?"

"I'm fine. And the other woman has regained consciousness."

"I gathered that. I heard another woman's voice."

Dep leaped down from the coffee table. Sitting on the floor beside the smeared Boston scream donut, she blinked up at me. "Meow."

I held the phone away from my mouth. "You did, you little heroine! You tripped him!"

The 911 dispatcher asked, "What's this about heroin?"

"Heroine, with an *e* at the end, a female hero. My cat is one."

"Okay." The dispatcher drew the word out. "Are you outside?"

"No, but there's so much cold air that I'm nearly freezing, so I think it's fresh."

"Go outside," the dispatcher insisted.

Dep lifted one dainty paw, gave it a swift lick, and shook it as if it had touched something nasty, like a donut. Or a murderer.

I pulled a crocheted afghan off the couch, took it outside, wrapped it around Cheryl, and told the dispatcher, "We're both on the front porch."

"If you can, go farther from the house."

"As soon as the victim can walk," I promised.

I asked Cheryl, "How did you and Steve get here?"

"We met at the Fireplug Pub and walked. We stopped at a few houses on the way and he got candy. But his pillowcase was already full when we got together at the Fireplug Pub. I think he probably filled it himself before he started out, but maybe I'm remembering it all wrong. It doesn't make sense."

"Not unless you want to hide a skillet in a pillowcase."

She twisted her mouth into a sort of grin. "Does that make sense? Was I hit harder than I thought?"

I told her firmly, "It doesn't make sense. None of it does."

Dep came out onto the porch with us, the pumpkins, the scarecrow, the unscared crow, and the goblins. I set the phone down on the porch floor, reached around the jamb for Dep's leash and halter, snapped them on her, and asked Cheryl, "Do you know where Steve parked his car?"

"Near the pub, I think."

"Do you know what kind of car he drives?"

"I'm not sure I ever saw it."

"You said you drove separate cars to Rich's party. Did you see it that time?"

She scratched her head. "I must have, but I was worrying about you and what had upset you, and I was focusing on the cars arriving so I could send them away."

Two police cars, an ambulance, and a firetruck stopped in front. I picked up the phone and told the 911 dispatcher that the first responders had arrived. She let me disconnect. Two EMTs from the ambulance ran up onto the porch. I pointed at Cheryl. "She was knocked out."

"I'm okay," Cheryl said.

One of the EMTs crouched beside her and asked quiet questions.

A crew of firefighters clomped onto the porch in their bulky firefighting outfits and heavy boots. I pointed toward the kitchen. "The gas was left on without flames, but my range turns off automatically. I made certain the burners were off, and opened doors and windows."

"We'll test the air inside your house and blow in fresh air if we need to," one of the firefighters assured me. "Wait outside."

As soon as he disappeared into the dining room, I grabbed the orange wicker jack-o'-lantern basket of candy, gave the EMTs a handful of chocolate bars, and gently placed my phone in the basket with the remaining chocolate bars. I hung the handle over my arm, pushed my witch hat with its attached frizzy silver hair more firmly onto my own curls, picked Dep up—leash, halter and all—and followed the firefighter's instructions.

Well, sort of. I went back outside, but I wasn't about to wait.

Dep and I were going ghost hunting.

Chapter 31

I wasn't going to confront Steve. If I saw him, I would stay back. With luck I would be able to tell the police which way he was going, and if he got into a car, I could describe that.

Cheryl had said that he might have left his car near the Fireplug Pub, which was close to Deputy Donut. Steve probably thought I was still lying on the floor in a house filling with explosive fumes. He wouldn't expect to see me out here. Trusting my hat with its attached hair and my trick-or-treat basket to disguise me, I turned left, toward downtown Fallingbrook, Deputy Donut, and the Fireplug Pub. Far up the street, trick-or-treaters were going house to house, but even by the light of the full moon, which was higher and no longer huge and orange, I couldn't make out what costumes they were wearing.

Dep squirmed in my arms. "Meow!"

"I'm not putting you down," I informed her. "Your usual pace might not be fast enough for us to see him before he drives away." I didn't want to think about the harm she might be doing to my lace sleeves, or the harm I knew she was doing to my arms.

Front porches were decorated with creative jack-o'-lanterns displaying every emotion known to man—or to pumpkin—plus some beautifully carved designs. The three football players who had been at my place earlier were ringing a doorbell.

Chilly, I hugged Dep closer. She reached up and batted at my hat. I tilted my head back. "Don't knock it off, please. I guess I should have made you a black cat costume to go with my witch costume."

She sniffed at my fake hair. Sooner or later, she was going to find a way to make me put her down.

At the end of my block, I had to decide whether to turn left and stay in the residential neighborhood for a little longer on our way toward the Fireplug, or take the quickest route to Wisconsin Street where no one would be trick-or-treating now that the shops were closed.

Far up the block to my left, a tall white ghostlike creature was among other trick-or-treaters heading toward someone's front porch. Was Steve mingling with trick-or-treaters to hide in plain sight as he fled my neighborhood? I turned left and walked a little faster.

Dep and I were only a few houses away when the trick-or-treaters ran down the porch steps. Carrying a bulging pillowcase, the tall ghost followed the other trick-or-treaters, glanced my way, and turned the other direction.

The back of the ghost's sheet was smudged with something that looked like fudge frosting.

I retreated behind a hedge next to the front walk of a house decorated with giant spiders. I set Dep down, looped her leash over my arm, and took my phone out of my basket of chocolate bars.

A car passed on the street I'd left moments earlier. The car was heading toward my house. It was a powerful black car with a kayak on top.

Instead of dialing 911, I called Brent's personal number. He didn't answer.

I left a message telling him where I was, and that Steve Quail alias Stanley Quentin Meadows had told me he'd murdered Rich. I also told him where Quail was and which direction he was heading. "At the moment, he's disguised as a ghost in a sheet, smeared in back with fudge frosting."

Feeling silly for not having pockets and for resembling a witch who'd stolen Little Red Riding Hood's basket, I put my phone back among the chocolate bars.

I bent down and scooped Dep into my arms.

"Merr-ow!"

Shivering, I held her close. "Shh!"

I stepped out from behind the hedge and peeked up the street.

The white ghost had stopped. He was facing me.

Hoping that he wouldn't notice the cat in my arms and also hoping that my tall conical hat with its cape-like veil and attached frizzy hair would fool him into thinking I was someone else, I headed back the way I'd come. Quickly.

An ambulance and a firetruck rumbled toward Wisconsin Street from the direction of my house. Neither used a siren, but the lights on the ambulance were flashing. The firetruck's engine roared.

No wonder Brent hadn't answered his phone. He had probably run up to my front door to find out what was going on. *Check your messages, Brent,* I thought silently.

Four costumed people ran across the intersection ahead of me. They were heading toward my house and were only about a half block from where I was trotting toward them. Two of them were exceptionally tall, one was almost as tall, and the fourth one was short. They had to be Misty, Scott, Hooligan, and Samantha, on the way to my party, and they were running because they'd seen the firetruck and the ambulance leave my section of the block.

Running too, I shouted, "Yoo hoo! Yoo HOO!" Would Hooligan, dashing farther and farther from me, hear the new nickname we'd given him?

A devil in a form-fitting leotard with a tail and horns sprinted behind my friends. She was carrying a pitchfork. She passed underneath a streetlight and looked my way. Even her face was red. She stopped in the middle of the street.

Footsteps were closing the distance behind me.

I ran faster. Dep howled her complaints about the bouncy ride.

Pitchfork in hand, the devil sprinted toward me.

Right behind me, Steve's voice said, "Did you think I wouldn't recognize you and that dress with all the sparkly things on it?"

I stopped and whipped around to face him.

Chapter 32

✁

Steve lifted that pillowcase, overflowing with candy and I didn't know what else, above my head. Clutching Dep firmly with my right hand, I raised my left hand to fend off the heavy pillowcase.

I shouted, "Rich didn't kill Patty!"

Steve's hand faltered, but he again raised it and the pillowcase.

I wasn't clutching Dep firmly enough. She sprang out of my arms and toward the eyeholes in the ghost costume. Steve yelped almost as loudly as Dep yowled.

Ducking the full pillowcase, I dropped my basket. I also accidentally stepped on one corner of Steve's sheet. That, plus the momentum of the overflowing pillowcase, the surprise attack of my cat, and the soles of the gymnastic devil's red sneakers striking a double blow into Steve's face sent him crashing to the sidewalk.

Spewing candy, the pillowcase thumped onto the ground beside the hedge.

Jocelyn completed her flip and landed upright without tripping over her forked tail. I thanked her.

"You and Dep did more than I did." She didn't seem the least bit out of breath.

Dep's leash was still around my wrist. "Good cat, Dep," I

said. She was a puff of fur, staring at Steve lying on his back on the sidewalk.

"Is he okay?" Jocelyn asked.

Steve's eyes were closed, but he was breathing. I wasn't sure if he was unconscious or merely stunned. "I don't know. Where's your pitchfork?"

"I left it back there. It's only cardboard."

"Can you help me roll him onto his stomach?"

Together, we rolled him over.

I took off my hat. Jocelyn held his hands together behind his back.

Slowed by Dep pulling at the leash looped around my arm, I wrapped my hat's veil around and around Steve's wrists. Despite its yardage, it wouldn't work well as handcuffs, so I sat, cradling my guard cat, on Steve's back while Jocelyn sat on his legs.

My phone was, fortunately, still nestled in the basket with the chocolate bars. I reached for it.

Headlights shined in my face. A low black car with a kayak on top purred to a stop beside me. Brent leaped out. He was wearing one of his normal, well-tailored suits, an enormous, floppy bow tie, and a tiny clown hat riding on clouds of bright red hair. He shouted, "Get away from him, Em and . . ."

"Jocelyn," I supplied. Still holding Dep, I jumped up, grabbed my basket with the candy and phone in it, and ran toward my street. Jocelyn kept up with me except for a second when she stooped to pick up her red cardboard pitchfork.

Four costumed adults raced up the sidewalk toward us—Misty, Scott, Hooligan, and Samantha.

Scott and Samantha reached us and stopped, arms out for hugs and protection. Misty and Hooligan passed us and sprinted to the tableau on the sidewalk. The headlights of Brent's car lit everything. Steve was still facedown with a witch hat at his side and a mound of spangled veil around his wrists. Crouching beside Steve, Brent removed the veil with, apparently, some difficulty and snapped real handcuffs on Steve's wrists. Although the situation was far from humorous, the bright silver reflective spangles on the veil and the fluffy gray hair attached to the hat looked so silly that I wanted to giggle.

"Are you okay?" Samantha asked.

Keeping a firm grip on Dep's leash, I set her down on the sidewalk. "Probably better than you. What are you supposed to be, Snow White?"

"Yes. Can't you tell?"

"Don't eat any apples."

"Don't worry." She pointed toward Hooligan bending over Steve. "Prince Charming has already awakened me from my deep sleep."

"What is he wearing?" He looked like a giant cardboard circle with legs and a head.

"He made his costume. He's a donut."

My giggles erupted, and Jocelyn joined in. "With pink icing and sprinkles," I managed. "It's a good thing he cut armholes in the front, or he wouldn't be much help to Brent and Misty. I think Brent is dressed as a clown, but I don't know what Misty's supposed to be. Something green, apparently."

"I'll let her tell you," Scott said.

I looked up at my tall friend in his pirate hat and cape. A toy garden hoe stuck out of one suspiciously long sleeve. "You're Captain Hook, I guess." Maybe Misty was Peter Pan.

A marked police cruiser pulled up behind Brent's kayak-topped car. Two uniformed officers jumped out. With help from Brent, Hooligan, and Misty, they got Steve to his feet. The uniformed officers put Steve into the back of the police car and shut the door. Instead of climbing into the cruiser right away, they returned to Brent, Misty, and Hooligan, and stood talking.

The pillowcase and the candy that had spilled from it were still on the ground. I picked Dep up again and told Jocelyn,

Samantha, and Scott, "I have to go talk to them." With the handle of the basket over one wrist and Dep firmly in my arms, I ran toward the five officers. Captain Hook, Snow White, and the she-devil came with me.

Seeing us barreling toward him, Brent closed the distance between us. He was still wearing the ridiculous hat, wig, and bow tie, and he was carrying my hat, complete with its veil and its hair. "Are you okay?" He held out his arms.

I placed Dep, still in her harness, into them. The leash was around my wrist with the handle of the basket. "I'm fine, but see that pillowcase and all that candy near the hedge? Steve was carrying it, so the officers need to take it as evidence."

Brent glanced down toward the hem of my black velvet dress. "Em, are you responsible for the hat and hair and whatever else is attached to it that we found tangled around Steve's wrists?"

I gulped. "They're mine. Including the tangling. Sorry about that."

His mouth twitching, he gave me the hat.

I put it on and tossed my head to straighten the veil and allow it to trail down to the hem of my gown the way it was supposed to. "My costume is elegant," I informed him. "You win the prize for funny."

He glanced toward our other friends. "Maybe." The grin won out over his attempt at keeping a straight face. He gave Dep back to me and returned to the uniformed cops. While the rest of us stood back, the uniformed officers put on gloves, picked up the pillowcase and the candy, slid it all into a supersized evidence bag, and shut the bag into their trunk. They drove away with Steve and his bag of loot.

Jocelyn, Scott, Samantha, and I joined Brent, Hooligan, and Misty beside Brent's car. The headlights were still on. Brent told us, "The injured woman was taken to the hospital to be checked out, and the firefighters said your range did what it was supposed to do, Emily. It shut itself off."

Samantha looked about to do a physical on me, right there

on the sidewalk in front of a porch full of gaping onlookers.

I quickly asked Misty, "What are you supposed to be?" She was wearing green-and-black plaid pants, a green-and-yellow-striped vest, a bright green jacket with huge white buttons, and an olive hat with an iridescent teal feather sticking out of it.

Misty piped in a squeaky voice, "I'm hurt that you can't tell. I'm a leprechaun."

"Of course," I answered. "You're just the right size."

Hooligan fretted in faked sad tones, "I bent my donut costume. I made it in your honor, Emily, and it didn't even last until the party."

"I have a worse complaint," I said. "A murderer sat in some of the donuts I was going to serve tonight."

Brent pointed out that my house was now a crime scene.

I wailed, "My party!"

Brent squeezed my shoulder. "Tom is among other guests waiting for you outside your house. He offered to have the party at Deputy Donut. I'll take you back so you can talk to him and the others."

"Do you mind if I walk? Dep isn't fond of riding in cars, and the little heroine deserves special treatment. Twice tonight, she slowed Steve down and made him easier to find and catch." I couldn't help a laugh that might have sounded hysterical. "She tripped him, and he sat in fudge frosting without knowing he was a marked man. I mean ghost."

Brent turned to Misty. "Can you drive my car to Emily's? I'll walk with her."

Misty accepted the keys he dangled in front of her. "Glad to."

"I'll go with you, Misty," Scott said. "To make certain you don't take Brent's car for a three-week joyride."

"Okay, only two weeks." She closed herself into Brent's car. Scott smiled at Samantha, Hooligan, Brent, and me. He took off the pirate hat, tossed it into Brent's car, folded himself into the passenger seat, and closed the door.

Brent asked me, "Are you warm enough?"

"That's why I brought Dep."

"Here." He took off his jacket and draped it around my shoulders.

Tilting my head forward to loosen the jacket's grip on my trailing veil and fake hair, I thanked him. "You'll be cold."

"I'll carry Dep."

"You already look strange enough without adding a cat to the effect. She goes better with a witch, even a witch with a blazer over her gown." Now that Brent had removed his suit jacket, his shoulder holster, complete with revolver, was plainly visible. It did not go well with the clown hat, the puffs of red hair, and the huge purple-and-yellow polka dot tie.

"Then I'll walk close to you." He slung his right arm, the one farthest from the holster, around my back and grasped my elbow through his jacket.

The five of us humans—Hooligan, Samantha, Jocelyn, Brent, and I—walked more quickly than we might have if we'd merely been out for a stroll.

I asked Hooligan and Samantha why they'd been walking to my place instead of driving.

"We changed at the police station," Hooligan told me. "And walked from there. Misty did, too. Scott was waiting for us at the fire station. He'd already put on his costume."

"Fallingbrook will never be the same," I moaned.

Hooligan explained, "We figured the walk back to our cars at the police and fire stations would be good for us at the end of your party."

Brent said, "I maintained my dignity. I hid in my car in the police station parking lot and put on my hat and bow tie."

"Dignity," I repeated, smiling up at the red fuzz sticking out above his ears. "I see."

"I walked from my house," Jocelyn said. "Except when I was doing cartwheels and flips."

Dep was becoming heavy, and carrying her and the wicker basket was awkward, but I liked her furry heat. Walking in the slinky gown and trying to match my steps to Brent's longer ones wasn't easy, especially since he seemed to be trying to shorten his steps. Without stumbling into each other much, we made it to my place.

Brent's car was behind my red car and the donut car in the driveway.

Yellow tape was draped around my porch. My front door was standing open. The living room light was on, and a uniformed officer stood in the doorway.

Tom, Cindy, Nina, Misty, and Scott were in my front yard. Dressed as a burglar, Tom held hands with Cindy, who was in a cat costume. Nina had made a gray plush Eeyore costume with drooping ears and baggy arms and legs.

Cindy told me, "You and Dep can spend the night with us and go to work with Tom in the morning if you feel up to it."

I thanked her. I didn't think anyone in the group knew that I'd been stunned by a skillet, and I wasn't going to let them think a little thing like chasing after a murderer in a fudge-stained ghost costume had been overwhelming. "I'm sure I will."

Brent asked me to go inside with him and show him where everything had happened. "And if you can without disturbing evidence, you can pack a bag for the next few days until we let you back in here."

He conferred with the officer who had taped off the house. I handed the basket and Dep and her leash to Jocelyn. She told Dep what a good kitty she was. Brent and I ducked underneath the crime scene tape and went inside. I showed him the skillet and the platter of smashed donuts on the living room floor. In the kitchen, I showed him where I'd played dead while listening to Steve confess what he'd done and why. We both double-checked the stove's burners. They were off.

"I'll take your full statement later," Brent said.

The firefighters had closed my back door and windows. Brent and I made certain they were all locked.

"Did Steve go upstairs?" Brent asked.

"No."

"Then you can go up and pack a bag. Let me know, though, if anything has been disturbed."

"Okay." I started up the stairs.

"Em?"

I stopped and leaned over the bannister. "Yes?"

"Pack some warm clothes for kayaking. The moon is full tonight, but if we don't make it tonight after your party, the moon will be almost full tomorrow night. And thanks to you, I won't have to work tomorrow night."

I smiled. "Okay." I packed enough clothes, including some warm ones, for several days and took my bag outside.

Tom and Cindy had parked Tom's SUV on the street. Tom was happy to drive the donut car, even with Dep howling in the cat carrier in the rear seat. I put my bag in the trunk. Samantha and I sat beside Dep's carrier. Our presence didn't seem to placate the meowing and obviously insulted cat. Hooligan rode in the front passenger seat.

Cindy took Scott, Jocelyn, and Nina in Tom's SUV.

Brent got into his own car, with Misty in the passenger seat. She appeared to be complaining about not being allowed to drive Brent's car again.

We left my car, still with the kayak on top, in the driveway.

Naturally, Tom turned on the car-top donut's sprinkle lights and set them to flash at their fastest rate. He dropped Hooligan off at the Fireplug Pub and let the rest of us out near the office door of Deputy Donut.

Samantha carried Dep, still muttering about her incarceration, to the back door. I took my bag and unlocked the office door. In the office, I let Dep out of her carrier. She ran up to the highest catwalk and looked down as our costumed guests paraded from the office to the serving counter and the tables closest to the kitchen. The office would have been nice for a party, but it wasn't big enough for everyone. I stuffed my bag underneath the desk with the cat carrier and followed the others into the shop. I dimmed the lights, giving the shop a party ambience. Still in her Eeyore costume, Nina made coffee while Tom-the-burglar offered soft drinks.

Jocelyn was supposed to join her boyfriend at another party, so Brent ushered her to a table near the front windows and took her statement first.

Samantha wasn't about to let me do anything. Her hands on her hips and her expression stern for someone wearing a Snow White costume, she cornered me. "The 911 dispatcher reported two injured women at your address."

"I wasn't badly injured, only a little shocked. And mostly scared because of smelling gas."

Samantha didn't let up. "Was there some reason that you couldn't stop the attacker from turning on the burners and blowing out the flames?"

"I fell on the kitchen floor."

She glared at me.

"Okay, he hit me with the skillet, too."

"Where?"

"The back of my head. If I lost consciousness, it was only for a second or two."

Samantha sighed. "Let's have a look."

She sat me down. The others, except Brent and Jocelyn, who were talking at a front table, must have decided that Samantha's use of the word "let's" meant they were supposed to have a look at my head, too. They crowded around while Samantha gently ran her fingers through curls on the back of my head.

"See?" I demanded. "No blood."

Samantha muttered, "It doesn't look too bad, but there's a lump. You should go to the hospital to have it checked out."

"And miss my party, on a Halloween that's on a Saturday night? When there's also a full moon?"

Nina understood. She went into the kitchen and came back with ice wrapped in a kitchen towel. I obediently held it against the lump on the back of my head.

Hooligan came in with wine and beer. Samantha gave him a big hug.

Brent finished taking Jocelyn's statement and told her she was free to go to her other party. He asked her if she wanted a ride.

She shook her red-hooded head. "It's near Emily's. I can run there in three minutes. What are the chances of two murderers trick-or-treating in that neighborhood in one night?"

I thanked her again for helping keep me safe from Steve.

"You and Dep did at least as much as I did."

We gave each other high fives, and I let her out the front door. She jogged south on Wisconsin Street.

Finally warm again, I gave Brent his jacket. He put it on. He and I sat at the table where he'd questioned Jocelyn, out of earshot of the party going on closer to the kitchen. Brent took out his notebook.

I told him everything that had happened before he drove up and illuminated the scene with his headlights. He sighed, put his notebook away, and squeezed my shoulder. "Sorry, but I probably won't return to your party tonight. I'll leave my car in the lot behind your shop, though, in case I finish before your party ends. I'll leave my hat, wig, and bow tie inside the car." I convinced him to take a donut along to eat during the short walk to the police station.

Samantha checked my head again. "It doesn't look bad. Continue icing that lump, off and on. And go easy on the alcohol tonight, okay?"

I agreed, although a glass of wine would have been welcome.

Heading toward the others, I called out, "Who wants to hear a ghost story?"

Chapter 33

❧

Everyone laughed at my offer of a ghost story, but, between stuffing ourselves with Halloween donuts and the chocolate bars I'd brought in my orange wicker basket with its grinning jack-o'-lantern face, a lot of our discussion was about the ghost who, thanks to his purloined sheet and my cat, had tripped and sat in a plate of Boston scream and other Halloween donuts.

Samantha called the hospital and reported that Cheryl did not appear to have been seriously injured and would probably be sent home after a few tests. Samantha checked the back of my head and told me not to be alone that night.

"I won't. I'm staying with Tom and Cindy."

"And bringing Dep," Cindy reminded me. "Dep will wake Tom and me up if Emily needs help in the night."

Samantha merely rolled her eyes.

She and Hooligan were scheduled to work in the morning. They left.

Misty and Scott offered to drop Nina off at her apartment. "If you don't mind walking to the fire station where my car is," Scott added.

"Or the police station where mine is," Misty said.

Nina answered, "I don't mind walking either place, but I usually walk home. I'll stay and help clean up."

Tom and I responded together, "No, you won't!"

"I'll help clean up," Cindy offered, "while I wait for Emily and Tom."

Nina accepted the ride with Misty or Scott. They went out the front and headed toward the fire and police stations.

I tried to get Tom and Cindy to act like guests instead of hosts. "There's not much to do when the partygoers are so neat."

Nevertheless, Cindy filled the dishwasher while Tom and I tidied everything for the Jolly Cops, who would be there in an hour or two. We were almost done when my phone rang.

"Where are you?" Brent asked.

"Deputy Donut. The party's about over."

"Sorry I missed it. Want to go kayaking?"

"Now?"

"Unless it's too late."

"I'd love to. I'll change while you're walking here."

We disconnected, and I asked Cindy and Tom if they would mind taking Dep to their house while I went kayaking with Brent. "Or if her howling while you drive will be too much, she can wait for me to come back here and I'll bring her later."

"We'll take her," Tom insisted. "What if one of the Jolly Cops arrives while she's still here, and he's dressed in a ghost costume? Dep might attack him."

Laughing at the image he conjured up, I thanked them.

"Have fun tonight," Cindy said.

I explained that we wouldn't be long and that we were hoping Lake Fleekom would be misty under a full moon.

Cindy made a pretend shiver. "Better you than me. That sounds cold."

"I brought warm clothes."

All three of us went into the office. Dep was snoozing on the couch. Tom picked her up. When she was securely locked in his arms, I dragged the cat carrier out from underneath the desk.

"Merow!"

Cindy spoke softly to her, and Dep became almost bone-less, making it easy for Tom to slide her into the carrier.

Wide-eyed, I looked at Cindy. "How did you do that?"

"I have no idea. Maybe after everything else that happened tonight, she just gave up."

I reached into the carrier and managed to touch Dep's warm fur with an index finger. "See you later, Dep. Be a good houseguest."

The answer was the tiniest *mew* I'd heard from Dep since she was a kitten.

Tom and Cindy left. I locked the door behind them, grabbed my bag, raced into the ladies' room, pulled off the velvet dress and put on warm leggings, a long sweater, a jacket, and socks and sneakers.

I went out through the office, locked the back door, and set the alarm.

Brent was waiting beside his car.

He stowed my bag in his trunk and opened the passenger door.

We got in and Brent started the car. "You were right," he said. "Derek drove his pickup truck to Rich's cottage on Thursday night. He claimed he was only trying to find Terri and help her, but we managed to get him to confess that Thursday night wasn't the first time he'd gone to that cottage since he was kicked out of it. He rode his motorcycle there after you sent him away from the party on Tuesday afternoon. He didn't know that Rich had been killed. He found the cottage's back door hanging open, so he went in. He stole that bowl. He wanted to get Terri into trouble, so he was going to report her for stealing the bowl from the cottage and leaving it at his place. After Derek heard that Rich was murdered, Derek didn't want to have that bowl in his possession. He drove back late Thursday night to put the bowl where he'd found it. By then, the place was locked, and crime scene tape was around it and he decided not to break in. The next day he dumped Terri's things in her front yard and put the bowl with them. He still hoped to get Terri into trouble for stealing it, but in the end, he admitted that he was the one who took it."

"Was he afraid that his being inside that cottage on Tuesday afternoon might make you charge him with murder?"

"Probably."

"Did anyone get Steve to confess to murdering Rich and attacking Cheryl and me?"

Brent turned south on Wisconsin Street. "Kim did. It didn't help his case that the pillowcase he was carrying around, the one Jocelyn saw him aim at your head, had several pounds of rocks in the bottom. Kim told him that testimony from Terri and from the owners of the Teddy Beddy Bye-Bye Motel, plus records from Rich's charge card had exonerated both Rich and Terri. Steve, that is Stanley, broke down."

"Didn't Stanley know that Patty's death was ruled as accidental?"

"He didn't believe it. He unearthed rumors about Rich's affair with Terri, so he was certain that Rich had killed Patty. He asked us why Rich's alibi wasn't public knowledge."

"Why wasn't it?"

"Delicate sensibilities and job security. Neither Rich nor Terri wanted anyone to know about their affair. And Terri was horrified. She ended the affair and switched jobs."

Folded in my lap, my hands were tense. I tried to relax them. "Rich might have broken up with Terri to preserve his own reputation."

"Could be. Anyway, Stanley was distraught just now in the police station, mostly about his half sister's death, but also about the way he'd spent years planning revenge for a crime that had never been committed, and about the way he'd now ruined his own life."

I exhaled. "He confessed in my kitchen when he wasn't sure I could hear him. I'm glad he confessed to you, too."

"It makes the case easier."

"Do you know if Rich signed a will between when his mother died and when he wrote the recent one naming Terri as his beneficiary?"

"We found no evidence of one. By the way, you guessed right about Stanley and the canoe. Forensics will check his car against the mold they made of the tire prints in that dried-up mud puddle, but he admits he parked beside that pathway. First, though, he drove to Rich's cottage, which he'd learned about from researching Rich. He parked at the log cabin next to it and hid his car among trees. He's a jogger. He jogged along the road to Rich's cottage where he broke in and stole the first weapon-like thing he found, that skillet. He figured no one would connect it with him. Then he saw Rich's canoe on the dock and used it rather than his car to transport the skillet to Rich's. The mist was wispy on the road to the cottages but heavy on the lake, and he thought he had a better chance of concealing himself and the canoe on the lake. He hovered behind a point with trees leaning out from it and watched Rich's place. He wasn't certain he would get a chance to attack Rich that day. He saw Terri canoe away, but the caterers were still there, and Terri only went as far as Hank's beach. After the caterers left and Terri paddled away from Hank's—"

I interrupted, "If Stanley was telling the truth about Terri, she really did go canoeing after she talked to Hank. And Hank lied. Why did he do that?"

Naturally Brent answered with a question of his own. "Any guesses?"

I shrugged in the darkness. "Maybe he was certain she didn't kill Rich, and he was trying to protect her?"

"Could be. Anyway, after Stanley saw her disappear in the mist, he took his chance and paddled to Rich's beach. Carrying the skillet, he found Rich inside the tent, and you know what happened then."

I shuddered. "Yes."

Brent made the turn onto my street. "The mist was still heavy. He paddled the canoe back behind the leaning trees to keep an eye on Rich's place and to try to figure out where Terri was so he could avoid her. He heard a car, probably yours, and decided he was dangerously close to Rich's. Sure that Terri was out on the lake, he didn't paddle all the way back to Rich's cottage or the cabin next to it. He paddled across the lake—"

"And he was so nervous that he banged his paddle against the gunwales."

"He didn't mention that. He pulled the canoe into the woods where you found it on Wednesday, and then jogged back to his car and changed his clothes. He drove partway down the road and parked beside it near the pathway that leads to where he'd left the canoe. He was supposed to meet Cheryl at Rich's party at noon, so he waited until two minutes till. He pulled into Rich's driveway right after Cheryl did."

"Where are his bloodstained clothes?"

Brent shot me a quick grin. "Trust you to think of that. We asked. They're weighted down with rocks in Lake Fleekom near the shuttered log cabin."

"Did he use his knowledge as a private investigator to find out what happened to Patty?"

"Yes, and to track Rich down. Rich must have known about Stanley's existence, but by the time of Patty's death, he must have had no idea where Stanley was, so Rich couldn't tell him that Patty was dead or about Rich's alibi. Stanley hadn't seen Patty since he was seven, and hadn't heard from her in years. The first time he met Rich was on Monday afternoon, at Deputy Donut."

"Stanley wasn't all bad."

Brent pulled into my driveway. "A lot of them aren't."

My front door was closed, but there were lights on inside and the yellow police tape was still draped across my porch. I felt like I might cry—for a blustery older man who had loved Boston and art, for a woman who had loved nature and canoeing, and for a small boy who had loved and lost the half sister who'd been like a mother to him.

We got out. A policeman opened my front door and stepped onto the porch.

Brent went to tell the officer I had permission to drive my car away. I put my bag into my trunk with my paddle and life jacket.

I drove my car, and Brent followed me in his to Lake Fleekom.

The full moon was high and bright, shining down on pale mist rising above the water.

No lights were on inside Rich's house.

I was glad that Terri hadn't murdered the man who had declared she was the love of his life. If she truly loved him, and I guessed she did, inheriting everything he'd owned was probably not much of a consolation, though.

I hoped she wouldn't go back to Derek.

Hank's house was dark, too. I liked Hank. I was also glad he wasn't a murderer. Maybe I would find out when he was giving another performance so I could attend it and hear him play.

With Brent following far enough back that his headlights didn't shine in my mirrors, I drove around the left curve and on, past the place where Stanley had ditched the canoe he'd stolen from Rich's dock.

I pulled into the parking area at the county park, got out, and unfastened my kayak. Because of the moonlight, which was almost doubled by the moon's reflection off the misty lake, I didn't need a flashlight.

Brent took off his shoulder holster and shut his revolver inside a case. He locked the case and put it into his trunk, which he also locked. We put on our life jackets and carried our kayaks and paddles to the edge of the water.

Mist blanketed the lake and writhed upward in long fingers.

Neither Brent nor I spoke, but I might have sighed.

As always, I managed to plunge one foot into the water. Then finally, there it was, that exhilaration of floating free, my kayak and paddle almost silent.

I meandered out toward the middle of the lake. I could hear the swish of Brent's kayak cutting through the water behind me.

When we were surrounded by white with the dazzling silver moon high above us in a sky too bright for stars, I stopped paddling and rested my paddle across the coaming in front of me.

Brent pulled up beside me and grabbed the end of my paddle. He placed one end of his paddle next to mine. I gripped it. He moved his hand to mine.

"Is anything wrong, Em?"

Brushing tears from my eyes with my free hand, I shook my head. "It's . . . everything." The moment was so beautiful that it hurt. I wasn't sure I ever wanted it to end.

Our clasped hands tethering our kayaks together, we drifted on the magical, mist-covered, moonlit lake.

Boston
Scream
Murder
Recipes

Boston Scream Donuts

Hint: Make the filling first so that it can be chilling while you make the donuts. Make the frosting while the donuts are cooling.

For the donuts:
1 cup less 3 tablespoons warm water
¼ cup unsalted butter, softened
2 tablespoons active dry yeast (yes, this is a lot!)
½ cup sugar
3½ cups all-purpose or bread flour
½ teaspoon salt
1 egg or 2 egg whites, room temperature
If frying your donuts: vegetable oil with a smoke point of 400° or higher (or follow your deep fryer's instruction manual)

In your mixer bowl fitted with a dough hook, combine the warm water, butter, yeast, and sugar. Let stand for 15 minutes to allow the yeast to work.

Add 2 cups of the flour, the salt, and the egg to the yeast mixture. Stir with the dough hook, stopping if necessary to scrape down the sides of the bowl. Add the remaining flour ½ cup at a time and knead with the dough hook. If the dough is too sticky, add ¼ cup of flour and knead with the dough hook. If the dough is still too sticky, carefully add more flour 1 teaspoon at a time. Continue kneading with the dough hook until the dough cleans the sides of the bowl, is satiny, doesn't stick to your fingers, and doesn't keep its shape when pinched. It should still feel slightly sticky. Too much flour will make the donuts tough.

Cover the bowl with a damp cloth or plastic wrap, place it in a warm area, and let the dough rise until it doubles in volume, about 1½ to 2 hours.

Punch down the dough and divide in half. For each half, roll the dough to about ½ inch thick between two sheets of parchment paper.

Remove the top sheet of parchment paper and cut rounds from the dough with a round cookie cutter, cutting them as close together as possible, and place them on a parchment-lined baking sheet (don't reroll the dough scraps.)

Cover the rounds with a damp cloth or plastic wrap and let them rise for about 30 – 60 minutes or until they are puffy.

Fry the donuts at 350°F, turning when golden, about 1 to 2 minutes per side. Lift them from the oil and allow them to drain on paper towels

OR bake on a cookie sheet lined with parchment paper or a silicone baking sheet in a 375°F oven for about 10 minutes until the tops are golden.

When cool, slice the donuts in half horizontally (you'll have two rounds to put together like sandwiches).

Frost the tops with fudge frosting (below) and carve screaming faces into the fudge.

Spread filling (below) on the bottom halves and gently place the screaming face on top.

Note: to make the donuts truly delicious and difficult to eat neatly, use lots of frosting and filling on each one.

For the fudge frosting:

This is a fudgy frosting that holds its shape if you want to carve screaming faces—or anything else—in the frosting. See below for a more traditional frosting for Boston Cream Donuts.

2 ounces unsweetened chocolate
1 tablespoon unsalted butter
½ cup milk
approximately 2 cups powdered sugar, sifted
1 teaspoon vanilla

In a microwave oven, slowly melt the chocolate and butter in the milk. Do not allow the milk to boil.

Transfer the chocolate mixture to a mixer bowl and stir well.

Let the chocolate mixture stand until it is lukewarm.

Stir in the vanilla.

Stir in, bit by bit, the sifted powdered sugar.

Test the frosting for spreadability and run a knife through it. If the gash fills in, stir in powdered sugar by the teaspoonful until the frosting is stiff enough to maintain the screaming faces that you undoubtedly want to carve into it for Halloween.

For the Traditional Chocolate Frosting for Boston Cream Donuts:

½ cup unsweetened cocoa powder
¼ cup granulated sugar
6 tablespoons cold water
1 tablespoon unsalted butter
powdered sugar, sifted
½ teaspoon vanilla

Sift the cocoa powder or press it through a sieve into a microwaveable dish.

Add the sugar. With a fork, blend the sugar and cocoa powder together well.

Add the water, two tablespoons at a time, and stir after each addition until you have created a thickish paste.

Add the butter.

Cover the dish and heat in your microwave oven for approximately two minutes on a medium-low to medium setting.

Stir until the butter has melted completely and is blended well with the paste.

Cool slightly.

Stir in the vanilla.

For the filling:

1 cup whole milk
3 egg yolks, at room temperature
3 tablespoons white sugar
1½ tablespoons cornstarch
2 tablespoons unsalted butter
1 teaspoon vanilla

Heat the milk in a small pot over medium heat until bubbles begin forming around the edges of the pot.

Reduce the heat to low.

With a whisk, combine the egg yolks, sugar, and cornstarch in a heat-proof bowl until mixture is pale and smooth.

Whisking constantly, pour the warm milk VERY slowly, teaspoonfuls at a time, into the egg yolk mixture. You want to warm the egg yolks without cooking them.

When all the milk has been added, place the mixture in the pot. Whisking it, heat it at medium heat. Whisk constantly until the mixture becomes thick. Remove it from the heat and fold in the butter and vanilla extract.

Place the plastic wrap right on top of the filling, with no air between the filling and the wrap.

Chill the filling in the refrigerator for at least 2 hours.

Scare-It Cake Donuts

These are baked, using a donut pan.

For the donuts:

1 egg
¼ cup orange or pineapple juice
¼ cup unsalted butter, melted
1 tablespoon orange zest
¼ cup brown sugar
1 cup all-purpose flour
½ teaspoon baking powder
¼ teaspoon baking soda
½ teaspoon cinnamon
¼ teaspoon allspice
¼ teaspoon nutmeg
¼ teaspoon ginger
1¼ cup finely grated carrots

Preheat oven to 350°F.

Beat the egg in a large bowl. Beat in the juice, butter, orange zest, and sugar.

Add the flour, baking powder, baking soda, and spices. Mix until blended.

Stir in the grated carrots.

Spoon the mixture into donut pan, filling each ring.

Bake for 9–11 minutes. Cool.

Frost with orange cream cheese frosting (below).

For the orange cream cheese frosting:

¼ cup butter, room temperature
4 ounces cream cheese, room temperature
1 tablespoon orange juice
1 tablespoon orange zest
2 cups sifted confectioners' sugar

Orange food coloring (optional)
Sprinkles (optional)
Up to 1 more tablespoon orange zest

Cream the butter and cream cheese together until fluffy.
Stir in the orange zest and orange juice.

Beat in 1 cup sugar. Beat in more sugar, a tablespoon at a time, until the frosting holds its shape.

Stir in the orange food coloring (optional) until desired shade is reached.

Spread the frosting on the donuts.

Decorate with sprinkles or orange zest (optional).

Connect with

Us

Visit us online at
KensingtonBooks.com
to read more from your favorite authors, see books
by series, view reading group guides, and more.

Join us on social media

for sneak peeks, chances to win books and prize packs,
and to share your thoughts with other readers.

facebook.com/kensingtonpublishing
twitter.com/kensingtonbooks

Tell us what you think!

To share your thoughts, submit a review,
or sign up for our eNewsletters, please visit:
KensingtonBooks.com/TellUs.